"Brandon...I think it would be best if you didn't come around anymore."

A line formed between his eyebrows. She opened the door and when he didn't take the hint to leave, she stepped onto the porch and waited for him to follow, then closed the panel behind them.

"Belle already loves you. Mason is getting attached. It's going to hurt them when you disappear. Lingering will only make it worse."

"Who says I'll disappear?"

"Me. I appreciate all you've done, but I can't forget...the past or how dangerous your job is."

His jaw and shoulder muscles bunched. "I promised Rick I'd look out for you."

"I'm relieving you of that promise."

He inhaled, long and slow, filling his chest and making it seem even broader. Then he dipped his chin once, sharply. "Take care of yourself, Hannah."

He pivoted and walked away. Seconds later his truck engine started. Tension drained from her. It left her empty. She walked back inside and locked the door. The engaging dead bolt sounded a lot like a gunshot echoing off the foyer walls. Cutting Brandon from their lives was the right thing to do. For her sake and her children's.

Dear Reader,

Sometimes life throws you curveballs. When it does, you have to find the courage to forge a new path—often one you've never contemplated before. That's what happens to Hannah Leith when all her plans and dreams are buried with her husband. For her children's sake, she must find the courage to start over. But she never anticipated that new beginning would include the man she held responsible for her husband's death.

As for Brandon Martin, police officer, he never expected to use his investigative skills for his dead best friend's son. He definitely didn't foresee being physically attracted to his friend's widow or suddenly wanting her to become his wife.

I hope you enjoy Hannah and Brandon's attempts to deny the inevitable.

Emilie Rose

USA TODAY Bestselling Author

EMILIE ROSE

—

A Cop's Honor

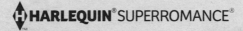

Recycling programs
for this product may
not exist in your area.

ISBN-13: 978-1-335-44911-5

A Cop's Honor

For questions and comments about the quality of this book, please contact us at CustomerService@Harlequin.com.

® and TM are trademarks of Harlequin Enterprises Limited or its corporate affiliates. Trademarks indicated with ® are registered in the United States Patent and Trademark Office, the Canadian Intellectual Property Office and in other countries.

Printed in U.S.A.

USA TODAY bestselling author and two-time RITA® Award finalist **Emilie Rose** lives in North Carolina with her own romance hero. Writing is her third career. She's managed a medical office and a home day care—neither offered half as much satisfaction as plotting happy endings. Her hobbies include gardening, fishing, cooking and traveling to find her next book setting. Visit her website, emilierose.com, or email her at EmilieRoseAuthor@aol.com.

Visit the Author Profile page at Harlequin.com for more titles.

For my dad.
Parkinson's took his mobility, his speech and his life, but it never took his sense of humor or his kindness.
He'll always be my hero.

CHAPTER ONE

HANNAH SANK DEEPER into her Adirondack chair and stretched out her legs. Her foot bumped the empty fire pit, and a few flakes of rust rained onto her ankles. She shifted again, hoping to find a more comfortable position on the hard seat. Her fingertips brushed across the chair's peeling paint and a sense of futility rose within her.

The furniture and fire pit, like everything else around the house behind her, needed work. A lot of work. More than she could handle or afford, yet she was tackling it one project at a time. But sometimes she felt like a hamster on a wheel, spinning 'round and 'round and getting nowhere.

The old house was home—the first real home she'd ever had. Not that the places she and her parents had lived as her father climbed the army's noncommissioned officer ranks had been bad, but they'd all been temporary. She hadn't been free to paint or make any changes in the rented accommodations. And she had never, ever put down roots until she and Rick had bought this fixer-upper.

Rick. She closed her eyes and let the loss roll

over her. Five years ago today he'd been taken from her. His death had robbed them of so many future plans as a family, and it had jeopardized their dream of turning this old house into the kind of home their children would remember fondly and always return to. She was trying to hold on to it, but life seemed determined to undermine that goal.

She took a deep breath of humid, hyacinth- and lilac-scented April air and tilted her head to stare at the full moon hanging like a fat beacon in the sky between towering oaks. A gentle breeze swayed the budding branches framing the orb. She pressed her bare soles against the still-warm brick pavers and endeavored to follow the advice she gave clients every day.

Inhale deeply to the count of ten, then exhale slowly. Release the tension by relaxing each muscle group sequentially: her forehead, her cheeks, her jaw, her neck, her shoulders. Knots loosened. Her pulse slowed and her grief settled back to a bearable level.

The click of the back door latch halted her progress. She'd thought both kids asleep before she'd slipped out for a moment of peace. Twisting, she leaned to look around the high back of her chair. The door eased open. Mason stepped onto the deck. Guilt pinched. Was he looking for her?

She opened her mouth to ask what he needed then noticed his backpack and remained silent.

Why was he carrying it at this time of night? Where was he planning on going? He turned the knob and silently pulled the door closed. An uneasiness pricked through her. The feeling amplified when he furtively glanced around then tiptoed down the steps, carefully avoiding the squeaky middle tread. He turned for the side gate and clicked on a flashlight.

He wasn't looking for her. Concern turned into alarm. "Mason, where do you think you're going?"

He jumped, dropping the flashlight with a clank. The beam flickered and died. "Mom! What are you doing out here?"

The dismay on his face and in his voice confirmed that finding her hadn't been his objective. Her heart thumped hard and fast in her chest. She rose and crossed the yard. "The question is where are *you* going at ten o'clock? You should be sleeping. It's a school night. Your bedtime was nine."

The sound of crickets filled the air.

"Mason Brandon Leith! Answer me."

His gaze skittered away. "I…um… I…was going to camp out in the treehouse."

Lying *and* sneaking out. Anxiety dried her mouth. She jabbed a thumb over her shoulder. "The treehouse is that way."

"I…um…was looking for frogs first."

Another lie. "Inside. *Now*."

"Mooooom," he wailed.

"Move it!" What had turned her sweet, easy-going ten-year-old son into trouble looking for a place to happen? He'd been suspended twice from school in the past three months for making inappropriate comments to other students then to his teacher, and finally, for sassing the school principal. She knew middle school kids were supposed to be difficult, but she hadn't expected sixth grade to change her little boy into someone she didn't recognize.

She followed him into the kitchen. "Where were you going?"

"I told you."

"You lied. Try the truth."

His chin jutted out. "I was going to meet a friend…for homework help."

"At this hour? Who?"

"No one you know."

That concerned her. "I've told you more than once that you're not allowed to go to anyone's house unless I've met them and their parents—and definitely not after bedtime and without permission."

"How's that supposed to happen? You work all the time. Even Grandmother Margaret says—"

"Do not throw your grandmother in my face. I work because I have to. And you're only required to spend a couple of hours a day in after-school care. It won't kill you. Anyway, you're supposed to use *that* time to get help with your homework."

But the guilt of not being there for them the way her mother had been for her, ate at her.

"You treat me like a baby. I'm not!"

She didn't bother arguing that he would always be her baby. "You know the rules, Mason. You're grounded for the week. No TV and definitely no video games."

"You're mean! I hate you!"

The dart hit home. Her heart ached and her eyes stung. She knew he was only striking out in anger, but his words still hurt. She stiffened her spine. "Go to your room."

He charged out of the kitchen and stomped up the stairs. His bedroom door slammed. She winced and hoped he hadn't woken his sister.

She had to figure out what had triggered the drastic change in his behavior before he ended up in serious trouble. But who could she turn to? Not to the school counselor who'd warned her that the next time her son misbehaved he'd be expelled. Not to her in-laws who'd insisted more than once that Hannah wasn't a good parent to their grand-children. Their constant criticisms were hard to swallow.

And she definitely couldn't turn to a professional—not only because of the cost. She feared her in-laws might warp whatever a psychologist learned into something that could be used against her to make good on their threat to pursue partial—if not full—custody. She didn't think they had a legal leg to stand on, but Mr. Leith had been golfing buddies with numerous lawyers and judges over the years. She couldn't even afford to hire an attorney if her in-laws took action. And after witnessing a coworker lose custody of her kids due to something her ex-husband had trumped up, Hannah was afraid to take chances.

She sank into a kitchen chair and dropped her head into her hands. She needed help. But who could she go to? Who could she trust? Only one name came to mind. Brandon Martin. She immediately rejected calling him. She was sure the only reason his name had popped up was because of his connection to Rick and because Rick was heavy on her heart today. But when no other names came forward, her thoughts circled back to Brandon. Would he—could he—talk some sense into her son? She'd recalled that he'd done some work with troubled youth in the past. Her stomach churned at the idea of contacting him.

Her anger and resentment toward Brandon over his part in Rick's death still festered inside her. As her husband's partner in the South Carolina Law Enforcement Division's Computer Crimes Department, he should have never left Rick alone in a suspect's house. But Brandon had been so focused on collecting evidence to keep his perfect conviction record that he'd failed to protect her husband.

She hadn't seen or spoken to him since Rick's

funeral where she'd lost control and screamed some harsh truths at him in front of God and everybody. Would he be willing to help her now?

For Mason's sake, she prayed he would.

BRANDON SPOTTED HANNAH the moment she entered the park on Friday afternoon. Judging by the scrub suit she wore, she was squeezing him in on her lunch break from the physical therapy office where she worked.

She paused at the wrought iron archway to scan the area. He rose from the picnic table on the neutral turf she'd designated for their meeting and lifted a hand to catch her attention. She spotted him, then after a noticeable pause, marched in his direction like a woman on a mission.

He assessed the changes in Rick's wife. Hannah had always been pretty—pretty enough to make even Rick's ugly mug look good. But the past five years had altered her. She'd cut more than a foot from her once-long hair. Shiny brown strands now feathered around her jaw, which happened to be set in a battle-ready, hard line. Her brown eyes weren't any softer he noted as she neared. She looked thinner. Tired. More fragile.

He nodded but didn't hug her as he once would have. She'd made it clear the last time he saw her that such gestures were no longer welcome from him. "What's wrong?"

She stiffened defensively. "Why do you assume something's wrong?"

"Because you told me you didn't want to see me again until hell froze over. It's eighty-five in the shade here. I doubt hell's any cooler."

Her gaze fell and her cheeks flushed peach. "I'm sorry I said that. I was hurting."

"We all were." Hell, he'd lost his best friend of twenty years. She hadn't known Rick nearly as long.

"Right." She perched on the edge of a bench seat.

He sat opposite her and waited, watching her pick at the table's rough surface with a short fingernail. Her wedding rings sparkled in the sun. Rick had been gone five years this week, and she still wore the set Brandon had helped his buddy pick out. She tucked a wispy lock behind her ear—all the while refusing to make eye contact. Whatever she had to say, it must be big to require this much courage. But a decade of practicing interrogation had taught him the value of silence and patience.

She swallowed, then her worried brown eyes found his. "Something's wrong with Mason."

Concern jolted through him. "Have you seen a doctor?"

"He's not sick. It's his behavior."

"What do you mean?"

"He's back-chatting, saying things he shouldn't. And he's become increasingly defiant."

"Mason's ten. Puberty's knocking. With hormones come attitude."

Her shoulders slumped. She shook her head. "He was such a good boy until…" She took a deep breath then blew it out again, fluttering her bangs. One lock tangled in her long eyelashes and he had to stifle the sudden urge to brush it away.

"He's been in trouble at school."

"What kind of trouble?"

Her cheeks darkened again. "He made inappropriate comments to other students."

"Kids talk junk, Hannah. Nothing unusual in that." He and his friends sure had.

"No." She glanced over each shoulder then leaned forward. "His comments were…sexual and crude. I don't even know where he heard the words he used. Definitely not from me."

"Movies? Internet?"

She shook her head. "I don't have cable TV and I'm very careful about what I allow him to watch, and I always supervise his internet time."

All good. "What about from the men you date?"

"I don't date!"

Her shock at his question seemed genuine, and the rings would be off-putting to most guys. How long would it take for Hannah to move on? He hated to think Rick would be replaced, but Hannah was attractive, in great shape and only thirty. It was inevitable.

"He probably has a girlfriend."

"He's ten!"

"They start early these days, Hannah."

Her gaze bounced to his then volleyed away again. She bit her lip. "I don't think it's a girl."

"What makes you so sure?"

"Because if I didn't make him do so he'd never brush his teeth, shower or change his clothes."

"Good point. Discovering girls would encourage him to improve his hygiene, and care about his appearance. Have you spoken to his teachers or the school counselor?"

"Yes. They don't have any idea of the cause. But… Brandon, they're threatening to expel him if he doesn't straighten up and I can't… I can't guarantee that he will. He's a handful. Even for me."

"Have you asked him about sexual abuse?"

She flinched. "Yes. I did. It was an…awkward conversation. He swears no one has touched him inappropriately. And I don't know where it could have happened…if it had. I don't leave him unattended or let him go anywhere that I haven't thoroughly checked out."

"There's always church and day care."

"Both places have excellent reputations, and there are always two adults in the rooms."

"If this has been going on for a while, why are

you calling me *now*, Hannah? What aren't you telling me?"

She swallowed, inhaled and glanced around again. "You can't say anything about this to anyone. Okay? It could…cause problems." He nodded, knowing if a crime had been committed he'd break the promise. "Mason tried to sneak out Wednesday night."

That could be cause for alarm, but it could also just be Mason acting like an adolescent. "I snuck out plenty of times as a kid—usually to go somewhere with Rick. What did he have with him?"

"His backpack."

"What was in it?"

She blinked. "I don't know."

"Didn't you look?"

"No. That's a violation of privacy."

"You're his parent, not his pal. Privacy is a privilege that must be earned." Or so his parents always claimed.

"I disagree. To teach respect you must show it."

"When he's thirty. Right now he's a kid with problems. You have probable cause and the right to search."

"You sound like a cop."

"Because I am one. Either you want my help or you don't."

She tipped her head back to stare at the dense leaf canopy. Then she swallowed and met his gaze. "Do you know how hard it was for me to call you? I wouldn't have if I'd had anyone else."

Regret twisted through him at the agony on her face. Talking to Hannah had once been almost as easy as talking to one of his sisters. She'd always been smart, informed and funny. "What about your dad or Rick's parents?"

Her mother had never been part of the picture. Rick hadn't told Brandon why.

"Dad's stationed in Italy right now. He's too far away to visit us more than once a year, and our parenting views...differ. Rick's parents think I'm a horrible mother. They fuss continually because my kids are 'ill-mannered and don't respect others' property.' Once a month we visit them or they come here, but...it's not a good relationship no matter how hard I try to fix it."

Some things never changed. On his few visits to Rick's house he'd learned not to touch anything. "I take it their house is still full of priceless collectibles?"

"Yes. In the Leiths' eyes I don't do anything right, and neither do my kids. Mason and Belle hate visiting them. But I want them to know their grandparents. I always lived too far away to see mine, and then they were gone and it was too late."

"What you're saying is, Rick's parents are still uptight pains in the ass?"

She grimaced. "Pretty much. They keep push-

ing me to move closer so they can watch the kids
when they're not in school. What they really want
to do is 'fix them.' But I don't want to leave our
home."

Her gaze bounced away. He waited, suspect-
ing the speech she was formulating in her mind
would be the core reason she'd called him.

Worry-clouded eyes found his. "The Leiths
miss their son, and they're clinging to my children as a replacement—especially Mrs. Leith.
When she heard about Mason's troubles at school
she insisted her precious Richard had never had
behavior issues, and if Mason did it had to be my
fault. She's threatened to 'call in a professional.' I
don't know if she means a psychologist or social
services, but neither would be good. Like you, she
assumed I was bringing unsuitable men into the
house, and when I assured her I wasn't, she said
he had to be learning his filthy language from
me. Which, she went on to tell me, made me an
unfit parent."

"She was always a vengeful bitch."

She'd tried to get Brandon fired after Rick's
death and throughout the follow-up investigation.
Because of the Leiths' clout with South Carolina's movers and shakers, it had been a serious
threat. He'd had to deal not only with his grief
over losing his best friend and the threat of losing the job he loved, but also second-guessing

his judgment because he'd let Rick talk him out of following protocol.

"I'm a good parent, Brandon. I do my best to provide for my children. I never leave them unsupervised, and I send them to the best after-school program I can afford. But I saw a friend who was an excellent parent lose custody of her children when her ex-husband manufactured things. What he accused her of wasn't true, but it cast enough doubt for her to end up with supervised visitation only. Like the Leiths, he's loaded and connected, and like me, my friend doesn't have the money to fight. I'm trying to give the Leiths as much access to the grandchildren as I can to keep them happy, but I'm afraid of what Rick's mom can do with the ammunition Mason is unwittingly giving her."

The fear in her eyes was genuine, and he understood her concern. He'd seen exactly what she described—great parents losing custody. "Hannah, I witnessed the way you 'mothered' for your first five years of parenthood. If that hasn't changed, there's no way you could be considered a bad parent."

"Thank you for saying that. But I can't risk it. In her grief Mrs. Leith doesn't always…think rationally. And her friends have clout. I don't."

Being a single parent with no backup had to be hard. His family was close. He had his mom and dad, two sisters and two brothers-in-law he could call on at any time for anything. Not that he had ever asked for help, but he knew they'd be there for him if he did—the same way he'd be there for them. No questions asked. He would have been that for Hannah and her kids—if she had let him. Maybe it wasn't too late. Which brought him back to the problem at hand.

"Was Mason running away?"

"He claims he was going to study with a friend."

"But you don't believe him?"

She worried her bottom lip with her teeth and took another one of those breast-swelling breaths. He jacked his gaze north. "No. It was an hour after bedtime. Mason doesn't make friends easily. And he refuses to tell me this supposed one's name or where he lives. I've asked his teachers, and none know of any new friends he's made."

Rick hadn't made friends easily, either. He'd been a late-in-life, surprise baby. The Leiths hadn't known what to do with the child they'd brought home from the hospital or how to interact with the brilliant boy he'd become. They'd raised him to be a little adult. Seen and not heard and all that crap.

And then Brandon had come along. He'd intervened on the first day of second grade when one of the fifth graders on the bus had tried to bully the prissy new kid on their route—Rick. Brandon had given the bully a bloody nose and gained a loyal friend. Rick had become Brandon's sidekick. He'd visited the Martins' orchard every time

Rick's workaholic parents had let him. Out in the peach groves Rick had learned how to be a kid, how to climb trees, get dirty and make noise—all the stuff he wasn't allowed to do at home. And Brandon had made sure his geeky buddy learned to defend himself.

Rick should have been here to teach those same lessons to his son. But he wasn't. And if Brandon had done things differently that day— He pushed aside the familiar weight settling on his chest.

"I'd offer to speak to the Leiths for you, but I'm not high on their good list, either." They blamed Brandon for turning their brilliant son away from a safe and lucrative, white-collar law career toward a dangerous, low-paying blue-collar law enforcement job. Mrs. Leith had said that if not for Brandon, her son would have gone to college and graduate school and he'd still be alive.

"I don't think they like many people. But they do love my children…in their own peculiar way."

"What do you want me to do, Hannah?"

"I need you to talk to Mason—unofficially, of course—and see if you can figure out what's going on."

Brandon leaned back. Here it was. The opportunity to fulfill his promise to Rick—to watch out for Rick's family. But he was ill-equipped for the job. What if he failed? "Hannah, I know almost nothing about kids."

"You're my son's godfather. You have to help."

Guilt torqued through him. He'd been a lousy godparent. Out of respect for Hannah he'd stayed out of sight and kept tabs on Rick's family from a distance. "How?"

"Come to dinner tomorrow—unless you have a date—and see if you can figure out what's going on with him."

The desperation in her face hit him hard—but not as hard as the jab about a date. Saturday night, and he'd be home alone. Again. He'd yet to find a woman he found more interesting than work. Sure, he dated. But not often. He was tired of the whole game. He met a woman. She pretended to be someone she wasn't and swore she didn't mind the danger of his job and didn't want kids. Then her true colors seeped through.

"Please, Brandon."

There was probably nothing wrong with the boy that some tough love wouldn't cure. "I'll be there."

He'd never live up to the gratitude in her eyes. But he had to at least try. He owed Rick that much.

HANNAH'S GARAGE GUTTER was sagging again. Brandon cursed and slowed his truck a hundred yards from the house Saturday evening. The fascia board behind the gutter, and possibly one or more rafters, would have to be replaced, but that meant removing the old ones, painting the new ones and getting it all reassembled without getting caught.

After Hannah had ordered him to stay away from her and her family and refused multiple offers of help from other officers from SLED, Brandon had covertly organized a team of Rick's coworkers. He and the guys were limited to working the one weekend a month when Hannah and the kids went out of town. That made complicated, multistep projects difficult to complete without getting caught.

Their clandestine activities were aided by the fact that her three-acre lot was heavily wooded, concealing the house on all sides from her neighbors, and those neighbors were the kind who minded their own business.

Privacy had been Rick's primary reason for choosing the fixer-upper in an older area, although he had planned to clear out more trees to make a bigger lawn for the kids to play on. But he hadn't lived long enough to finish that project or many of the others on his long list. Brandon kept the small patch of grass in the front yard weeded and fertilized, but he couldn't do much more without revealing the team's secret work.

He parked beneath the basketball goal "Santa" had left last Christmas then scanned the house as he traversed the walk, noting the white clapboard siding was still clean from the last pressure washing, and the shutters still looked good, too. He climbed the stairs to the small porch and pushed the button. A bell chimed inside. Seconds later the door opened. A miniature version of Hannah with big blue eyes—Rick's eyes—stared up at him and regret gnawed his gut. Rick would never get to see how much his baby girl had grown.

The heavy humid air clogged Brandon's throat. He cleared it. "Hello, Belle. I'm Brandon. Your mom's expecting me."

A rustle of movement behind her preceded Hannah's appearance. She looked flustered. Color tinted her cheeks and upper chest. She opened the door wider, revealing an outfit identical to her daughter's short denim skirt, pink T-shirt and sparkly sandals. But Hannah wasn't shaped like a six-year-old. Her curves rounded out her clothing nicely, and her legs—

Eyes north, dumbass. "Hey."

"Hi. Belle, Officer Martin is joining us for dinner. He's the one you set the extra plate for."

"Did you know my daddy? He was an occifer, too."

"Your dad was my best friend. We grew up together. We met when we were just a little older than you."

"I have a best friend. Her name is Sydney. She sits beside me at school. Mommy packs extra snacks for Sydney because her family can't 'ford them and the Bible says we hafta share with those less fort'nate."

He—a master interrogator—had no idea what to say. He glanced at Hannah. Pride and love for her daughter glistened in her eyes. "That's uh… nice," was all he could muster.

"Let's see if Mason remembers Brandon, Belle."

Rick's little girl curled her fingers trustingly around Brandon's then she pulled him inside, towing him across the scarred hardwood floor that Rick had once planned to refinish. A strange feeling, similar to the sixth sense that prickled up his spine before a dangerous encounter, crawled over him. But there was nothing to fear from this house, Hannah or her children. He attributed the weirdness to the fact that he hadn't been inside since before Rick's death, and being here now without his buddy felt wrong somehow.

From the moment Hannah had laid eyes on the place she'd wanted it, and with Brandon's help, she'd sold Rick on the idea of turning the old house into a dream home for him and the big family the two of them had planned to have.

The foyer was clean but worn. A dark wood intricately carved banister curved upward. Rick had wanted to paint it all white. Correction: he had wanted to con Brandon into doing it or pay someone else to. Rick hadn't been much on manual labor. He'd been more of an egghead who could visualize the most efficient way for others to implement his plan unless it was a computer program. With those he'd been a tireless genius at building them or picking them apart.

But Brandon had been tied up with his first rental property and couldn't help, and hiring someone required cash—something cops didn't have a surplus of. Which meant that jobs had to be prioritized and spread out. So Rick had drawn up a five-year renovation plan and been killed two years into it.

Belle released his hand to grab a toy pony. "This is Molly. I'm going to have a horsey like her when I get big."

"I like horses, too. We have them in the orchard where I grew up. Your dad and I used to race them between the trees."

"Daddy could ride?"

"Yeah. I taught him how."

Brandon spotted a dark-haired boy sitting at a desk in the den, staring into a laptop. He didn't turn when they entered.

"Mason, come and meet Officer Martin."

The kid jumped, then punched buttons and quickly shut down the computer. Too quickly? He twisted their way and *déjà vu* hit Brandon hard, hurling him back to his childhood. Mason was a miniature Rick. Those familiar blue eyes were wary. The cop in Brandon immediately asked why and if it was related to his school issues? But he dismissed the questions. Hannah had introduced him as an officer and a lot of people were uncomfortable around cops.

Brandon crossed the room and stuck out his hand. "Mason, you probably don't remember me. I'm Brandon, a friend of your dad's."

Mason showed no sign of recognition. His expression soured. "My dad's dead."

Brandon suppressed a flinch at the inevitable stab of pain. "I know. I'm sorry."

He was sorry in more ways than the boy would ever know.

Hannah cleared her throat. "Mason."

"Nice to meet you, sir," Mason added at the prompt and shook Brandon's hand.

"Your dad was good with computers. What do you like to do on them?"

The kid froze then snatched his hand back. His gaze slid left. "Nothing. Just look at stuff."

That warning prickle intensified. "What kind of stuff?"

Mason swallowed and shrugged. He focused on a point beyond Brandon's ear.

"Games? Instant messaging? Chat rooms?" Brandon prompted, endeavoring to keep his tone friendly and casual, but red flags were flapping wildly in his subconscious.

Mason shook his head vigorously. "Mom doesn't allow any of that. It's just research. For papers I have to write."

Hannah patted her son's shoulder. "Mason's in the accelerated Language Arts class."

"Your dad was smart in Language Arts. He really liked to read. Sometimes he helped me with book reports."

The kid rolled his eyes. "Is dinner ready? I'm starving."

Hannah opened her mouth as if to protest her son's rudeness, but Brandon caught her gaze and shook his head. No point in alienating someone he was here to study. "I'm hungry, too. Lead the way."

Hannah's expression turned apologetic. "I hope you don't mind baked spaghetti. It's one of the few things my picky eaters like."

"Sounds good." He stopped on the threshold of the dining room. The once dark walls and wainscoting gleamed white. "You painted in here."

"We're working our way through the list, slowly, but surely."

"We're going to paint my room 'morrow," mini Hannah chirped.

Brandon heard opportunity knocking. "Oh yeah? Maybe I can help. I like to paint."

He glanced at Hannah for confirmation. She nodded.

"I'll be here first thing in the morning."

Hannah shook her head. "We won't get home from church until 12:30."

"I'll be here when you get home."

"Don't you go to church, Occifer Brandon?"

Was the half-pint channeling his mother? "I'm usually working. But tomorrow I'm off. And I can't think of a better way to spend the day than painting with you."

Belle beamed. Hannah and Mason looked less than thrilled. But Hannah had asked for his help, and she was going to get it.

CHAPTER TWO

HANNAH WAS HAPPY to see the end of the meal. Belle had chattered almost nonstop, but that hadn't been enough to cover Mason's monosyllabic responses to Brandon's questions. Even though Brandon had appeared relaxed, Hannah doubted he'd missed her son's rudeness, and she was sure she'd hear about it—the same way she heard about it from her in-laws—as soon as they left the table.

"Mason, go take your shower. Belle, pick out your pajamas and a book."

The children left the room, Belle skipping, Mason moving at a slower, rebellious pace. Hannah missed the days when they both raced up the stairs like a thundering herd and all she had to worry about was one of them falling and getting hurt.

After the footsteps faded Brandon hit her with a somber look across the table. "He wasn't thrilled to have me here."

Hannah bolted to her feet and started stacking dishes. "It takes him a while to warm up to strangers. Just like his father. But I really appreciate your efforts to draw him out." When Brandon rose and grabbed what she couldn't carry she protested, "You don't have to do that."

"In my house, if you eat, you clean." He followed her into the galley-style kitchen and set his load in the sink.

She hadn't had a man in this room since Rick's death. And even then, preparing the meal and cleaning up afterward had been her job while Rick had played with the children or watched TV. Brandon's shoulders were broader than Rick's had been, and he took up more space. His presence made her feel claustrophobic in the narrow area between the counters.

Brandon rinsed a dish and offered it to her. She jumped into action. Her hip bumped his as she bent to open the dishwasher, and her pulse blipped erratically. Nerves over what his take on Mason's attitude might be. That was all it was. She was certain.

"Brandon, I'm sorry, but until I renovate this kitchen there's only room for one of us in here, so…if you don't mind…"

He scanned the room. "I forgot you wanted to knock out some walls."

"Just that one." She pointed to the wall dividing the den and kitchen.

"Did Rick ever get that structural engineer's report he talked about?"

"Yes, but kitchens are expensive projects, so

it's pretty far down the list." And now it was off it completely because one salary would never be enough to cover the cost.

"Could I see the report?"

She sighed. If it would get him out of the way, she'd give it to him. Crossing to the built-in desk, which she rarely used, she opened the file drawer, flipped through the folders and extracted the file.

"You're still organized, I see."

"Yes. Here you go."

"Thanks. I'll read it after I take a look at the computer."

Anxiety burned in her chest. "You won't find anything. Like I told you, I have all kinds of parental controls on it, and—"

"Then you don't have anything to worry about." He retrieved the laptop from the den and brought it to the kitchen table then pushed a button and the machine hummed to life. "Do each of you have separate log-ins?"

"Yes. That way the programs we use are on the desktop and my bill paying is out of the kids' reach."

"Do you ever sign in as Mason to see which sites he visits?"

"No. I trust him." She didn't need to see Brandon's lips compressing to know he didn't like her answer—especially given she'd demanded his help. "I don't know his password."

"No problem." Long fingers moved rapidly over the keyboard.

She rinsed the remaining dishes and loaded the dishwasher, trying hard to ignore him clicking away. What if he found something? If she confronted Mason with it he'd know she'd gone behind his back and invaded his privacy. How would he react? The way her mother had? She tamped down the fear. Brandon wouldn't find anything on the computer. She was too proactive for that.

"I'm in," Brandon stated.

She stilled, water dripping from her hands into the sink. "How did you get in without his password?"

"I signed in as the administrator." He looked back at the screen then frowned. "Mason's history has been deleted. Did you show him how to do that?"

Her anxiety level climbed. "No. Maybe the computer is set to automatically delete the browsing history?"

Click. Click. Click. "His account is." More taps. "Neither yours nor Belle's is. It's not the computer's default. If you didn't set it up this way, then Mason did."

"But why…?"

"Exactly."

Acid burned the base of her esophagus. She dried her hands. "I…could ask him."

But if she did, then he'd know she was spying

on him. And spying on someone was a violation of trust that couldn't be forgiven or forgotten.

"You think he'd tell you the truth?"

"Yes."

"Your hesitation says differently. Hannah, he's a kid doing something he wants hidden. Let me talk to him."

"No! I don't want you interrogating him like a criminal. He's a little boy."

His jaw shifted. "Then let me take the computer with me so that I can find out what sites he's been visiting. I'll bring it back tomorrow."

"That's spying."

"That's parenting. If you want to know what's driving his behavior and you won't let me take the computer, then at least let me install some software that'll track his activity. He'll never know it's there."

Fear tightened her chest. "I'm not violating his trust like that."

He shut down the computer, set it aside and stood. In three strides he was by her side. Close. Too close. She had to tip back her head to look at him. He wasn't as tall as Rick, but he was... imposing in his breadth. Dark evening stubble shadowed his jaw and his eyes were...intent. She shuffled backward and nearly tripped over the open dishwasher door.

He reached out, but she caught herself and held up her hands before he made contact. "I'm fine."

"Hannah, I can't help you if you won't let me. Mason is probably nothing more than a curious boy looking at porn, and he's picked up some of the language. But it could be more. And software is the easiest way to find out what's going on."

"You're just paranoid because of your job chasing cyber criminals. But my son isn't a criminal." Then another thought dried her mouth. "He won't be able to tell you logged in as him, will he?"

"No. Think about a tracking program. It's your best bet."

"No software. I want you to promise me you won't do anything to violate his trust."

Frustration radiated from him, pleating his brows and making his shoulder muscles bunch. "Hannah, we've covered this."

"Promise me, Brandon. I want Mason to feel he can come to me with anything, and if I go behind his back he won't feel that way." She saw opposition in his face. "If you can't make that promise, then leave and don't come back. I have enough problems with the Leiths trying to undermine me. I don't need you doing the same."

A muscle ticked in his jaw. "Fine, I agree. But only as long as I don't think he's in danger or a crime's being committed. If I suspect either of those, then I'll do whatever it takes to keep your son safe. I owe Rick that."

Mason wasn't committing a crime. As his mother, she'd know if he was. Brandon's half promise wasn't the unconditional one she wanted, but it would have to do. "Okay."

"I'll see you tomorrow. And while I'm here I'm going to check out the gutter over your garage. It's sagging and it needs to be repaired before you have water damage."

He swung around and left the kitchen before she could protest. The old adage "give 'em an inch and they'll take a mile" came to mind. She'd invited Brandon back into her life. She hoped she didn't regret it.

BRANDON RETURNED HIS ladder to the bed of his truck on Sunday morning. He had come over early to work on Hannah's gutter. As he'd suspected, the gutter repair was going to involve more than hammering a couple of nails. Good thing he'd gone ahead and brought the necessary materials.

He bent to check his face in the side mirror and winced. The mug reflected back at him wouldn't win any beauty contests. His right eye was swollen almost shut, his upper lip looked ready to burst and an assortment of other bulges puffed out his cheeks and chin. He gingerly touched the worst spot beneath his eye and swore. It hurt. Hell, his whole face hurt. But a promise was a promise. He hoped he didn't scare Belle.

He checked his watch. Hannah should be home from church any minute. As if on cue, her minivan came up the driveway. Hannah parked outside the garage. Mason bailed out of the side door, scowled in Brandon's direction then did a double take and smirked. "How bad does the other guy look?"

The kid thought he'd been in a fight. He decided to play along. "There were about fifty of them. And *I'm* still standing."

The boy's mouth dropped open and his eyes widened.

Hannah stopped as she rounded the hood, a horrified look on her face. A flowery sleeveless dress fluttered above her knees, displaying long, tanned legs. She looked good. Really good. He squashed that thought and noted that Belle wore an identical dress.

"Fifty yellow jackets," he elaborated. "They nest in the ground. I ran over their hole this morning with my lawn mower."

Belle tugged his hand and pointed at his face. "Does it hurt?"

He wasn't going to lie. "Yeah. But not as bad as it looks."

Hannah moved closer, concern puckering her forehead. "Have you removed the stingers?"

"The ones I could reach."

"You have more?"

"Some of the bast—*buggers* got in my shirt."

"Have you taken an antihistamine or put anything on the wounds?"

"I didn't have anything but antiseptic."

"I have a first-aid kit. Come inside. I'll fix you up then you can go home."

"I promised to help paint, and I don't break promises." Except for the one he'd made to Rick. But he was righting that now. Hannah had reopened the door. He wouldn't let her close it again.

"I don't think you should exert yourself."

"I'm fine, Hannah. I'm not allergic. Just ugly."

"Did you pour gas in the hole and set it on fire?" Mason asked, his eyes gleaming with excitement.

Was Mason a firebug? That would suggest even bigger problems. "No. You have to do night ops to kill yellow jackets."

"How come?"

"Yellow jackets return to their nest at dusk. After dark they can't see as well and they're less likely to attack. I'll hit all of them at once with chemicals that'll fog them to death."

"Can I watch?"

Bloodthirsty little rascal.

"No," Hannah replied before Brandon could. "It's a school night." Ignoring Mason's "*Moooom*," she swung her gaze to Brandon. "Come inside." He followed her in. "Wait in the den. I'll get the first-aid kit. Mason, stay with Brandon and watch for…anything unusual. Belle, put on the painting clothes I laid out for you." Hannah left. Two sets of footsteps ascended the stairs.

Mason studied Brandon's face as if he'd never

seen anything like it before. "There are bites all over. You look like you've been beaten up."

"You ever been in a fight?"

The boy's expression turned defensive, cagey, putting Brandon on alert. "Maybe. You're not going to like, die or something if I leave the room, are you? I'm hungry. I need a sandwich."

"Go ahead. If I was going to drop dead from anaphylaxis I'd have done it by now."

Mason headed for the kitchen. His actions confirming what Brandon suspected. The boy was evading providing a direct response. So Brandon followed him and leaned against the doorjamb. "Do you know how to defend yourself, Mason?"

Wary blue eyes whipped his way. "Why?"

"Because your dad didn't. I had to teach him."

"Why?" he repeated and grabbed a loaf of bread and a jar of jelly from the fridge.

"He was having trouble with a bully. I don't like bullies."

Mason paused with his knife above the peanut butter jar while he mulled that over. "Would you teach me to fight?"

"To fight? No. To defend yourself? Sure. There's a big difference in the two. Hand-to-hand combat is always a last resort for when you have no other choice. It's better to walk away if you can."

The answer earned him an eye roll. Mason returned to assembling his sandwich. "You're only saying that cuz you're a cop. I'd be called a pussy if I ran."

"Name-calling doesn't break bones but fighting can. I'm saying it because you're built like your dad. Not a lot of muscle yet. I don't want you to get your butt kicked or to get suspended from school. You'll have to use your brain instead of brawn."

Another eye roll.

Hannah returned with a small box. She took in the situation. "Did you offer Brandon a sandwich?"

"Want one?" Mason asked with his mouth full.

"No, thanks. I ate before I came over."

Hannah aimed a dark look at her son for talking while chewing, then turned to Brandon. "Pills or cream? I'd recommend both."

Brandon recognized the pink bottle she displayed. "Antihistamines knock me out. I'll stick with the topical."

"Take off your shirt and have a seat." He did as directed then sat at the table. By the time he had his shirt fabric bunched in his hands, she'd set down the box and held a playing card. Her gaze ran over him. She blinked, hesitated, then licked her lips. He caught himself watching her pink tongue and mentally kicked himself.

"Where are the ones you couldn't reach?"

"Back." The word came out gruffer than intended. She whirled a finger, signaling him to turn.

He twisted in the chair. "There are three and two stingers are still in."

He felt the rasp of the card across the first bump, then the second. A moment later the coolness of the cream hit his inflamed skin, accompanied by a twinge of pain caused by the light pressure of her touch. Then the warmth and slow caress of her fingertip registered.

"Turn around," she ordered before he could figure out what was causing him to have difficulty breathing. Was he having a delayed reaction to the venom?

He turned and found himself at chest level. The neckline of Hannah's sundress dipped low enough to reveal smooth skin and a fine gold chain that disappeared between her breasts. His lungs locked. He swallowed—*hard*—then closed his eyes and forced a breath into his tight chest. Her scent, combined with a hint of flowers, filled his nostrils. His mouth dried. He opened his eyes and searched for safer territory. He spotted a quarter-inch thread standing out from the seam of her dress on her left shoulder and fixated on it. But then his mind took an unexpected detour. *What would happen if he pulled that thread? Would the dress fall from her shoulder?*

"You're lucky you're not allergic. With this many stings this could have been a life-threatening situation."

His attention lasered in on the gentle stroke

of her finger on the thin skin beneath his eye, then she moved on to the sting on his cheekbone, smoothing small circles over the puffy flesh. His pulse jackhammered with near-deafening force against his eardrums.

Delayed reaction to the venom.

She rubbed the lump beneath his earlobe and the one under his chin, and his respirations shallowed and quickened. The pressure descended from his chest to his groin. What in the hell was wrong with him? This was Hannah. *Rick's Hannah.* And getting a woody in response to her was unacceptable. But there it was, straining against his zipper. He held out his hand to take the tube from her.

Ignoring his silent request she squeezed out more cream. "Sit still, Brandon."

He gritted his teeth against the pleasure/pain and gripped the T-shirt in his lap so tightly he'd probably imbed permanent wrinkles into the cotton. He hoped like hell Hannah didn't notice his condition.

She brushed the tender, swollen flesh of his upper lip and a lightning bolt of sensation shot south. He jerked out of reach, sucked in a sobering breath and snatched the tube from her hand. "I'll get the rest."

She stilled. "I'm sorry. Did I hurt you?"

What was that song lyric? *Hurt so good*? "No.

But we need to get painting. Put on your work clothes. I got this."

Looking as relieved as he felt, she stepped back. "Well…if you're sure. The guest bathroom is—" She shook her head. "You know where it is."

"Yeah. I do." His momma had raised him to stand whenever a lady entered or left the room. He did so, but he kept the T-shirt in front of his crotch until Hannah left.

What in the hell had just happened? And how could he make sure it didn't happen again? He mentally shook himself and caught Mason watching. "Put on your painting clothes, kid. After we knock out this job I'm going to wipe up the basketball court with you."

The kid glanced toward the den. "I need to work on my project."

"More online research?" The computer was in the den.

"Yeah."

If Hannah was going to paint upstairs and Mason was going to be on the computer downstairs, then the kid wasn't as supervised as Hannah thought. Brandon filed that away and went into the bathroom to treat the remaining stings.

Once that was done he climbed the stairs. As he reached the landing the spare bedroom door opened. Hannah, wearing a T-shirt that had seen better days, cut-off jeans a thread longer than indecent and sneakers, stepped out. She'd changed clothes. Behind her he spotted the dress she'd been wearing draped across the corner of the bed he'd slept on a few times when Rick's renovation projects had run late into the night.

He assembled the clues. "The master bedroom is downstairs."

Her gaze flicked away then returned—evasive, like her son's. "I can hear the children better up here."

"What happened to that fancy monitor I gave you when Belle was born? Camera, sound and the whole deal?"

She shifted, drawing his attention to her legs. He hoisted his gaze north. "I'd have to come up anyway if they needed me during the night. It's easier not to have to race up the stairs when I'm groggy."

She no longer slept in the downstairs master suite she'd shared with Rick. "When did the move take place?"

"Does it matter, Brandon? We have work to do. Belle's room will probably take several coats… unless you're not up to it."

A challenge to distract him. He recognized the technique but followed Hannah into Belle's room without comment. The six-year-old stood in front of an easel with a paint-by-number set attached. "What's that?"

"While we're painting the walls Belle will be creating artwork to hang on them."

"It's going to be a ballerina," the girl said and twirled, making her little plastic paint smock fan out. "Like me."

"I'm sure it'll look great." He turned his attention back to Hannah, who'd bent over to open a can of paint. The pose hiked her shorts up, revealing even more leg, and caused her shirt to gape. Her bra was pink. The knowledge paralyzed him.

"Honey, run down and eat your lunch. I left it in the refrigerator for you. You can paint when you're done."

Belle skipped off.

Brandon pulled himself together. "Mason says he's going to work on his project instead of helping."

"That's right. He has a paper due Friday."

"But you'll be up here."

Her eyebrows dipped. "Yes."

"That means he'll be unsupervised on the computer."

She bit her lip again then took a deep breath, stretching the worn-thin shirt. "Only for a little while. Your point?"

"You can't watch your kids one hundred percent of the time. No parent can. Let me install the software."

"No. Absolutely not. Do not bring it up again, Brandon. I'm going to grab a sandwich. You can get started or wait for me." Then like Mason, she walked away, deftly avoiding the conversation.

Which left Brandon back at ground zero. With nothing. He was certain the boy was up to something, but pushing would get him booted out and ruin any chance he had of keeping his promise to Rick.

CHAPTER THREE

HANNAH SWALLOWED THE last of her sandwich and tried to diagnose her reluctance to return upstairs.

Touching Brandon had been…unsettling. And that made no sense. As a physical therapy assistant she touched people all day, five days a week. She'd dealt with plenty of men as attractive, if not more so, than Brandon, but none of her patients had ever elicited a frantic pulse or the shakes.

Maybe her jitters had been caused by low blood sugar. She hadn't eaten since before Sunday school. And if that was the case, then she'd have no problem with him while they painted.

Satisfied with her explanation, she released a pent-up breath and directed her attention to her daughter. "You all set, sweetheart?"

Belle scrambled up from the table. "Yes, Mommy."

"Then let's go paint your room."

Together, she and her daughter climbed the stairs. Brandon had taped off the windows in their absence. When she met his hazel gaze her heart thumped an extra beat and her pulse kicked up. Then her hands started shaking. If it continued she wouldn't be able to paint straight lines along the ceiling and baseboards. She needed to give her blood sugar time to level out before attempting something that meticulous.

"I'll roll if you'll cut in," she suggested.

"Got it," he replied and positioned the stepladder in the far corner.

She took one final look around the room. The last time she'd decorated in here had been a month after Belle's birth. She and Rick hadn't wanted to know their baby's sex before delivery. That meant no personalization. Afterward, caring for two children with Rick's hectic schedule, not to mention their tight budget, had limited Hannah's decorating to hanging a border of pastel merry-go-round horses on the builder-beige walls. Now her baby girl wanted pink walls with ballerina pictures. That was no surprise considering she'd started dance classes this spring.

"Are you starting here?" Brandon stood beside her, one dark eyebrow cocked.

She startled over his proximity. How had he crossed the plastic drop cloth she'd spread on the floor after removing most of Belle's furniture so quietly? "Yes. I'll go clockwise if you'll go the opposite."

She winced when she looked at his face. He had to be hurting. Each time she'd touched him he'd flinched. When she'd finished he'd been one big knot of muscles. The professional side of her had wanted to massage the kinks loose, but the personal side of her had rejected the idea. He wasn't her patient.

Brandon was a trouper to work through the discomfort, and for that, she was grateful. But he had a point about Mason being on the computer. Under the guise of checking her email while she was downstairs, she'd ensured her parental controls were still in place before letting Mason have the laptop.

"You washed the walls after removing the border?" Brandon asked.

Of course he'd remember the border. He'd loaned her his level and shown her how to mark a straight line for hanging the paper. "Last week."

Brandon lifted the lids on each of the paint cans and poured all three into an empty five-gallon bucket. Nine years ago she'd messed up Mason's room because one of the batches of paint hadn't been mixed correctly. She'd ended up with a streaky mess of slightly different shades of the same color paint on the walls. After she'd bought replacements, Brandon had shown her the trick of mixing all the buckets beforehand to ensure a uniform result. It had been an expensive lesson— that was the only reason she recalled it so clearly.

His muscles bulged as he lifted the heavy bucket and carefully poured some of the pink liquid into a rolling pan for her and then a smaller pail for himself. The veins lining his hair-dusted forearms and biceps were a sign of his good muscle tone. He'd always been brawnier than Rick, and more adept at doing the physical stuff that this old house required. And he'd never been stingy with his time even though he had his own projects.

He expertly used his brush to catch any drips then looked up and caught her watching him. "You okay?"

She blinked and felt her cheeks warm. "Yes."

Why was she so focused on him? She had a job to do and a limited amount of time to get it done before the children needed attention. She slid a roller onto her handle and pushed it through the thick liquid and then onto the wall, but the mindless back and forth action wasn't enough to erase the realization that Brandon had been a part of every major project she and Rick had completed together on this old house.

Brandon had been the one who'd taught both her and Rick how to paint, build swing sets, plant shrubs and grass and to safely replace faulty outlets and faucets along with countless other chores. If Brandon hadn't known how to do it, he'd been the one to liaise with the contractors for them because he spoke their language. She and Rick would have been lost without him. They never could have taken on this house without him.

So even though she'd banned Brandon from their lives for five years, he'd been here all along, embedded into the walls and the soil around her home. But that didn't mean she could forgive him for not watching Rick's back—no matter what the preacher had said this morning.

"Mommy!" Belle's panicked cry almost made her drop the roller.

"What is it, baby?"

"I messed up. I painted the wrong color in the nine spot."

"It's okay. When it dries you can paint over it."

"But I want to do it now!"

Tired eyes filled with tears. Because they'd moved Belle's furniture yesterday, Belle had stayed in Hannah's bed last night. That meant her baby girl hadn't slept well and was cranky today.

Brandon descended the ladder to survey the disaster then cut his eyes Hannah's way. "If you'll get me a cotton swab I'll show you how to fix it."

Hannah hurried to retrieve one from her bathroom. Brandon took it. Their fingers brushed, and that unsettling sensation swept through her again. If her sudden agitation wasn't caused by low blood sugar, then what was it? The only other time she'd felt like this was when Rick had—

No. It was *not* desire. Not for Brandon. She staggered back a step—away from the man and the idea.

"You fixed it, Occifer Brandon!" Belle's excited cry yanked Hannah out of her unpleasant thoughts. Her daughter threw her arms around Brandon and hugged him.

Hannah blinked. She'd completely missed his magical fix. Her confusion must have shown in her face because Brandon winked and displayed the paint-stained cotton swab with a smile on his swollen lips. That smile/wink combo made Hannah's stomach flip.

"The acrylics are water-soluble. A little dab'll do ya'. Knock yourself out, kiddo." He ruffled Belle's hair and she beamed.

Hannah marveled at how good he was with her daughter. Not many single men would be. He returned to the ladder and Hannah's gaze followed, fixing on the muscles stretching denim as he climbed. She flushed hot all over and her palms moistened. Her tongue felt thick and dry, then panic quickened her heart as she acknowledged the undeniable. Her reaction to Brandon Martin was...*sexual*.

Her libido had been buried with Rick. It was a sick, cruel joke that her womanly needs had been resurrected by the man responsible for putting her husband in his grave. The one man she could never trust with her future because he'd already ruined her past.

BRANDON POINTED THE water hose at a paint tray and absently surveyed Hannah's backyard while he formulated a plan. He had to build a rapport with Mason if he wanted the boy to trust him enough to confide in him. Putting some distance between him and Hannah wasn't a bad idea, either.

Three hours confined to the same small room with her had totally screwed with his usual ability to block out distractions. He'd been aware of every move she made, every sigh and every sound. The only time he'd been able to relax was when she'd left the room to check on Mason. Even then he'd wanted to follow and observe her interaction with the boy to see if the kid was hiding something. But he was trying to respect the boundaries she'd marked.

He finished washing up the painting gear and debated going home. But he had a job to do, and cutting corners on an investigation had never been his way of dealing with complications. He stored the materials in the garage and reentered the house. He found Hannah in the den standing behind the sofa and reading the laptop screen over her son's shoulder.

"I need Mason for an hour."

She turned, a furrow between her brows. "For what?"

"To help me remove your sagging gutter then replace the fascia board and paint it."

"Do I have to?" Mason asked with a put-upon expression.

"If you help, you get to use my nail gun."

Mason perked up. "For real?"

"Yes."

"No," Hannah replied simultaneously and shot Brandon then Mason a dark look. "Nail guns are dangerous and you are not allowed on the roof."

"Mooooom."

Hannah ignored her son's protest and turned back to Brandon. "I don't have the board, and the building supply stores close early on Sunday. Maybe we should call it a night."

She wanted to get rid of him. Not happening. "I brought the materials with me, and Mason can do what I need from the ladder. No need to get on the roof. And I wouldn't let him use the nail gun if I couldn't teach him how to use it safely."

Reservations filled her eyes. "Brandon, I don't think that's a good idea."

"Hannah, he'll be fine. Trust me."

The corners of her lips turned down.

Belle tugged his hand. "What can I do, Occifer Brandon? I want to help, too."

He couldn't help but smile at those big, earnest eyes. "You can make sure we rehang the board straight when we get to that part."

Belle nodded enthusiastically. "I can do that."

He glanced at Hannah and caught a look of such unadulterated love in her eyes for her daughter that it made his chest ache. He'd seen the same look in Rick's eyes—like he thought his kids were miracles. Brandon had never felt that way about anyone and wasn't sure he wanted to. Seemed like keeping a door open for pain and disappointment to slip in. He shook off the negative thought.

"Whatdaya say, Mason? We're burning daylight."

The boy bounded off the sofa, ditching the laptop with no reservations. He wouldn't have done that if he had something on it to hide. He raced to the garage.

"Stay off the roof," Hannah called after him.

Brandon stepped closer to Hannah and bent his head so Belle wouldn't overhear. "You asked for my help, remember? Let me do what I do best."

"But—"

"The only way I'll get him to open up is by spending time with him and building a rapport."

She hesitated, then nodded.

Brandon tracked after Mason. When he reached the garage, the boy rolled his eyes. "She treats me like a baby."

"Get used to it, kid. I'm thirty-two and my mom still does the same thing."

"For real? But you're a cop."

"Moms only do it because they love us. And your mom has to be mother *and* father for you, so she's trying twice as hard to be a good parent. Cut her some slack. Let's get the gear from the truck."

When they reached his vehicle Brandon donned his tool belt then lowered his small compressor to the ground. He slung the hose over his shoulder and hefted the nail gun. He could carry everything himself, but he wanted Mason to feel as if he was part of the process. "Loop the extension cord across your shoulder like I did the hose and grab the other end of this board."

They carried their load to the garage and dumped it. "Now we need the ladders. I'll get one if you'll get the other."

Mason did so without argument. Together they set up on opposite sides of the open door. Brandon climbed the ladder. "I'm going to pull this end of the gutter down and lower it to you. Hold it and try not to let it crimp while I release each section. That way we can reuse it."

"If you were such good friends with my dad, why'd you quit coming around?" Mason asked while Brandon was trying to pry the first gutter spike free. The question jarred him so much that when the spike broke free suddenly he almost fell from his perch.

Did the boy not remember the funeral fiasco? Maybe not. He'd only been five. Brandon formulated an abbreviated version. He met Mason's gaze. "Because I remind your mom of your dad, and that hurts her. She asked me not to visit."

"Why'd you show up now?"

He couldn't tell the truth. Lying was a slippery slope. "Because I missed you."

"Well, don't get the idea I need a dad now. I've been fine without one."

The false bravado wasn't a surprise. He descended the ladder and handed Mason the end of the gutter. "I'm sure, as man of the house, you've had to be fine. I still have my dad. But he has a disease. I worry about losing him every day, and I can't imagine life without him. It must be tough."

"What's your dad got?"

"Parkinson's. It steals a little of his strength at a time. And eventually, it'll take him entirely. What's worse is that his mind is as sharp as ever, and he's aware of every inch of ground he's losing. I'm fortunate to have him, and I make sure he knows that."

He moved the ladder, climbed and repeated the process with each additional spike. Mason kept silent until Brandon removed the last one, then he blurted, "Have you ever shot anyone?"

A vision of the perp standing over Rick's body and the blood pools spreading across the floor flashed across his brain. The sudden pressure on Brandon's chest felt as if a beam had dropped on it. "Once. I try to avoid that."

"Are you scared to?"

That day he'd wanted to empty his clip into the guy who'd killed Rick. The only reason he'd managed to stop after one shot was because he wanted to see if Rick was still alive. "No. I value life—mine and others'—and my job. Shooting someone without cause jeopardizes both."

"Have you ever beat up anybody?"

Another tough answer, but truth often was.

"Yes. But never for the sport of it. When I've hit someone it's because I was defending myself or someone else. Again, fighting is—"

"I know, I know. A last resort. Jeez. I heard ya' the first time."

Brandon lowered the last end of the gutter and helped Mason carry it to the grass beside the driveway then stopped beside the boy. "Is there someone you think needs beating up *now*?"

A darting glance was a telling glance. "Who, Mason?"

"Nobody."

"C'mon, everybody wants to pop someone sometime. Is a kid bothering you?" No answer.

"At school? On the bus?"

Mason hustled to the compressor. "Are you gonna show me how to use this thing or not?"

The refusal to answer was an answer. But the kid wasn't ready to talk. Brandon let it go and offered Mason a hammer. "We'll get to the power tools soon enough. First, we need to remove the rotten fascia board and check the rafters for decay. If we find any we'll have to cut the bad board away and sister on a good one."

"Huh?"

Success. Confuse the subject then offer assistance. Gaining trust, whether it was a suspect's or a boy's, was all about strategy. And Brandon had his mapped out. It wasn't the best or fastest option, but it was the only one Hannah's restrictions permitted.

"That's what your dad said the first time I asked for his help. I'll teach you what you need to know. Just like I taught him. But you have to listen, follow instructions and trust me. Then and only then will I let you use the saw and nail gun. Can you do that?"

The question was about far more than carpentry, but Mason wouldn't know that.

"Yeah, I guess."

Over the next hour Brandon guided Mason through replacing and repainting the rotten boards, with Belle's occasional input, and then he stood back. "Not bad for your first day wielding a nail gun."

Mason offered the first genuine smile Brandon had seen from him. "It was pretty cool. I'm hungry. You hungry?"

Progress. Mason was asking about his welfare. "I don't think your mom's expecting me for dinner. But let's ask her about me coming back later in the week to show you how to rehang the gutter."

"Okay." Mason hustled inside.

They found Hannah and Belle in the kitchen. The smell of bacon filled the air and Brandon's stomach grumbled.

Hannah glanced up from the frying pan, and the wariness in her eyes engaged his protective instincts. "Thank you for letting Belle hold the level. She's talked nonstop about it since she came in."

"No problem. She was a big help." He winked at Belle, making her giggle, then pulled out his phone and hit the calendar app. "If weather and my case load permit, I can come back Wednesday to finish the job."

Hannah shook her head. "We can't do Wednesday. Belle has dance lessons."

"Where does Mason go?"

"With us."

"To dance lessons?"

"There's a quiet place for him to do his homework," she defended.

Poor kid. "Let me keep him here so he can help me with the gutter."

Hannah pulled one corner of her bottom lip into her mouth. It was a habit he'd noticed too many times today.

"Please, Mom? Brandon's teaching me to use his tools, and I really want to learn."

She looked surprised by Mason's enthusiasm. "Okay. But you have to promise to do your homework."

"I will. I swear."

Her gaze swung back to Brandon. "Do you um…want to stay for supper? It's breakfast night. We're having bacon, eggs and pancakes."

Hannah's forced smile couldn't hide her lack of eagerness for his company. And he couldn't blame her. He needed some time to get his head back on straight. "Thanks, but I'll have to take a rain check. I need to get a few things done before work tomorrow. See you Wednesday," he offered to the room in general.

Belle slid off her stool and rushed him. She wound her little arms around him and squeezed. "Thank you for painting my room, Occifer Brandon. It's bootiful."

"You're welcome. Your picture is going to be perfect on the wall." The urge to stay hit him hard. But he had to go. This wasn't his family. It was Rick's.

No matter how much he'd enjoyed spending the afternoon with Hannah and her children, there were too many risk factors attached to him. If his job didn't get him killed, he'd still have the cloud of Parkinson's hanging over his head.

Brandon had read extensively about the future his father faced as the disease progressed, and having loved ones wipe his butt was not in Brandon's plan.

He could never be a family man.

CHAPTER FOUR

BRANDON HAD SPENT Monday and Tuesday convincing himself that his out-of-line thoughts about Hannah had been a fluke. He arrived at her house Wednesday evening, determined to prove his point.

The front door opened. Belle, wearing a pink headband, leotard and tutu and her sparkly sandals, darted out toward him. She hurled herself at him. "Occifer Brandon!"

He swung her into the air then set her down. She weighed more than the twins, his four-year-old niece and nephew, but squealed the same. "Hey, kiddo. How's the room?"

"Prettiful!"

Her made up words were…cute. Mason stepped onto the porch. The sour expression he usually greeted Brandon with was absent. "Mom's inside. She's all in a tiz about leaving me here. Like you're gonna kill me or something."

"I'll try not to." Brandon fist-bumped Mason then followed the kids through the foyer to the den.

Hannah hustled around the room, gathering

her purse, a sweater and a tiny pair of dance slip-pers. The pink band in her hair matched Belle's, as did the shoes on her feet and the fitted T-shirt skimming her slender curves, but the resemblance ended there. A khaki skirt hugged Hannah's hips and revealed her long legs. There was nothing girlish about her figure.

The inappropriate reactions he'd hoped were a one-time deal shot through him like an Am-trak train. His heart *clickety-clacked* against his sternum, and adrenaline sped through his veins. *Déjà vu*. Damn.

She glanced up, spotted him and stopped. Her lips parted and her breasts rose with a quick in-halation. Color tinted her cheeks. "Hi."

"Sorry I'm late. Last-minute conference call."

"Thanks for texting and letting me know. We're still okay for time. Are you sure you don't mind staying with Mason?" Her words came out in a breathy rush—the kind that made him think of urgent middle-of-the-night whispers. And that was just *wrong*.

"Nah. I need his help. It's a two-man job."

Behind her back Mason gave him a thumbs-up. Teamwork. Progress.

"We usually grab dinner after dance lessons, but there's sandwich stuff if y'all get hungry be-fore I get home. Make yourself comfortable. If there's anything you need, anything at all... Except I don't think I have beer and I know I don't have anything stronger, but—"

"Hannah." He held up a hand to stop the flood of words. Despite what she'd said, she wasn't at ease giving him full run of her home. Her hit-and-run glances and the pink-painted toenails curling in her sandals revealed her agitation. "I'll get dinner for Mason and me, and I don't mix alcohol with power tools. Take your time. You and Belle should have a girls' night out dinner."

"Oh. Well… I don't know."

"Do it, Mom. Go to that dumb salad place," Mason encouraged. "You know…the one I hate and you love."

Smart. The kid was trying to get them some extra tool time.

"Okay then… I'll see you in a couple of hours." Her attention shifted to Mason. "Listen and behave." Then she hurried Belle out the door.

"You owe me, kid," Brandon said.

Mason's gaze turned wary. "For what?"

"For getting you out of going to dance with your sister."

"Oh yeah. Thanks." Mason scuffed his shoe on the floor. "Sisters suck."

"Not always. Wait until she starts learning to cook. You'll have more cookies and cakes from her experiments than you ever dreamed of, and most will be edible. Then when she's a teenager she'll bring home her friends. Pretty, datable girls, paraded right through your door. What's not to like?"

Mason's face turned red. "How do you know?"

"I have two sisters." He checked his watch. "I'm ordering a pizza. You interested?" The magic word could make most males smile.

"Pizza! Heck, yeah."

"Who delivers here?"

Mason shrugged. "We never get pizza delivered."

He couldn't have scripted a better answer. "Boot up your computer and let's look it up."

"Can't you do it on your phone?"

He'd anticipated the question. "It's easier to see a menu on a larger screen."

"Why do you need a menu for pizza?"

"Because I want to order more than just pizza. Hang with me, kid. I'll teach you a few things."

Mason bought his excuse and quickly logged on. The boy executed a search without any instructions from Brandon. Then he pivoted the screen for Brandon to see. "These are our choices."

Brandon pointed to a familiar name. "Your dad and I used to eat here. Food's good. It's not a chain. May I?"

At Mason's nod, Brandon reached across him and used the touchpad to open the restaurant's menu. "Large, all-meats okay with you?"

"Sounds great!" Mason said enthusiastically. "Whenever we get pizza we have to get plain cheese. That's all Belle will eat. And it's cheaper."

Brandon hated the idea of Hannah having to watch every penny. He deliberately closed the window and straightened, then stopped, feigning a puzzled expression. "Wait. Did the phone number end in two six or six two?"

"Uh... I don't know."

Brandon clicked on the arrow that would bring up the search history. As he'd expected, it came up blank. "The URL's not there."

Mason's fingers poised over the keys. "I can get the website back up."

"Is your computer set to delete histories?"

Tension invaded the boy's face and body. "Um...yeah."

"How do you know how to do that?"

Mason hunched over the keyboard, ducking his chin. "I learned at school. I have to take a computer class every year, and they make us erase our histories so the next class can't cheat and use our answers. So I do it at home. Out of habit. Because I do it every day at school. That's all. Nothing else. Just habit."

Plausible answer. But it didn't explain Mason's sudden wariness or why he'd used so many words and spoken so fast. Excessive explanations usually meant the subject had something to hide.

Mason found the page. Brandon dropped the subject. There was a time to press for more info and a time to ease up. If he didn't want Mason on the defensive, this was the latter. He dialed the number and placed the order for pizza and the garlic knots Hannah used to love.

"Pizza won't be here for forty minutes. Let's see if we can get the gutter hung before the rain or the pizza arrive."

Mason abandoned the computer easily and followed him outside. The lack of hesitation made Brandon question whether the computer was the root of the problem. No, there were too many clues implicating the device as a link.

The air was thick and heavy with a pending storm. They gathered the tools and set up in front of the garage. Brandon talked about anything but computers for half the job then asked, "You keep looking at the woods. Are you expecting company?"

Mason dropped his hammer. It clattered loudly down the aluminum rungs. "Ummm. No. I'm never here on Wednesday nights. Nobody would be looking for me."

The kid sounded a little defensive. Brandon searched for a neutral subject. "Right. Ballet. Do your mom and Belle always dress alike?"

Mason's face screwed up like he'd bitten into a lemon. "Yeah. Belle's idea. She loves it. I think it's stupid."

"It's kind of cute."

Mason faked a vomiting sound.

"Could be worse, bud. They could make you wear the same color."

"I'd shoot myself first."

"You have any guns in the house?" Rick had owned several.

"No. Jeez. It's just a sayin'."

Brandon held the level and waited for the boy to retrieve the hammer and get back into position. "Do you have any friends in this neighborhood? I didn't see bikes, toys or basketball goals in the other yards when I drove in."

"Nah. Only old people live on our street."

That shot down one theory. "What about behind you?"

Mason stiffened. "I don't know."

Looked like the friend he'd been going to study with wasn't fictitious. "I just wondered if you have anyone to shoot hoops with."

"Nah. Somebody left the net here one Christmas. Mom says it was Santa." The sarcasm in his voice and the accompanying eye roll silently voiced his opinion about that.

"Not buying that, huh?"

"No."

"You ever shoot?"

"Sometimes. I'm not very good."

"Your dad and I used to play together." Mason said nothing. Brandon let a few more minutes pass, then asked, "Do you like computers?"

"I guess."

"Your dad was good with them—probably the best I've ever known."

"Why do you keep talking about my dad?"

"Because he was my best friend for more than twenty years. More like a brother. He was a big part of my life. I miss him."

"Well, I don't even remember him, and he wasn't a big part of mine. So stop it. Okay? Pizza's here." Mason scrambled down the ladder and headed for the delivery vehicle just entering the driveway, ending the discussion.

It pained Brandon to hear that Mason didn't remember his father. Rick had been too great a guy to be forgotten—especially by his own son. Brandon resolved to find a way to rectify that situation. That meant he now had two assignments: figure out where Mason's bad behavior originated, and help him remember his father.

"I WAS ABOUT to call you," Lucy said when Hannah bustled Belle into the dance studio's waiting area. "You're never late."

Hannah checked her watch. "Hi, Lucy. We're not late, but we are cutting it close. Is Ella feeling better?"

"No. That stomach flu has knocked her out. She's staying with my mom while Celia gets her groove on."

Hannah glanced through the window overlooking the dance floor to Celia, Lucy's youngest. She'd worn her dress-up tiara tonight. Belle would be begging for one on the way home.

"I hope you and Celia don't come down with it." Then she turned to Belle. "Hurry and put on your slippers, sweetie. The other girls are already lined up."

Belle did as asked then dashed through the door and galloped across the room to the barre to greet her friend Celia. Hannah scooped up her daughter's sandals and sank onto the bleachers provided for parents. Her pulse was racing, but only because she'd been rushing and because she was having second thoughts about leaving Brandon in charge at her house. It had nothing to do with the man himself. Nothing at all.

Lucy scanned the room. "Where's Mason?"

"At home."

Red eyebrows shot skyward. "Alone? Given what's been going on, is that wise?"

Hannah took a long, calming breath. Aside from Brandon, Lucy was the only one who knew about Mason sneaking out. Her friend's question was understandable. "I left him with a former colleague of Rick's."

"A cop?"

"Yes."

"Then I guess Mason won't get into anything."

Hannah glanced around to make sure no one was listening. "Hope not."

"So who is this colleague?"

"Brandon Martin."

Lucy's green eyes and mouth rounded. "It's-his-fault, Brandon Martin?"

Hannah put a finger to her lips and nodded. She didn't want her business shared.

"I thought you hated his guts," Lucy whispered.

"*Hate* is a strong word." But accurate. For years she'd channeled all of her anger from grief toward Brandon. "He's Mason's godfather. And I didn't know who else to ask. He and Mason are fixing the sagging gutter over my garage door."

"Ooh. He's a handyman? Is he single?"

She shot Lucy a level look. "What does that have to do with anything?"

"If you're determined to keep your fixer-upper, you have to admit, you could use a man around."

"For repairs, yes. For anything else, no."

"But—"

"Even if I didn't hold him responsible for Rick's death, the fact that he's a cop makes him off-limits."

"That's only two strikes."

The third was that Brandon made her feel things. Womanly things. She would never let herself fall in love again. Falling meant landing—hard—when it ended. And sex…well, for her, love and sex went hand in hand. "This isn't baseball. Two strikes is enough."

"Girl, you don't know what you're missing."

Lucy was a single mom with an active social life. She fell in and out of love every few months and shared all the juicy details with Hannah. At first, the guy was Mr. Perfect and she'd extoll his virtues. Then she started to see his flaws and Hannah heard about those, too. She was convinced her friend was more in love with the idea of love than the practice of it. It seemed like she always wanted romance's version of new car smell.

"I'm not missing anything. I love my kids. I love my job. I love my house. Life is good."

"C'mon." She leaned closer. "Don't you miss sex?"

Embarrassed, Hannah again checked to see if any of the other parents were listening, but they were too engrossed in their cell phones to care.

"No." *Yes*. But it wasn't just the physical act she missed. It was all the rest: the companionship, the adult conversations, having someone who shared her hopes and dreams and understood her need to put down roots—deep roots. But no matter how great her relationship with Rick had been, nothing could fill the gaping hole his death had left behind. Her children had been too young to suffer much then. They weren't now, and she would never put them through the loving and losing hell she'd endured. Which meant that bringing a man in—one who might leave—was out of the question.

"But—"

"Lucy, watch the girls."

The peace lasted five minutes. "Maybe if you

did something at church besides volunteer for nursery duty you'd meet a guy."

"I know you find it hard to believe, but I'm not looking."

"Men with babies have wives," she continued as if Hannah hadn't spoken. "If you'd teach the older kids' class you could meet some single Christian dads who no longer have that wife attachment."

"News flash. I don't go to church to pick up men."

Lucy rolled her eyes. "Girl, you are blind to so many opportunities. Just think who you'd meet if Mason played sports."

"He doesn't like sports."

"Then sign him up for a scout troop or a science club."

Hannah stuck her fingers in her ears. "*La la la.*"

"Scoff if you want, but I'm worried about you. You spend too much time alone."

"I'm with people all day."

"I meant in your downtime." She paused briefly before her next question. "So, is Brandon attractive?"

Hannah's ears burned. She shot her friend an end-of-my-patience glare that would have silenced her children.

"That blush answers my question, but FYI, I meant for me, not you. I'm in the relationship Sahara right now. Invite me over after dance tonight. Introduce us."

"*No!*" Hannah spoke so loudly that the other mothers looked up from their gadgets. She didn't know why she felt so strongly against the introduction. "He's not your type. He doesn't go dancing or hang out in bars."

At least he hadn't back when he and Rick had been friends.

"He's a desk jockey?"

With that body? Not likely. "He's a cop who worked with Rick, remember?"

"Then he's my type. And who are we kidding? I'll consider any man who is relatively intelligent, gainfully employed and in decent shape."

The problem was, Lucy might do more than date Brandon. And then Hannah would have to hear about the physical side of their relationship in excruciating detail. No, thanks. She turned away from Lucy. "Oh look. They're practicing pirouettes. Aren't they adorable?"

She could feel Lucy watching her, but she didn't turn or do anything else to encourage the conversation. This class couldn't end soon enough. But once it did, she'd be going home to Brandon. *To Mason*, she hastily corrected. *To Mason*. Brandon was just a temporary affliction she must endure until she figured out what was going on with her son.

THE STORM THAT the day's humidity had promised broke loose on the drive home. As if she wasn't stressed enough about seeing Brandon again,

Hannah had to fight through almost zero visibility and pounding water on the roads, grabbing and pulling her tires. She needed new wiper blades and tires. Pushing that worry aside, she pulled into the garage, heaved a sigh of relief and wiggled her fingers. They were cramped from having a death grip on the wheel.

Belle sprang from the car and sprinted into the house. Her daughter ran everywhere. Where did she find the energy? Hannah followed more slowly, pausing a moment to register the lack of water falling over the open door before she pushed the button to close it. She passed through the laundry room and dropped her purse on the kitchen counter.

The aroma of Italian food assailed her, making her wish she'd eaten more than a salad after dance class. She hustled to the den where Belle was chattering nonstop and demonstrating the new steps she'd learned tonight for Mason and Brandon. Both males reclined on the couch with an open, empty pizza box on the coffee table. Mason was wearing different clothes now and looked like he'd had a shower.

Brandon's smiling gaze transferred from Belle to Hannah, and a surge of…something…shot through her. Relief that Mason looked relaxed and content instead of combative. That was all it was.

Brandon rose. "She's quite a talented ballerina."

"Yes," was the only thing Hannah could squeeze

out through her tight throat. Why did his smile and gentlemanly manners make it hard to breathe? Then she realized it was because his jeans were damp and clinging to his—*Ahem*.

"We saved some garlic knots for you. They're keeping warm in the oven," he said.

She looked at the box and recognized the familiar logo. Her stomach rumbled in anticipation and her mouth watered. "From Giuseppe's? I haven't eaten there in years."

He turned to Mason. "Your mom was bloodthirsty. She used to threaten me with bodily harm if I ate the last garlic knot."

The pressure in her chest increased. "That was a long time ago."

He shrugged. "They're as good as they used to be."

Mason perked up. "Brandon said we had to save the rest for you. But if you don't want 'em…" He started to rise.

"I do."

"Dang." Her son flopped back down, a picture of total dejection.

Brandon cut him a look. "How can you have room for more food?"

Mason grinned, looking so much like the sweet child she loved that it choked Hannah up all over again. "I'm a growing boy. And man, you worked me hard."

Which reminded her... "I see my gutter is fixed and draining properly."

"You should have been here, Mom. Right after we finished, a big bolt of lightning lit up the sky, then it thundered so loud it sounded like a bomb went off. The ladders rattled. We barely got the tools into Brandon's truck before the bottom fell out. We got soaked!"

That explained the shower and clean clothes. Her son's sullen attitude was gone. Brandon had managed a miracle. "Thank you for your work. Both of you."

"I put the wet towels in the washer," Brandon added. "Added to the stuff you already had in there, it was enough to run a load. So we did."

"The machine's pretty easy to work," her son, who had never done a load of laundry in his life, volunteered. "Brandon showed me how. And he says I can help him with more stuff if you'll give him a project list."

It took a moment for her brain to recover from the shock of her son being eager to do chores. "Um... I'll work on that."

She didn't want to be beholden to Brandon or have him hanging around her house or washing her clothes. Asking for help with Mason had been hard enough. And that was all she wanted from him. But how could she refuse when her son sounded so happy about being included? And then the guilt kicked in again. He needed a man's influence. And she couldn't give him that.

"Did you finish your homework?"

Mason's crestfallen expression revealed his answer before he mumbled, "Most of it. All I have left is math."

"Get to it."

He slouched out of the room. Thunder shook the house, drowning out the sound of Mason's heavy footsteps tromping up the stairs. The lights flickered.

Then because she couldn't handle more of Brandon's silent smiles she turned to her daughter. "Belle, you need to have your bath and get ready for bed. Go on up. I'll be there right after I see out our guest."

"But, Mom, can't Occifer Brandon tuck me in?"

"No."

"Sure," he replied simultaneously.

Hannah shook her head. She needed him gone. "You don't have to do that. I know you need to get ready for work tomorrow."

"I can stick around until after you give Belle her bath. A few more minutes won't kill me. It might even give the worst of the storm time to pass."

Suddenly, she felt mean for wanting to throw him out into the deluge. "You don't know what you're getting yourself into."

"I have a niece and nephew, twins who just turned four. I can handle reading a bedtime story."

"Yippee!" Belle charged upstairs before Hannah could come up with an excuse.

The lights blinked again and Brandon frowned. "Do you have frequent outages?"

"Enough."

"Where do you keep your flashlights? I'll get them out in case you lose power while you give the ballerina a bath."

"In the laundry room drawer, but I usually use the hurricane lamps on the mantel. Matches are with the flashlights. What did you find out from Mason?"

"Very little. Gathering info is a finesse job. It'll take time, but I'll get to the bottom of it. Do you know the families who live on the street behind you?"

"No. Why?"

"Mason kept checking the woods. I'll see what I can get on your neighbors."

"Why?"

"Just a hunch."

"What kind of a hunch?"

"Nothing concrete."

The lights went out before she could press for more. Belle cried, "Mommy!"

Brandon pulled his cell phone from his back pocket and hit the flashlight app. Hannah had left hers in her purse on the kitchen counter.

"Wait here. I'll get you a light." He left and returned a moment later with a box of matches. "Your flashlight batteries are dead. Do you have more?"

"Mason dropped the flashlight the night he tried to sneak out. I suspect it's the bulb."

After lighting the kerosene lamps, he handed her one. "Take care of Belle. You have city water and a gas water heater. She can still have her bath. I'll check on Mason."

Of course Brandon knew all the details about her house. He'd been a huge part of the purchase process. If not for him, she would never have been able to convince Rick to buy the old home she'd fallen in love with the moment she'd seen it. Brandon had been the one to shadow the inspector, and when Rick had been daunted by the amount of work the house needed, Brandon had pointed out that the previous owners had already done all the expensive renovations, leaving only cosmetic projects incomplete. He'd helped Rick make and prioritize the renovation list.

That Brandon had been such a huge part of their lives had made his failure to protect Rick even more difficult to comprehend.

They climbed the wide stairs side by side. Wind rattled the windows and whistled under the eaves. It was comforting to have someone else here to help with the weather this nasty. And that was crazy, because she'd handled every previous outage just fine by herself. She pushed that feeling aside, and on the landing, they went in opposite directions—her to her daughter, him to her son.

After giving Belle her bath and dressing her for bed, Hannah left the lamp on the table and headed for Mason's room. Brandon had one hip parked on the corner of her son's desk. Both he and Mason looked comfortable together. Even though she hadn't made a sound Brandon looked up. "He has Rick's head for numbers."

"Yes. He does. Belle has picked out her book. She's waiting for you. I'll take over here."

He rose and crossed the room. Their shoulders brushed as he passed, and static electricity zapped her, making her gasp. Brandon paused and their gazes met in the darkened room. The electricity between them had to be due to the storm. She hustled to Mason's side and settled in to check homework, but her thoughts were anything but settled. She kept listening for sounds from Belle's room.

Finally, Mason closed his book. "He's pretty cool. Brandon, I mean. I can see why Dad would have wanted to be his friend. He knows stuff."

She didn't want her son comparing the men and have Rick come up short. "Yes. He does. But your daddy did, too. He was smart in a different way."

"If you say so."

"I'm going to leave the light with you. Be careful. It's an open flame and fuel—"

"Moooom, I know!"

She returned to Belle's room but paused outside the door to listen as Brandon read a much-loved tale using different voices for each character. Undetected, she observed the reflection of the man and child in the bed via the mirror hanging over Belle's dresser.

Brandon was propped against the headboard, book in hand, looking as if he belonged there. His long legs, crossed at his ankles, were on top of the quilt revealing his sock-covered feet. Her daughter lay trustingly beside him with her folded hands beneath her cheek, eyes heavy lidded and close to sleep. A pang of yearning hit Hannah so hard it took her breath. Rick used to read in bed, and Hannah had often fallen asleep at his side.

How would it feel to be curled against Brandon's side as trustingly as Belle? She shook her head. Thoughts like that were disloyal to Rick. Her husband had never known the simple joy of reading stories to his daughter. He'd been killed on the eve of Belle's first birthday. Pain and regret rolled through her.

Then she realized Brandon had gone silent. She caught him watching her in the mirror and she couldn't look away. Her pulse quickened. Why? Why did *he* have this effect on her?

He closed the book and eased from the bed. After gently covering Belle, he gathered his boots off the floor and the lamp from the table and joined her in the hall.

"She's out, but she fought it," he whispered. Lamplight and hushed voices engulfed them in intimacy.

His attention shifted behind her—to her bedroom. It lingered, scanned. Lightning flashed, illuminating her bed and the half-dozen throw pillows that hadn't been there when he'd last slept in that same bed. Lord, she didn't need to think about him between those same sheets.

Then his gaze swung back to her. The flickering light picked out the golden flecks in his irises. She felt vulnerable even though he couldn't possibly know that her obsession with pillows was because she couldn't bear to sleep in an empty bed.

He lifted his arm, the one holding the light. Her breath caught. An image of Brandon propped against her headboard flashed in her mind. Only in this picture his chest was bare and his legs were beneath the covers. Heat rushed through her.

The atmosphere changed, becoming as electrically charged as the storm raging outside. Her heart pounded harder, but it was barely audible over the thunder rumbling the house.

"After you," he said.

What was wrong with her? He was indicating the stairs, not the bedroom. She blamed her unwelcome thoughts on her conversation with Lucy.

She did not want Brandon. Not in that way. She had to get him out of her house. She turned and quickly descended the stairs. On silent feet he followed her, the edge of his circle of light nipping at her heels. In the foyer he set the lamp on the console table and stepped into his work boots.

"So you've read bedtime stories before," she said to break the awkwardly intimate silence.

"I read to the twins sometimes when they stay with my folks to give Mom a break. And, once in a while, I get suckered into reading at the library on Cops and Kids day."

She'd like to see that. *No! She wouldn't.* "Why aren't you married with children of your own by now, Brandon?"

He finished tying his laces then straightened, looming over her in the murky light. The corners of his mouth curved downward. "Two reasons. My job—you, more than anyone, know the risks that entails—and my dad."

Yes, she knew the dangers of police work. And she needed to remember them. Right now. "What does your father have to do with anything?"

"He has Parkinson's disease. It's not believed to be hereditary, but the doctors can't be certain of the cause. One day he'll need 'round the clock care for his most basic needs. I wouldn't wish that on anyone."

She was familiar with the disease and had

worked with several afflicted patients in the past. "What stage is he in now?"

"Stage two. He's still mostly independent, but he's starting to need help. Not that he's willing to admit that."

"I'm sorry."

"It is what it is. You play the hand you're dealt. You've done a good job of that, Hannah. Mason and Belle are great kids."

The praise, something she heard so rarely, choked her up, made her eyes burn. But she would not cry in front of Brandon. "I wish Rick was here to see them."

Brandon's flinch stabbed her with guilt. She hadn't intentionally used the spiteful barb to push him away, but distance between them was for the best. When she'd seen him so comfortable with Mason and then again with Belle he'd made her ache for something she would never have again. A partner, someone with whom she could share the joys and burdens of parenthood.

That wind-down period at the end of the day when you rehashed what had happened and planned for the future was tough. That was when loneliness enveloped her. And, yes, as much as she'd tried to deny it, she did miss intimacy. But taking a lover as casually as Lucy did just wasn't part of her makeup.

Brandon's lips compressed. "Make your project list, Hannah. I'll be back. And we'll get to the bottom of what's troubling Mason."

CHAPTER FIVE

BRANDON THREW DOWN his pen in disgust late Friday afternoon, pushed back from his desk and stabbed his fingers through his hair. He had shit for brains today. He'd tried repeatedly to focus on the case files on his desk, but no matter what he did, he couldn't wipe what he'd seen Wednesday night from his mind.

For a split second while standing on the landing outside Hannah's bedroom something hotter than the hurricane lamp's flame had flickered in Hannah's eyes. Want. Need. Hunger. And for the span of a dozen racing heartbeats, he'd been tempted to give her what she desired. Because he'd wanted it, too. Then he'd come to his senses. He'd tried blaming the heat in her eyes on the reflection of the lamp's fire. But he wasn't buying it.

Circumstances were throwing them together and causing the craziness. It had been five years and she didn't date. That meant she didn't have sex. She needed a man. Any man. Except him— the man she blamed for her husband's death. It didn't matter that she needed his help with Mason right now, a basic distrust—because he'd let her down, because he'd let Rick down—lay just below the surface.

His dry spell hadn't been nearly as long as hers, but it had obviously been too long if he was looking at Rick's wife that way. He needed to rectify the situation. He reached for his phone but didn't pick it up. He had no interest in dialing any of the numbers in his contact list, and he wasn't interested in a casual pickup.

As if his thoughts had activated the device, his cell phone vibrated on the desk. He glanced at the screen. He had a text message from his mother.

Hello, dear. Jessamine and Logan are flying into town for the weekend. We're going to have an impromptu cookout. Are you able to attend?

His mother's habit of always texting in complete sentences and with proper grammar made him smile. His youngest sister and her new husband lived in the Florida Keys. He didn't get to see them often. He liked Logan, his brother-in-law, but a guy always had to keep an eye out for his baby sister's welfare.

Depends on day and time. Helping Hannah, he tapped back.

Hannah? Are you dating someone new?

He cringed. He could practically feel her excitement even though they were miles apart. She'd made it clear she wanted more grandchildren. He'd also made it clear they wouldn't be coming from him. But she wasn't listening.

Rick's Hannah.

I thought she wasn't speaking to you?

His parents had been at the funeral and witnessed the blowup.

She needs help with a project.

What kind of project?

His mother had been a schoolteacher until she'd quit at the end of the last school year to help his father around the orchard, and she understood kids better than anyone he knew. He would like her advice. He debated filling her in. But that was a face-to-face conversation. Not a texted one.

Home maintenance.

Truth, just not the whole truth.

You could bring her and the children to the cookout. They are welcome and we would love to see them.

Given Rick had practically grown up at their house, the sentiment was no surprise.

I'll relay message. When's dinner?

Saturday night. Come early. Your father will need assistance, but don't let on that you're helping.

Will do.

He put down the phone. It immediately vibrated again, but this time "Hannah Leith" flashed on the screen, sending a jolt through him.

Need u 2 come over. NOW.

A freefalling sensation hit him, not unlike what he'd experienced the one time he'd stupidly let Rick convince him to try skydiving. He grabbed the phone and hit her number. This wasn't texting material, either.

"Hello?" The whispered response was almost inaudible.

Adrenaline pulsed through him. People whispered on the phone when they were in danger. "What's wrong? Are you okay?"

"It's me. Mason. Mom doesn't know I swiped her phone. There's water all over the kitchen floor. Something busted. She wants to call a plumber, but she told her friend Lucy we can't afford it this month. She's kinda upset. I think she might cry."

Relief doused panic. Water and tears he could handle. "The cutoff valve is in the pantry. Bottom left corner. Turn off the water. I'm on my way."

He grabbed the file he'd been working on and shoved it into his briefcase. Thankful the rest of the team had already left to begin whatever their Friday night entailed, he signed out and headed for Hannah's. Twenty minutes later he pulled into the driveway. Mason was waiting for him on the porch.

Brandon grabbed the toolbox he kept in his truck. "Did you turn off the water?"

"Yeah. I umm…didn't tell Mom I called you. She might be mad."

"If she is, I'll handle it. You did the right thing. Let's see what we have." The kitchen floor resembled a soggy quilt of multicolored, saturated towels. Hannah stood over the sink wringing out one. Her drooping shoulders screamed defeat. Her lavender scrub suit was wet at the bottom and down the front. The thin fabric clung to her—

"Occifer Brandon," Belle cried out when she spotted him. Brandon welcomed the distraction.

Hannah stiffened and turned. "What are you doing here?"

"I heard you needed help."

Hannah shot Mason a scolding look then nodded. "Clearly, I do."

Oblivious to the tension in the air, the little ballerina sprang from her stool and splashed across the wet floor to wrap her arms around Brandon's hips. He set his tools on the counter and hugged her back. She was, of course, dressed in the same hue as her mother. He liked that. But he couldn't see his sisters ever doing it.

He crossed to the sink, squelching on wet towels with each step, and stopped beside Hannah. Her breath caught, her head tipped back and her lips parted. Standing only inches from her, her scent infiltrated his nostrils, addled his brain. He mentally shook himself. "I need to check under the sink."

"Oh. Right." She jumped out of the way, landing with a splash on a wet towel.

He opened the cabinet. "Dry here. That leaves the dishwasher and the refrigerator as water sources."

He straightened and addressed Mason. "My dad taught me to check the easy fixes first. Since fixing the dishwasher means pulling it out from under the counter, I'm going to start with the fridge."

"I'll help."

"First, try this." Brandon cupped his hand beneath the water-in-the-door spout and pushed. It clicked but didn't dispense anything. "This looks like the guilty party. Now I need your help, Mason."

He didn't really, but including the boy was a calculated move. Mason sprang forward, and together they rolled the fridge away from the wall. Brandon spotted the problem immediately, but instead of reacting, he asked, "What do you see?"

It took Mason a quarter minute. "The icemaker thingy is on the floor."

"Bingo. Hoses don't usually detach by themselves, but this one did."

Hannah groaned quietly. "It might not have been by itself. I dropped Mason's field trip permission form between the counter and fridge this morning. I pushed the fridge aside to retrieve the paper."

"You might have jiggled the waterline loose. Grab my tools, Mason. I'll show you how to fix it."

Five minutes later the job was done. "Kids, carry the towels to the washing machine for your mom. Then Mason, you can turn the water back on."

They hustled into action. Hannah stood with her hands wrapped around her middle. The gratitude in her eyes hit Brandon square in the solar plexus. She made him feel like a rock star when he was only a guy with a wrench. "Thank you for finding the leak. But more than that, thanks for making it a teachable moment and letting Mason fix it."

"No problem. It's what my dad would have done. He put tools in our hands as soon as we were able to carry them and taught us how to repair rather than replace. Besides, if the hose came loose once, it might again. He'll know what to do next time."

"We both will." She shifted on her feet. "I'm sorry he called you. I hope he didn't interrupt a date or something."

Brandon stifled a wince over his lack of a social life and ducked into the closet to turn on the water without waiting for Mason. "I'm glad he did. It was past time for me to leave the office, and it's important that Mason knows he can ask for help. I want to help, Hannah. But like Mason, you have to be willing to ask. Mind reading isn't one of my skills."

She ducked her head and plucked at her damp shirt. "I'm not very good at asking. My father raised me to be independent."

"With him deployed as often as he was, I'm sure you had to be. Good thing you're not too old to learn new tricks. Although you are pushing thirty-one. That's cutting it close," he teased.

Her gaze snapped back to his, surprised at first, then filling with amusement. A self-deprecating smile twisted her lips. "Thanks for making me feel ancient. My birthday isn't for a few more weeks, and I'm still younger than you."

He laughed. That was the old Hannah—quick with the comeback.

"Can Occifer Brandon stay for dinner?" Belle asked.

Hannah's expression filled with dismay. "We're only having hot dogs, sweetie, and I'm sure Officer Brandon has other plans."

A smart man would go home. He, apparently, wasn't that man. "I love hot dogs, and somebody needs to man the grill."

He waited to see how Hannah would get out of that one. "The grill probably won't work. I haven't used it since Rick… Cooking outside was his domain."

"Do you have propane?"

"I don't know."

"Mason's old enough to take over. We'll check it out."

"Okay, then," she replied with a noticeable lack of excitement. "Brandon, I need to pay you for what you've done and for the boards and whatever else you bought to repair the gutter."

After hearing she couldn't afford a plumber, the last thing he would do was take her money. "I had extra supplies laying around from fixing my rental houses."

She shook her head. "They still cost you something, and your time is definitely worth—"

"Hannah, I don't want your money."

"I insist—"

Once again, opportunity knocked loud and clear. "There's a way you can repay me. My parents are having a cookout tomorrow. I want you and the kids to come."

He knew her answer before she opened her mouth. Refusal was stamped all over her from her puckered brows to her folded arms and even the curling toes of her bare feet. "No. I… I wouldn't be comfortable."

He held up a hand. "Hear me out. I told you my dad has Parkinson's. He needs help. But he refuses to admit it. He's losing ground, but he hates the physical therapist his doctor recommended. That means he doesn't go. I want your professional opinion on his status. If you could evaluate him without him knowing what you're doing and give me suggestions for managing the changes overtaking his body, it would be a great help."

Compassion filled her eyes. She bit her lip. "Denial of the diagnosis is common. I guess we could drop by for a bit."

EVEN THOUGH SHE'D been a guest at Rebecca and Thomas Martin's home more than a dozen times, Hannah didn't want to be here. She didn't know how to act without Rick. But she followed Brandon's instructions and circled the backyard, trying to keep up with her eager children.

A white board fence enclosed the large grass area. Beyond that border row upon row of peach trees, laden with fruit, stretched as far as she could see. Off to one side outbuildings, including a barn and a chicken coop, blocked her view.

"Ponies!" Belle squealed and tugged on Hannah's hand. But Hannah held tight.

"Four-wheelers," Mason called out with equal enthusiasm.

"We'll pet the horses later. Mason, you are not getting on the four-wheelers."

A chorus of "*Awwws*" greeted her.

Most of the faces in the Martins' backyard were familiar, but Rick had been the honorary family member. That left Hannah feeling like an outsider without him here. She spotted Brandon in the back corner of the yard, tossing a tennis ball for a golden retriever. The dog sprinted after it. A boy and a girl about four chased the dog. The boy tumbled down and rolled around in the grass. The little girl did the same. Doggie kisses and peals of laughter ensued.

"Can I go play with them, Mommy?" Belle asked, tugging again.

The dog returned the ball to Brandon and dropped it at his feet, dancing in anticipation of another throw. Then the pooch stilled and lifted his nose. His head swiveled in their direction. Brandon turned, spotted them and waved. Hannah's already rapid pulse pounded faster. Then suddenly they were the focus of his entire family. The last time she'd seen the Martin clan had been at Rick's funeral. They'd silently stood by during her outburst.

Brandon headed toward her. Simultaneously, his mother broke away from the group on the patio and did the same. The children and dog galloped after their uncle. All were smiling, even the dog who went straight for Mason. Panting happily, the animal sat at her son's feet and lifted a paw.

"Boomer wants to shake," Brandon explained.

"Neat." Mason shook hands with the dog and patted him on the head. Then Boomer lay down and rolled over. Mason laughed. "How many tricks does he know?"

"A lot. He's asking for a belly rub. But let me warn you, Mason, if you show him any attention he'll follow you around for the rest of the day. He's a sucker for it," he said with an affectionate smile. Clearly he didn't mind the dog's demands.

Her son dropped to his knees and rubbed the dog. "Is he yours?"

"No. He's my dad's. It wouldn't be fair for me to have a dog with the crazy hours I work. Out here he has all this." His gesture encompassed the acreage. "My yard's a lot smaller."

"I want a dog. But Mom won't let us have one." Mason's resentment came through loud and clear.

All eyes swung to Hannah, making her feel like the world's meanest mom. Then Brandon crouched beside Mason. "Did you know that one dog visit to the vet cost about the same amount as a month's groceries?"

Mason's eyes widened. "Really?"

"Yes. Around two hundred and fifty bucks. And that's if he's healthy and all he needs is a checkup. If he's sick it's worse. Then there's the food, the flea and heartworm medicines and a bunch of other stuff. Dogs aren't cheap. There's a lot more to being a responsible dog owner than just playing with him. So until you're old enough to get a job and help pay for a pet, you need to respect your mom's decision."

Mason's shoulders and mouth drooped. "Yeah, I guess."

Hannah marveled at the way Brandon had handled Mason's whining, and how well her son had accepted his explanation. She had explained that they couldn't afford a dog until she was blue in the face and all Mason did was argue with her.

Brandon's mother swept forward and enveloped Hannah in a hug. "Hannah, we are so glad you and the children are here. We've missed you and your little darlings."

She turned to Belle and offered her hand. "Hello, Belle, I'm Ms. Rebecca. The last time you were here you hadn't yet learned to walk."

"I can walk now. And I can do this." Belle displayed her best pirouette.

"That is lovely." Rebecca shook Belle's hand

as if they were at a formal party, then crossed to Mason, greeting him with the same handshake. "Mason, I know you probably don't remember me, but I remember you. You were always so smart and so polite and a joy to have around. Now, children, I think I made too much chocolate ice cream. After supper I'll need some volunteers to help me eat it. Are either of you willing to do your part if I add sprinkles?"

"Yes!" the pair shouted in unison.

"Wonderful. Let me introduce you to Eva and Evan. They're only four so they're not quite in your league yet, but if you'd play soccer with them until the food is ready it would make me very happy, and it would give me time to duck inside and find those sprinkles."

She led the children away, leaving Hannah alone with Brandon. "Your mother's very good with kids."

"She misses teaching. But she's needed here."

"FYI, Mason's already asking about the ATVs. The answer's no."

Brandon grinned so boyishly her stomach fluttered. "It's a guy thing. I'll respect your wishes, but if you change your mind, know that I'd be careful and make him wear protective equipment."

"Excuse me? A guy thing?" one of his sisters called out as she approached. "Do I need to show you how much better I can handle the ATV than you?"

"In your dreams," Brandon grumbled good-naturedly.

The blonde faced Hannah. "In case you don't remember me, I'm Leah—the one in charge of keeping this guy's ego in check. And those are my rug rats your kids are playing with." Turning to the woman beside her, Leah said, "This is Jessamine. She and her husband are newlyweds and the reason for our get-together."

"Not that we've ever needed an excuse to eat," Jessamine replied. "Welcome back, Hannah."

None of them acted as if they remembered the funeral or the accusations she'd shouted at their brother. Hannah said her hellos, then Brandon touched her arm to draw her attention. "Let me reacquaint you with the rest of the crew and introduce you to Jessamine's husband. How he puts up with my mouthy sister, I'll never know."

The sister in question punched his arm. "Because he's smart and can carry his end of the conversation unlike a certain knuckle-dragging Neanderthal cop," she sassed back.

As an only child, Hannah had no experience with their gentle teasing and even envied it a little.

The women pivoted and walked toward the patio. When the doubts returned and Hannah hesitated, Brandon added, "I'll get you a glass of sweet tea, then you can kick back on the patio and observe my dad."

The reminder of why she was here prompted her forward. She had a job to do, and she was very confident in her professional abilities. Not only could she could handle this, she also wanted to help Brandon's father because Mr. Martin had been so good to Rick. And Rick would want her to repay him for his kindness.

"By the way, I rode through the streets surrounding your house this morning and I checked the incident reports," Brandon said. "Crime is minimal."

"That sounds good, but from your tone, I gather it's not?"

"I was hoping to see signs of a kid or two that might give us a clue where Mason was headed when he snuck out, or at the very least, to have a troublemaker to finger as a likely conspirator. Finding neither means we're back to nothing."

When they reached the others he dropped the subject and made the introductions. And she actually had some nice conversations. Leah offered her a glass of tea and a plate of jalapeño hush puppies then went off to chase children after asking permission to give Belle a pony ride once they'd all had dinner. And Mr. Martin asked about Hannah's work and progress on the house. No one mentioned Rick.

Brandon steered her toward a chair with views

of the lawn and the orchard but also of his father. He pulled his chair closer, so close she wanted to protest that he was in her personal space. "See what I mean about Dad? He stutter steps. What do you think?"

Happy for the distraction, she pried her attention from the man beside her to the one at the grill. "Definitely stage two. He's affected bilaterally and is having trouble initiating movement. I'm assuming he's taking his medications?"

"Yes. But like I said, he's refusing physical therapy."

She recalled an article she'd read recently. "Do you still have speakers out here?"

Brandon's eyebrows dipped. "Yes. Why?"

"There are some studies that support the idea of music helping with movement. I haven't used that modality, but you could try it on your father, and see if it helps. I doubt he'll suspect what you're doing if you turn on the radio."

He nodded. "Mom and Dad used to love to dance."

Brandon rose and went into the house. Moments later country music filled the air. His father tilted his head to listen, then resumed turning the chicken, but Hannah noticed his foot tapping. When he crossed to the table to retrieve his sauce bottle his movements were more fluid. Music therapy worked.

Brandon returned to the patio. He said a few

words to his brother-in-law, who nodded then swept his wife into his arms. Jessamine let out a surprised squeak then fell into step with him. Brandon grabbed his mother, twirled her around a few times then dropped her off beside his father.

His father hesitated, then laid down his grilling tongs, took his wife into his arms and two-stepped around the patio. His steps were smooth.

Brandon reached for Hannah's hand and pulled her out of the chair. Shocked, she resisted, but his grip and strength were unrelenting. She found herself wrapped in his arms. "Work with me or Dad will know something's up."

Hannah endeavored to relax, but the heat of Brandon's palm seared hers, as did the fingers he'd splayed on the small of her back. She tried to hold herself away from the warmth emanating from him, but it didn't cool her chaotic response. Breathing became difficult instead of autonomous. She had to concentrate on the mechanics of inhaling and exhaling. He smelled good—not like cologne, but more of a spicy soap.

"Well, I'll be damned," he said, his breath tickling her ear. "Look at him go."

She felt the stir low in her belly. Alarmed, she tried to pull away, but Brandon held fast then swung her around so she faced his parents. Their thighs brushed and it was all she could do to keep her feet from tangling with his. She forced herself to focus on the Martins, on the way they shuffled together as if they did this every day.

"Yes." Her voice came out as little more than a whisper.

"I have to admit, when you suggested music I was skeptical, but you've proved me wrong."

Focus. On work. "If you can get him to play music throughout the day, it might help."

"I will."

"And get him to change therapists."

"Do you have openings?"

Another frisson of alarm skittered through her. She didn't want to get tangled up with Brandon's family. "It's over an hour ride to my office. I'll recommend someone closer."

"He might be willing to drive that far to see you."

Desperate, she scrambled for an out. "Not with harvesting time approaching."

"Good point." And then his eyes shifted beyond her and took on a twinkle that wreaked havoc with her equilibrium. "Belle has an audience."

He swung her around again, making her dig her fingertips into his shoulder muscles for balance. Her daughter was teaching ballet moves to the twins. The four-year-olds' attempts at mimicking were comical. Mason sat nearby, laughing at their antics and petting the dog. It was everything a family outing should be. But this wasn't her family. It never would be.

The song ended. She pulled free and backed away. Ignoring Brandon's questioning expression, she returned to her chair when what she really wanted to do was gather her children and race home. But she would not make a scene. Not this time.

She was losing control of her life. She'd opened the door a crack and Brandon had forced his way in. Last night was a perfect example. Mason had called him behind her back then Belle had invited him to dinner. Brandon had tinkered with the grill until he got it to light, and he even taught Mason how to cook the hot dogs.

Mason had been so proud of himself that when he'd brought in their dinner Hannah hadn't had the heart to protest that Brandon had outstayed his welcome. Then Belle had demanded equal time, begging him to read her a bedtime story, and he'd done just that. It wasn't that she didn't appreciate his help, but she had to do what was best for her family and what was best for her. Avoiding him and the unacceptable reaction he caused topped that list.

Her children liked him. They looked forward to his visits and talked about him when he wasn't there. If she didn't find a way to keep some distance between Brandon and her family then Mason and Belle would become even more attached to him and they'd suffer the pain of losing him. Because even if Brandon didn't get killed like Rick, he was a temporary visitor in their lives. As soon as she figured out why Mason was misbehaving, Brandon would be gone. She couldn't have it any other way.

THE AFTERNOON HAD been perfect—so perfect it made Hannah uncomfortable. The children would want to attend Martin family gatherings again. But they couldn't. This wasn't their family.

She hated being the bad guy, but it was time for them to go home. While she searched her brain for the words to make their excuses, she scanned the group clustered around the patio tables and found Rebecca Martin's empathetic gaze on her. For a moment Hannah thought the woman could see inside her head. Then her hostess's lips curved upward.

"Who wants homemade ice cream?" Rebecca asked before Hannah could put her plan into action. The children shouted in the affirmative and clamored from the table. The remaining adults even raised their hands. "Hannah?"

"I'll have to pass. I didn't save room. But thank you."

Rebecca's gaze swung to her son. "Brandon?"

"I'll pass, too. Could you watch the kids a few minutes, Mom? I want to show Hannah some of the orchard."

"Of course. Run along," Rebecca replied, and Hannah was stuck.

Alarm raced through her. "I don't think—"

"Go, dear. Thomas and I have everything under control. And the orchard is so full of promise at this time of year. It's the calm before our storm."

Hannah reluctantly rose from the patio table. Brandon jerked his head. "This way."

She didn't want to be alone with him. "Brandon—"

"It's only a bike ride, Hannah."

A bike ride meant yards between them, and being out in the open meant no privacy. But still… "I haven't ridden in years. I can't even remember the last time."

"Nobody forgets how to ride a bike. It's a short trip over soft grass. If you fall you won't get hurt. And it's a one-speed. No gears. It's not complicated."

Against her better judgment, she followed him to the barn. Inside the shadowy interior he grabbed an old-style blue bicycle propped against a wall, then pointed to a red one. "Climb on and see if you can keep up."

He pushed it out of the building then mounted and pedaled off. She did the same, wobbling at first, but slowly regaining balance and confidence. He dropped back beside her and stayed there, checking her progress and leading her between rows of trees with peach-laden branches. He named the varieties and the harvest dates, but she was so busy trying to stay upright on the uneven ground that the facts rolled right over her head.

It smelled different out here. The peaches didn't smell sweet like fruit yet. It was more of a leafy scent. And it was quiet. Other than birds and the swish of the grass against their spokes, there was little noise. If she wasn't with a man who made her jumpy, the setting would be peaceful.

They came upon an irrigation pond. The dozen or so ducks on the water shattered the quiet. Quacking loudly, the fowl quickly paddled toward them.

"Do they bite? Or peck or whatever ducks do?"

"No. They're moochers looking for food. Dad fed them this morning. If we overfeed them they won't keep the pond clean."

"Ducks clean ponds?"

"They're omnivorous. They eat all kinds of amphibians, insects and plants."

She filed that tidbit away for the children. It was the kind of nature fact that both kids enjoyed. She looked over her shoulder and couldn't see the house anymore. "Shouldn't we turn back?"

"Not yet. There's a barn at the end of this field. Rick and I used to hang out there."

Rick. He'd ridden this path, possibly even on this old bicycle. A pang of loss slipped through her.

Brandon cut her a sideways glance. "Race you

to the end of the row. I'll even give you a three-tree head start."

She shouldn't accept his dare, but she needed to get away from thoughts of her husband. She took off, pedaling as fast as she could. Wind whipped her hair and exertion quickened her breath.

"I'm gaining on you," Brandon called out.

Gritting her teeth, she pedaled harder, faster. Her thighs burned but she kept going. Moments later an old wooden structure, its siding bleached by the sun, came into view. Brandon shot past her and reached it first. He jumped off his bike, laid it down and did a victory dance around it. She couldn't help laughing at his silly antics. She reached his side, climbed off the bike and tried to catch her breath.

"You could have been a gentleman and let me win."

"No way. You'd tell my sisters and they'd never let me live it down. I have a reputation to uphold." His endearing boyish smile erased her fatigue.

"You like my parents, right?"

"Of course. They're wonderful. Why?"

"And Rick? He was a great guy. Straight as an arrow, right?"

Where was he going with this? "Yes."

He crossed to the door and shoved it along the metal track, opening it to expose the building's dark interior. "C'mon."

"You didn't answer my questions."

"I will."

She checked out the grass between her bike and the building. It was tall, as if no one had been here recently. "Are there snakes?"

"If there are they'll leave before you see them."

"That's not exactly comforting, Brandon."

His grin brought back the rubbery feeling in her knees. "I've been coming here for decades and I've never been bitten."

Scanning the ground at her feet, she carefully picked her way to the open door but stopped just shy of entering. Dust motes danced along the sunbeams streaking through a few gaps in the wood. The splotchy light shone on piles and piles of dusty and disintegrating boxes, farm implements and old furniture. "What is all this?"

"Our neighbor's long-forgotten storage shed. Come in."

"No way. There's bound to be snakes hiding in there."

He pulled a flashlight out of his pocket and swept it around the interior of the barn. The visible cobwebs didn't add to the attraction. "All clear. I need to show you something."

"Bugs, snakes and creepy crawlies aren't my thing."

He held out a hand and his gaze locked on hers. "Trust me. The last thing I'd want is for something to happen to you."

Her breath hitched at the sentimental statement and the sincerity in his eyes.

"I'm Mason's godfather, remember. If you're out of commission then I become an instant father, and trust me, I'm not qualified for the job."

The comment doused her warm fuzzies. But Brandon was better with children than he realized. All four kids back at his parents' adored him. And he seemed to be perfectly comfortable with them asking endless questions and crawling all over him. The big ketchup smear on his shirt, compliments of one of the twins, testified to that. Brandon hadn't complained once.

She put her hand in his and heat flashed up her arm. One step over the door track and she stopped and pulled free. The musty, dusty smell was almost unbearable, but it wasn't nearly as disturbing as his touch. And suddenly she felt like a teenager who'd slipped off to be with her boyfriend.

"What's so special about this barn?" she blurted to derail the thought.

"Rick and I found the courage to enter it when we were about nine. After that we'd sneak out here whenever we could."

"I don't see the appeal." She couldn't imagine wanting to be in this dark, dirty place.

He swung the beam to the back corner, illuminating two old, aluminum folding chairs. "All kids are curious. That corner's where he and I learned about girls."

"You brought girls here? I'm sure that impressed them."

He chuckled at her sarcasm. "Give me a little credit. The box on the floor is full of old girlie magazines. Rick and I practically dog-eared the pages."

Stunned, she stared at him. "You're telling me you and Rick looked at porn? Here? In this barn?"

"I'm telling you even good kids are naturally curious. Not everyone who looks at porn grows up to be a pervert."

He meant Mason. And Rick. And him.

"And Hannah, not every parent who raises a kid who looks at porn is a bad parent. So even if we discover Mason's into something he shouldn't be, you've done nothing wrong. You are a great mom. Don't let the Leiths or anyone else make you doubt that."

Emotion welled in her chest, clogging her throat and making her eyes sting. She shouldn't be so needy for praise, but apparently, she was. "Thank you."

He lifted an arm as if to offer comfort then lowered it and shoved his hand into his pocket. "The magazines date back to the fifties, including the first *Playboy*, featuring Marilyn Monroe."

"That must be worth something."

"The owner probably doesn't remember they're here, and I know he doesn't need the cash. After he passes away I'll tell his daughters. He has four. They could probably use the money."

"Why not tell them now?"

"Because I respect the old man's privacy. Dear ol' dad was married to their mother when he was looking at naked ladies."

"That's considerate of you." Brandon was a genuinely nice guy. That explained why Rick had loved him. But it completely contradicted the way he'd let down his best friend. Who was the real Brandon Martin? The thoughtful guy or the get-the-job-done-regardless-of-the-costs cop? She didn't know anymore.

Something growled behind Hannah. Startled, she practically jumped into Brandon's arms. Whatever *it* was, it was between her and the door.

"Whoa." His breath stirred the hair on her forehead, and his arm banded around her.

"What is it?"

He swung the flashlight. "Looks like a raccoon sow and three kits."

She twisted to see and his biceps abraded her breasts. Desire shot to her core like a bolt of electricity. Her nipples popped to attention. Only then did she register that she'd plastered herself against him from knee to shoulder. But she was too afraid of the angry creature to let him go.

Ignoring her body's betrayal, she focused on the collection of glowing yellow eyes peering at them from the rafters near the door. Lots of eyes.

Set in black fur. And the mother had teeth. Very sharp teeth.

"Will they attack?"

"Not if we leave them alone. Sows can be aggressive when they have young." His voice had an odd note to it. She studied his face. Tension stamped his features, tightening his mouth and jaw. She couldn't see his eyes in the shadows, but she noted his lowered eyebrows.

Something hard and hot nudged her hip. It wasn't the flashlight. The realization of what it was made her gasp. Her mouth dried and her heart raced. Her lungs felt tight, and it wasn't due to the musty air. She was stuck between an aroused man and a possibly rabid animal. Her brain urged her to go one way, her body another. Being turned on by him was wrong on so many levels.

She needed space. Acres and acres of space. Keeping a wary eye on the raccoons, she eased away until a few inches separated their torsos. Their legs were tangled. No surprise since she'd practically climbed him. Where he'd pressed against her hip continued to burn.

"How will we get out? She's really, really close to the door." Her breathless voice gave away her involuntary response.

His jaw shifted. "I'll scare her out of the way. Then you go."

She shook her head. "What if she jumps on me? Or you?"

He gripped and squeezed her shoulder. She felt every finger and the heat of his palm. "Hannah, you're going to have to trust me."

Trust him? That was the crux of the problem.

He shifted, stepping into a shaft of light puncturing through a gap in the wall. The ray illuminated the upper half of his face. Their gazes met. Held. Desire shone in his eyes. Her pulse quickened in response and her blood simmered. Trusting him and wanting him were apparently two different things. "Won't she just leave?"

"Not until tonight. Raccoons are nocturnal. And if there are enough mice in here, she may hunt here."

She gulped. There was no way she'd be in the barn after sunset. She had to trust him. And that was a tall order.

But more than anything, she had to avoid dark places with Brandon, because they brought out needs she could not and would not satisfy with him.

CHAPTER SIX

HANNAH PUSHED THROUGH the glass door of the physical therapy office just after noon Wednesday. She took a deep breath of hot, humid air, and reached for her sunglasses. It might only be mid-April in South Carolina, but it already felt like August. A dark figure suddenly pushed off the wall in her peripheral vision. Heart leaping, she pivoted toward it.

Brandon stood only a couple of yards away. He wore an open collar black polo and pressed black tactical pants with his badge clipped to his waistband. His dark hair had been freshly trimmed, and he looked…good. Good and professional, she amended.

"You scared me half to death." She was not glad to see him, and she had not missed him. And she most definitely was not concerned about his well-being.

"If you'd answer my texts I wouldn't have to surprise you."

A guilty flush heated her neck. He'd messaged her twice since Saturday and she hadn't responded. After her crazy reaction to him in the barn, she'd needed space and that meant not having Brandon be a part of her day. "I've been busy."

His hazel eyes filled with disbelief. "I'm taking you to lunch."

"I can't. I only have thirty minutes."

"I know."

"What do you mean, 'You know?'"

"Your receptionist told me your morning appointments had run late."

She was going to have to speak to Jan. Hannah lifted her paper bag. "I brought a sandwich."

"Eat it tomorrow. Lou's is only a half block away."

She loved the mom-and-pop-style burger joint he'd mentioned, but if she wanted Belle to be able to take dance lessons, eating out more than once a week wasn't in her budget, and she and the kids would be eating out tonight after the lesson. "We won't be able to get a table. The place is standing room only at lunch."

"Lou's holding one for us. I need to talk to you about Mason."

"What about Mason?"

"Over lunch."

Not thrilled by the prospect of spending even thirty minutes with the man after she'd vowed to keep her distance, she hesitated. But his resolute expression told her she couldn't get out of this, so she began walking. "We couldn't have had this conversation Saturday?"

"We had other things going on then."

She kept pace beside him. People stood by the door waiting for a seat, but Brandon headed for a table in the back corner with a discreet Reserved sign and two menus already on it.

"How did you rate a table with no wait?"

"I've been coming here for years. Their onion rings are still the best in the state," he said. "I recommend those and the Lou Special."

She flipped the menu and didn't see the item. "What is the Lou special?"

"Whatever Lou feels like cooking. You can ask the waitress, but it's always good and it's fast."

The waitress appeared. Hannah made the safe and less expensive choice and ordered a salad. Once their orders were placed, Hannah turned to Brandon. "What about Mason?"

"He doesn't remember Rick."

She blinked. Whatever she'd been expecting, that wasn't it. She'd been bracing herself for... something else, and had even been hoping Brandon had figured out what was going on with her son. "Of course he does."

"He told me he didn't. I want to take him by SLED and show him how important his father's job is—was—and next time you come to my parents' house, I'd like to show him Mom's photo albums. Rick's in almost as many pictures as I am."

She wouldn't be returning to the Martins'. That entire afternoon had been too...cozy. She fiddled with her silverware and tried to find the words to explain her reluctance to let Brandon take Mason to the SLED offices. Would he understand that she feared he'd ignite an interest in law enforcement in her son? She wanted Mason to do something safer with his future, something that wouldn't take him from her. In that, she understood her in-laws concerns for their son and their anger with Brandon for "leading him astray."

"I'll introduce Mason to the team and give him an abbreviated description of what each does. I'll watch him for tells."

"Tells?"

"He'll give a physical sign if I hit too close to home or if something makes him uncomfortable."

She should have known this wasn't just about reminding her son about his father. Brandon never forgot his assignments. Rick had often remarked about his partner's single-minded determination.

"I forgot you're a body language expert. But you're assuming his problem is computer-related, and I'm not convinced it is."

"It's hard to get convictions without being able to read the clues. And I'm following the clues now. If I'm wrong, I'll be the first to admit it. The team is ready for Mason. I'll pick him up from school today and return him home when we're done. Could you call the school and relay the plan?"

"Belle has ballet tonight."

"That's why tonight is perfect for him to hang out with me. I'll get his dinner, too." Again, she hesitated. More bonding wasn't in Mason's best interest long-term, especially after Saturday. Both of her children had talked nonstop about their trip to the Martins'. But in the short-term...?

"Hannah, I won't let anything happen to him."

"You've made that promise before." About Rick.

Brandon went rigid then opened his mouth as if to speak but closed it again. His nostrils flared. He remained silent while the waitress set their plates on the table and refilled their cups. "If you want my help with Mason, then this is my strategy."

Did she have a choice? No. "I'll call the school when I get back to the office and ask them to tell Mason you'll be picking him up."

Hannah looked from her salad—a very nice colorful salad with dressing on the side—to Brandon's plate of hamburger steak, mushroom gravy and a pile of inch-wide onion rings. Her salivary glands kicked into overdrive, and for a moment she wished she'd ordered the calorie-rich special, but she dutifully dug into her healthier meal.

"Try this."

Before she realized his intent he'd reached across the small table and nudged her lips with the golden onion ring. The delicious aroma prompted her to take a bite. The ring was crisp and a little spicy and so juicy she had to grab her napkin to mop her chin. Then the flavor exploded in her mouth, and her absentee appetite returned full force. He carried the remainder to his mouth and devoured it in two bites. She realized she'd fixated on his actions—specifically, his lips—and averted her gaze.

"Now try this." He held out a bite of hamburger steak dripping with gravy.

The act of him feeding her seemed…intimate, a thought reinforced when she caught an older woman watching them with a smile softening her face. Hannah's cheeks heated. She pushed his hand away. "I don't need you to feed me."

The heat of his skin permeated her palm and sent an electric current up her arm as if she'd grabbed a TENS unit pad. She sat back. But unlike the electrical stimulating device she used on patients, when she broke the connection with Brandon the tingle didn't subside. It just relocated to swirl in a most unsettling way in her lower abdomen.

Brandon made her feel things she shouldn't. And she didn't like it. She didn't ever want to feel desire again and definitely not for a cop—not for Brandon.

He shrugged. "I wanted you to know what you're missing. Lou learned to cook in the navy like his father did before him. He takes his job seriously. Next to my mom, he's the best cook I know. I've never had anything bad here. Next time we come, do yourself a favor and get the Lou's special."

"There's not going to be a next time, Brandon. I can't afford to eat out often."

He frowned. "This is on me."

"I'm not letting you buy my lunch."

"How many times have you fed me in the past week?"

"That's different. You're helping me and it's repayment."

"Helping you. That's right. Because that's what friends do. And taking you to lunch where we can discuss Mason without being overheard is part of that."

Frustrated, she stabbed her salad. How could she fight a man who made an illogical action sound logical?

"JEEZ, WOULD YOU take off the badge," Mason grumbled to Brandon and slouched as they walked through the middle school halls. Mason's initial happiness to see him had vanished when he spotted the badge clipped to Brandon's belt.

"Why?"

"People are gonna think I'm a snitch. Why didn't you go through the carpool line like a normal person?"

"Because the cars were backed up a half mile down the street. We don't have all day. The team's waiting for you."

Mason's gaze turned wary. "What team?"

"The guys who worked with your father."

His expression turned even sourer. "Aw, man. I'd rather go to after-school care."

"Then you'll miss out on the wing restaurant tonight, and you'll have to go to ballet with your sister."

Mason groaned. "Can't you just tell me about my dad's job? I don't want to go to the station."

"It's important for you to know how important your father's work was and how much his team members respected him."

They exited the building. Mason scanned the parking lot then grimaced. "Please tell me you drove your truck."

"I'm in this unmarked vehicle." He pointed at the sedan by the front entrance.

The boy looked ready to make a run for it.

"Mason, you'll be sitting up front, not in the back. No one will think anything of it."

"Right," he mumbled, sounding unconvinced, and looked around.

"Are you searching for someone in particular?"

"No."

"I wanted to make sure you didn't have a friend you needed to say goodbye to."

"I don't."

Brandon unlocked the vehicle. Mason quickly ducked into the passenger seat and slid down until he'd be invisible to anyone outside. He didn't speak as Brandon navigated his way out of the busy lot. Keeping one eye on traffic and one on the boy, Brandon watched to see if Mason reacted to any of the kids they passed. He didn't. But then he probably couldn't see over the door.

"Does your mom ever talk about your dad?" he asked as he pulled onto the road.

"No. I used to ask about him after he died, but it always made her cry. So I quit."

"That's pretty perceptive of you."

Mason shrugged. "I'm not stupid."

"No. You're not. Your dad was one of the smartest people I know, and you take after him. You can ask me anything about him."

"And you won't cry?" A trace of sarcasm laced the words.

"Probably not. I won't lie. I cried when your dad died. More than once. Rick and I had been friends for so long I never thought he wouldn't be here. It didn't help that I knew if one decision had been made differently, he probably would be."

"Are you saying it was your fault he got shot?"

Brandon hesitated. He couldn't reveal the whole truth. It was better for Hannah to blame him. "It was a combination of unfortunate decisions. Sometimes you make a choice that seems harmless at the time. And then it blows up in your face. And no matter what you do, you can't make it right. You know what I mean?"

Mason stared out the window. "Maybe."

I'll take that as a yes. "Need me to act as a sounding board?"

"No."

"If you're hungry, I have cookies and bottled water in that cooler at your feet."

Mason dove for the insulated carrier. "Oh man, are these the ones your mom had on Saturday?" He shoved one into his mouth—whole.

Brandon nodded. "She sent a bag home with me."

"She makes the best cookies," the boy muttered with a full mouth. By the time they reached the red brick building holding the SLED offices, Mason had consumed a half dozen of Brandon's oatmeal cookies and guzzled a bottle of water. When Brandon parked Mason stilled then gulped.

Brandon reached into the backseat and grabbed two jackets. He passed one to Mason. "Put this on."

"Why? It's like eighty degrees out there."

"We keep the computer lab cold to prevent static charge from frying the equipment." He shrugged on his jacket and waited for Mason to do the same then led him inside the building. A couple of security doors and a guest badge later they stood outside the computer forensics lab. "Ready for the meat locker?"

"Huh?"

"Cold room. Where we find evidence to arrest guilty people." He reached for the door handle.

Mason moaned and rubbed his stomach. "I think I ate too many cookies."

Brandon searched his face, noting his pasty complexion. "Need a minute?"

"I'm gonna throw up."

Shit. "Bathroom's this way."

He clamped a hand on Mason's shoulder and hustled him down the hall and into the men's room. The boy barely made it into the stall before puking.

Brandon had zero experience with vomiting kids. He waited by the sinks. Had Mason really eaten too many cookies? Or did he have a virus? "Need anything?"

"No," the boy groaned then hurled again.

Brandon fingered the phone in his pocket and debated calling Hannah. But she hadn't wanted Mason to visit the lab, and this would only reinforce her hesitancy.

Finally, the toilet flushed and the stall opened. Mason wiped his mouth with the sleeve of Brandon's jacket, making Brandon wince. "You okay?"

"Can you take me home?"

"I don't have a key."

"Mom keeps one hidden. I know where."

If Mason had a virus then Brandon couldn't expose the team or take Mason to after-school care. That left two choices: call Hannah or take him home and stay with him until Hannah arrived. Not thrilled with either option but not knowing what else to do, Brandon nodded. "I'll take you home."

THE UNMARKED SEDAN in the driveway raised Hannah's anxiety level from a six to a nine as she returned home from work. Rick had driven one of the vehicles home often enough that she recognized the make, model and plates that SLED used. Brandon was supposed to have Mason. Was Brandon driving this car? Why was it here? Was he so convinced Mason's issues were computer-related that he'd brought equipment to examine the laptop without telling her? Brandon always put the job first—ahead of anything and anyone else.

She scanned her yard and porch. Nothing seemed out of place. With her mouth dry, she didn't even bother pulling into the garage. She parked in the driveway and hurried Belle to the front door. It wasn't locked. She never left the door unsecured and had taught her children the same precaution. She pushed it open, heard an unfamiliar male voice in the den and followed the sound. Brandon and Mason sat on the sofa watching a baseball game on the television. They looked...normal. The strange voice was the announcer's.

"Belle, honey, go to the kitchen and get out your homework."

Both males turned at the sound of her voice. "Hey, Mom."

Brandon rose and nodded. "Hannah."

"I thought you were taking him to work then dinner today after school?"

Brandon's features froze. "I took him to the office. Then I brought him home."

There was something in his eyes that she couldn't identify. What wasn't he telling her? "In your work vehicle?"

"I'm off today, but on call."

"I barfed my guts out," Mason announced with relish, filling in the blanks.

Alarm shot through her. "What? When?"

She rushed forward and pressed a hand to his brow. He wasn't feverish and his color was good.

"At his office." Mason jerked a thumb to indicate Brandon.

Hannah scowled at Brandon. "Why didn't you call me?"

He shrugged. "There was nothing you could do. He ate too many cookies."

"Cookies? What cookies?"

"I brought a bagful that my mother sent home with me. I remember how hungry I always was after school, and I packed him a snack. Mom's cookies have never made anyone sick before. He only vomited the one time. He didn't need a doctor and there was no reason for you to miss work."

She tried to appreciate his consideration and failed. "That wasn't your decision. You should have let me know."

"He's fine, Hannah."

She pushed her hair off her face. "I'll call Lucy and see if she can take Belle to dance."

"Aw, Mom, Brandon promised me wings."

Brandon's head whipped toward Mason. "You're hungry?"

"Heck, yeah. I mean, I blew everything. My stomach's empty."

A deep chuckle rumbled from Brandon's chest. It sent a shiver of *something* through Hannah. Then his wide grin hit her with a double whammy that weakened her knees. "You heard the boy, Hannah. Take Belle to her lesson. I've got Mason."

"What happens if you get called in?"

"Then I'll drop him off at the dance studio."

"I don't think he should go out if he's been sick."

"M*ooooo*m, I'm starving."

"He's kept his ginger ale down for a couple of hours. I'm willing to risk it."

She didn't know many men who would volunteer to keep a vomiting child or who'd be smart enough to give them ginger ale. But parenting was her job. Not his.

"Wings are too greasy for an upset stomach. You'll have to wait until another night for those." She turned a stern gaze to Brandon. "And no greasy pizza, either."

"M*ooooo*m," Mason wailed predictably.

"Get your homework done. You have a presentation to give Friday, and I know you're not finished. I'll see what I can rustle up for dinner."

Mason turned "save me" pleading eyes toward Brandon, who merely shook his head. "You heard her, kid. How about I make some banana sandwiches and we finish watching the game?"

"You promise you'll take me for wings another night?"

Brandon lifted a hand, his expression as solemn as if he were about to testify in court. "I swear I will take you out for all-you-can-eat wings another time."

"Deal." Mason flopped back down on the couch without argument.

Hannah blinked. Once again Brandon had handled her son perfectly. She had to be careful. She could get used to his help.

CHAPTER SEVEN

MASON MET HANNAH at the door when she returned from Belle's dance class. He was bright-eyed and didn't look as if he'd been sick again in her absence. "Brandon makes the most awesome banana sandwiches ever! He puts peanut butter and potato chips in 'em."

So much for a bland meal. Her gaze lifted to the man standing behind her son in the kitchen. "Potato chips? Really?"

Brandon's wide shoulders lifted. "Salt keeps you hydrated."

"I ate two," Mason added. "I wanted three, but he said he didn't want me puking again."

Her son clearly didn't have the stomach flu that had been going around. "It's a wonder you didn't make yourself sick again. Did you work on your presentation?"

Mason's shoulders slumped and he rolled his eyes. "Yeah."

"Good. I'm sure it'll be great. You can practice on me later." She turned her attention to Brandon. "Thanks for staying with him. I need to get them ready for bed, so if you'll excuse us…"

Belle tugged on her shirt. "Can't Uncle Brandon read to me?"

"Not tonight, sweetie," Hannah replied before Brandon could volunteer. *Uncle Brandon*? Who had told Belle to call him that? Definitely not Hannah. She hiked an eyebrow at him. He shrugged again. She wished he'd stop doing that. Each time he did it made her notice the breadth of his shoulders. Rick had been tall, thin and wiry. Despite working out with Brandon, her husband had never developed the muscles his partner had.

"Officer Brandon needs to go home and get ready for work tomorrow, and you need to go pick out your pajamas and get ready for your bath. You, too, Mason."

Mason's face puckered up in protest. Brandon clapped him on the shoulder. "I'll bring the materials to fix the treehouse next time I come over."

"Tomorrow?" Mason asked, his face filled with anticipation.

"Tomorrow you'll need to finish your project," Hannah interjected.

Brandon's gaze swung her way. "Friday?"

She shook her head. "Friday we leave for the Leiths'."

Mason moaned. "Do we have to?"

"Yes. Your grandparents look forward to your visits."

Mason snorted. "Yeah, right."

"I'll come by one day next week, bud. Work

on your plan and email it and any other ideas you have to me before then."

"Okay, I will. G'night." Then her son sprinted up the stairs behind his sister, leaving Hannah marveling once again at Brandon's way of relating to her children. Part of her rejoiced at seeing the return of Mason's old attitude. Another part was a little jealous that Brandon had been the one to resurrect it. Admitting that made her feel petty.

"How did you get him to cooperate so easily?"

Brandon shrugged. "Simple negotiation tactics. I offered him something he wanted in exchange for compliance."

He'd applied his work techniques to managing her son. She shouldn't be surprised. "He hasn't used that treehouse in a couple of years."

"He claims it's babyish. We checked it out, and it's still structurally sound. I gave him some ideas for converting it from a playhouse to a hangout. Rick and I spent a lot of time on that thing. I hate to see it go unused, or worse yet, become unsafe."

Rick had been so proud of his part in building the structure. "What were your ideas?"

"Put up a hammock, add screen to the windows to keep out the mosquitos, add a climbing wall and rope and run a power cord... Stuff like that. He wants to be able to camp out up there."

"He's mentioned sleeping in the treehouse a few times." Including the night he'd tried to sneak out. "But he can't exclude his sister."

"He came up with a pretty cool plan to build her a wing of her own and give her a separate entrance. If you recall, Rick and I designed it so it could grow with them."

"I can't afford all the additions you're talking about at once. Maybe we can add one item a month."

"Hannah, I have most of the materials on hand for my rental houses."

Why did he make it so hard to say no? "How many rentals do you own now?"

"Six. I buy fixer-uppers, make the repairs then either flip them or rent them. I've been flipping longer than it's been trendy. When the time comes to retire, I want to have a good income from the properties."

Yet another way he differed from Rick. She'd always wanted to sock away money, but Rick had wanted to invest every spare dime in their home. The memory brought regrets. If Rick had invested a few dollars each month in life insurance then keeping the big house wouldn't be such a struggle. But the house was all she and the kids had left of him and their dream.

"I'd like to take Mason with me to do maintenance sometime. It'll teach him a few skills."

She took a deep breath. "We'll discuss it when the time comes. Thanks for your help today, but I need to get them to bed on time tonight."

"Mason's smart, Hannah, and a problem-solver.

You've done a good job with him. Whatever blip was on his screen, we'll figure it out."

She clung to his words and his praise, soaking them up and tucking them in a little corner pocket of her heart, because she knew the criticisms she'd face from her in-laws this weekend.

"I'm still putting my money on him being nothing more than a boy curious about girls," Brandon continued. "It wouldn't take five minutes in the computer lab to figure out which websites Mason visited to satisfy his curiosity. Probably the same sites where he learned the foul language."

Then it hit her. His kind words to her were nothing more than him using work techniques to get permission to search the computer. She yanked open the front door. "No, thanks. Good night."

"What about Monday? Can Mason spare an hour to work on the treehouse?"

"Monday we will be playing catch-up from the trip. Probably Tuesday, too. Visiting Rick's parents takes a lot out of us—them."

That telling little crease appeared between his dark eyebrows. "Call me if you need me. For anything."

The sudden inclination to lean on him was so strong it blindsided her. Why him? Because it felt as if she finally had someone on her team— something she hadn't had since Rick's death. But she had to stand on her own two feet. Brandon was temporary. She'd be solo again as soon as they resolved Mason's issue.

"I'm ready for my bath, Mommy," Belle called down the stairs.

Brandon stepped over the threshold then paused and faced her with one foot in her house and one outside. "Mason trusts me now. I could talk to him, man to man, and see if he has any questions about sex."

"Mason and I have had 'the talk' and he gets sexual education at school."

"Rick would have—"

"You're not Rick." The words sprang from her mouth—as much a reminder to him as to herself. Brandon was being nice. Too nice. What strategy was he employing now?

He held her gaze, his hazel eyes somber. "Don't let the Leiths get to you."

Then he nodded and headed out into the night. Hannah closed the door, locked it and sagged against it for a second before quickly pushing off. Her night was far from over. As soon as she got Belle settled, she needed to talk to Mason.

She usually enjoyed giving Belle her bath and tucking her into bed, but tonight that twenty minutes stretched on for an eternity because of the suspicion circling Hannah's brain like a pesky mosquito. On autopilot, she kissed Belle's forehead and pulled up the sheet. "Good night, love bug."

"Mommy, can Uncle Brandon go to church with us?" Belle asked.

Hannah was used to Belle's odd questions, but this one was stranger than usual. "I think he has his own church."

"Could we ask him?"

Proud of her daughter for wanting to share her faith with others, she smiled. "I suppose. Why is it so important to you?"

"Cuz Sydney has an uncle, and this weekend he and Sydney's mommy went to church and now he's her daddy."

Hannah's heart slammed her sternum. "Hannah's mom and her 'uncle' must have gotten married."

"Can you and Uncle Brandon get married?"

"No!" Eyes wide, Belle shrank back against the pillow at Hannah's vehement reply. Hannah took a calming breath. "Honey, I was married to your daddy, and he was the best daddy in the world. I could never find one as good as him."

"But don't you want me to have a daddy so I can be like the other kids?"

Hannah's heart ached. "You don't need to be like the other kids. You're special just as you are."

"But I want Uncle Brandon to be my daddy!" The tired whimper tugged at Hannah's emotions. "And you said if I want something real bad then I hafta keep trying."

"That's not going to happen, Belle. Brandon

was a friend of your father's. He can be your friend now. But that's all."

Belle's rosebud mouth turned into a frown and her bottom lip poked out. Fat tears rolled down her cheeks.

"I'm sorry, sweetie. You know I do what I can to make you happy, but marrying Brandon is something I just can't do."

"Why not?"

"Because I don't love him."

"But we're s'pose to love everybody."

Lord, give me the answer to this one. "The love a mommy feels for a daddy is a different kind of love than loving everyone else."

"Can't you try harder?"

"No, Belle. I can't."

She kissed Belle's forehead and left her pouting. What she feared had come to pass. Belle had become attached to Brandon.

Hannah made her way to Mason's room and knocked. She heard rustling and quick footsteps then when he called out, she opened the door. He was propped against the pillows. He very deliberately lowered his book when she entered and looked up with exaggerated curiosity. But his respiratory rate was too fast for someone at rest. What had he been doing before she'd knocked? Anxiety tightened her chest. The hope that Mason's issues had resolved themselves evaporated.

Hoping this conversation went a little better

than the one she'd just left, she sat on the edge of his bed. "Everything okay?"

"Yeah."

"Good book?"

"Yeah."

"It's part of that series you like, isn't it?"

"Uh-huh." Edginess radiated from him.

She wanted to ask what he'd been doing, but memories of her parents' screaming matches when her father had been caught listening to her mother's movements outside the bedroom door kept the words locked away. "Did you feel sick at school?"

"Nah."

"Because you could have called me if you did."

"I didn't. Anyway, I know you can't miss work unless you really have to."

Fighting a wince because her kids shouldn't have to worry about money, she reached out to touch his cheek, but he leaned away. Lowering her hand, she tried not to let him see how much his rejection hurt. She missed the little boy who used to hold her hand and snuggle.

"Were you uncomfortable about going to the SLED offices with Brandon today?"

He stiffened and his eyes turned wary. "Whatdaya mean?"

"Sometimes your stomach acts up when you're anxious—like it did the first day of middle school. I wondered if that's what happened today."

His cheeks reddened. "No! It was the cookies! I ate six. Really fast. Then I chugged a bottle of water. I guess it all expanded in my stomach and erupted like a volcano!"

The rapidly spoken protest seemed a little too exuberant. She searched his face. "Mason, if you don't want to visit SLED just tell me, and I'll tell Brandon."

He pondered that a moment. "Would he still take me for wings?"

"He promised he would."

"I don't want to go to the office. Why would I want to look at a bunch of old geezers staring at computer screens?"

The geezer comment made her wince. But it also told her Brandon was right. Mason didn't remember Rick's job. Maybe he'd been too young to understand how much his father loved his work. "There's a lot more to it than that. Your dad loved his job and he was very good at it. He helped catch a lot of criminals. But I'll tell Brandon the trip's off."

"'Kay."

"I love you."

"I know." He picked up his book and ducked his head. Her heart cracked a little. He used to throw his arms around her and say it back. She missed that. Life had been so much simpler before Mason had entered middle school.

Brandon makes things easier.

No. He makes things more complicated.

She sprung from the bed. "You know you can tell me if something or someone is bothering you, right? And that I'll still love you no matter what."

He flicked her a wary look. "Yeah."

But he didn't believe it. The fissure in her heart widened. How was she going to get her baby boy back?

And what was he hiding?

BRANDON CLOSED THE file Wednesday afternoon, checked his phone for the tenth time and then cursed himself for doing so. Hannah hadn't answered his text.

"You finished the report?" Toby, his partner, asked.

"Yeah. Just emailed it to the boss."

"What'd you do? Work all weekend? You trying to make the rest of us look bad?" Toby delivered the question with a grin, no malice attached.

"You don't need my help," Brandon zinged back.

Toby flipped up his middle finger. "We still on for wings tonight?"

"I'm waiting to hear from Hannah. I want Mason to meet you guys."

"You figured out why she banned you from bringing him here?"

"I'm guessing because he tossed his cookies the last time I tried."

Toby's brow puckered. "Poor kid. Sounds like he inherited his daddy's nervous stomach."

The hair on the back of Brandon's neck prickled. He gave Toby the squinty eye.

"Didn't you say Rick barfed before every big game in high school and before his wedding? He sure as hell did before every major raid we had."

Brandon mentally kicked himself. How could he have failed to connect those dots? He'd dragged Rick into sports: baseball and football, and while Rick had loved playing, he'd always had gut-heaving jitters before important games, and as Toby said, before other momentous occasions. "Yes. He did."

Mason hadn't wanted to come to the office, but he'd been fine in the car. He hadn't acted sick until after they'd cleared security and slapped the visitor badge on his chest.

"You think meeting us made the kid nervous?"

Not unless Mason had a guilty conscience or something to fear from a room full of cops. Brandon hadn't shared Hannah's concerns about Mason's behavior with the team, and he wouldn't do so now. "Some folks are anxious around cops."

"True. So we'll meet y'all at the wing place if Hannah gives the go-ahead?"

"That's the plan. I want this laid-back. No pressure. Just food and talk. Mason needs to know what a great guy his dad was, but I don't want anyone to mention Rick until Mason's comfortable."

Brandon's phone buzzed on the desk. A text message from Hannah.

Mason would love to do wings tonight.

He met Toby's gaze. "We're on. Pass the word."

HANNAH OPENED THE front door Wednesday evening before Brandon could ring the bell. One look at her foreboding expression and he knew she wasn't happy to see him. He braced himself for the anger in her eyes to spill from her mouth.

"Uncle Brandon!" Belle, wearing her pink dance costume, skirted around her mother, wound her arms around his hips and squeezed like a baby boa constrictor.

"How's my favorite ballerina?" he asked and she beamed, missing one of her top front teeth. "Hey, where'd your tooth go?"

"I lost it at Grandmother and Grandfather's house. But the tooth fairy couldn't find me there. She waited till I came home to visit."

"I guess her GPS was broken."

"That's what Mommy said, too."

Hannah tucked a loose hair into Belle's tiny bun. "Go get your brother, sweetie. He's upstairs doing homework."

Belle skipped off, and Hannah turned her glare to Brandon. "I told you I couldn't afford to spend much on the treehouse."

"And I told you I had the—"

"Don't lie." She shook a long strip of paper in his face. "Mason found the receipt stuck to the bottom of the slide. Two hundred dollars, Brandon!"

Damn. That was where the receipt went. He'd looked everywhere for it. He took it from her. "I have the basics: boards, nails, window screen… But at lunch on Monday one of the guys caught me looking at the drawing Mason emailed. I told him what we were planning and he told the rest of the team. They wanted to pitch in and went a little overboard with the curly slide and the military-grade climbing rope. I picked it up yesterday and dropped it off on my lunch hour today."

He didn't mention that he hadn't thought she'd see the items where he'd stashed them behind the treehouse.

Her eyes narrowed even more. "Let me guess. These are the same guys who've mysteriously done maintenance on my house when I'm out of town. Or was that all you?"

Busted. "We all thought a lot of Rick, and we look out for our own."

Arms folded, her chin jacked up. "I have never asked for your help before now."

"No, you haven't. But you can be gracious enough to accept it—for your kids' sake and for the men's. If you want to thank them, make 'em a cake or something. The guys miss your baking." Rick had brought in something Hannah had baked a couple of times a month, much to the team's delight.

"You should have asked before dumping those parts in my yard where Belle and Mason would find them. That makes me the bad guy when I return them."

"Then don't return them."

He could see the steam building as her face flushed darker. "Hannah, tell me something. Wouldn't you help another team member's family if the positions were reversed? And didn't you and Rick contribute whenever we took up a collection to help one of our own?"

She deflated as if he'd stuck a pin in her. "Yes. We did. Rick and I gave as much as we could afford. But Brandon, this is too much."

"Let the guys do this. We deal with scum every day. The treehouse gives everyone a common purpose, makes them feel good."

She averted her face and blinked away the tears he saw pooling. She was still angry. The stiffness of her spine gave that away. He braced himself. Living with his sisters had taught him that when a woman was angry enough to cry you had real trouble on your hands. But then she huffed out a breath and nodded.

"Okay. But this is the end of it. You understand?" She poked his chest. The impact hit his sternum like a flaming arrow. "I don't want to be anyone's charity case. I will paint my own shutters, trim my own shrubs and buy my kids their basketball goals and bicycles."

She hadn't missed much. "I'll relay the message. No more help. At least, not without asking first."

"No. Just no more help. Period."

Mason peered around her shoulder. "Wing night?"

"You bet. Feel like you could eat a couple dozen?"

"Yes, sir!"

Hannah stepped aside. "Have him back before 8:00."

"I will. Let's go, bud. Wings are waiting."

Mason hustled toward the truck, piled in and buckled up. "The rope is cool. We have one like it in the gym."

"Can you climb it?"

"Not yet. But I will."

Brandon laughed at his determination and drove toward the restaurant. "Now you sound like your dad."

Mason rolled his eyes.

"Hey, how was the trip to your grandparents'?"

"Horrible. All they do is nag. *Sit up straight. Don't talk with your mouth full. Get a haircut. Speak up. Be quiet.* And they upset Mom. She keeps her lips mashed together, like she's biting her tongue or something, the whole weekend. She hates going, too, but she'll never admit it. They don't like us. And I don't like them. They're mean. I don't know why she makes us go."

"It's not you, Mason. The Leiths have always been difficult people. That's one of the reasons your dad spent so much time at my house. And they didn't like that, either. But your mom makes you go because she wants you to know your grandparents. Family is important."

"Yeah, well, the only good part is that Grandfather has a neat train set in the basement. Sometimes he lets me play with it. As long as I don't touch anything except the switch."

"Your dad had a train set."

Mason shot him an end-of-his-rope look. Brandon changed the subject before the kid shut down. "What about your mom's father? Do you visit him?"

"We almost never see him except on video chats. When he calls on the regular phone I can tell from Mom's side of the conversation that he wants her to send me away to a military academy. I heard him offer to pay for it once. But she said no."

"Do you want to go to a boarding school?"

"No way! I need to stay here and take care of Mom."

"That's admirable of you. I want to help, too. I promised your dad I would."

"You heard her. She doesn't like help."

"Yeah. But this was a deal between me and your dad." Brandon drove in silence, then said to himself, to hell with it. He had to help even if it was against Hannah's wishes. "Do you have a girlfriend?"

"I'm ten."

Was that a yes or a no? "Just askin' because if you have questions about sex—"

Mason's face turned red. "I don't!"

"Okay. But I know how hard it is for a guy to talk to his mom about sex, so I'm offering. If there's anything you need to know, just ask."

"Jeez," Mason muttered under his breath. "Can you turn on the radio or something?"

"We're almost there. Is your dad's dartboard still hanging in the garage?"

Mason nodded cautiously. "Why?"

He ignored the evasion. "You ever play with it?"

Mason shifted in his seat and looked out the window. "Mom says I'm not supposed to."

More evasion. "But you do?"

A shrug lifted his narrow shoulders. "Sometimes I get bored. And yeah, I do." His chin and tone reeked defiance.

"Are you any good?"

Eyes, narrowed with suspicion, swung Brandon's way. "Maybe. Why?"

"They have dartboards at the restaurant." The building came into view. Brandon noted the guys' vehicles were already in the parking lot. Would Mason get nervous and be sick again when he met them? There was only one way to find out. "I was going to test your skills. Your dad was a great dart player."

Mason groaned. "Do you ever let up?"

"Not when something's important. And it bothers me that you don't remember him." He parked the truck and shoved his keys into his pocket.

The plan was to get Mason to relax around the team. Once they'd eaten and played a few rounds of darts each member would share his favorite story about cases they'd worked with Rick. Brandon hoped in the process Mason would learn what a great guy his father had been and how valuable he'd been to stamping out cybercrime. It would be a bonus if Brandon picked up clues to Mason's recent behavior problems.

"How did you find this place? It's a dump."

"It's not much to look at, but it's clean inside and they have the best wings in the county. My buddies and I meet here on Wednesdays."

Mason's eagerness turned to wariness. "Your buddies?"

"Yeah. You'll like them. We have dart matches. Two teams of three. One of the guys couldn't make it tonight. You're taking his place. First team to five hundred points wins. Losers pick up the tab."

Mason's brow puckered. The leather seat squeaked as he squirmed. "I don't have any money."

"I'll cover you."

Silence stretched in the cab. "Are they cops?"

Brandon noted Mason's stiff posture. "They're the guys who bought the slide and climbing rope."

"Are they cops?" Mason repeated.

He wouldn't lie. "Yes."

Fear flashed in Mason's eyes. "I don't want to play darts or meet your stupid friends."

"You have nothing to be afraid of. They're good guys and they were friends of your dad's. Let's go."

"I want to go home."

"I can't take you home. Your mom's not there."

"Then take me to the dance place. I'd rather be stuck there watching a bunch of bed-wetters than eat with old geezers who live in the past."

Ouch. "It's just wings and darts and friends, Mason."

"Your friends. Not mine. I'm not going in there."

"What are you afraid of?"

"Nothing. Let me out. I'll walk home." He yanked on the door handle, but it was locked by the control on Brandon's side.

"You can't. It's ten miles. And we have to eat."

Mason's face took on a mutinous set. "You eat with your dumb old friends. I'll make a sandwich when I get home. I'm not a baby. I can feed myself."

The kid had shut down. "I know you can. But believe it or not, I actually enjoy your company."

"Well, I don't like yours. You lied to me."

"I didn't lie. I told you we were going to get wings."

"Unlock the door now. I'm outta here and neither you nor your friends will find me." More frantic jerks on the handle accompanied his words. Brandon could feel Mason's panic rising.

Shit. "You don't want to do that. Running away is a punishable offense in South Carolina. Not only would that bring in cops, you'd have social services and a busload of other officials up in your business. Do you want that?"

Mason stilled, his eyes becoming more fearful. He gulped. Brandon was going to lose any chance of helping the kid if he didn't retreat. He'd have to abort the mission. But he couldn't take Mason to Hannah and let her see how much he'd upset her boy. She'd never let him near her children again.

"If you don't want to meet the team, we'll go someplace else."

"Right, and you'll text 'em and tell 'em to ambush me there."

"No. I won't. Let's hit the burger place that has the good milkshakes."

"You're bribing me with ice cream? How dumb do you think I am?"

"Not dumb at all. But we both need dinner. You choose the restaurant. Afterward, I'll take you home. No tricks. But you have to swear not to run. Deal?"

Mason mulled that over a full minute. "Yeah. Whatever."

Brandon might be able to regain Mason's trust, but he wasn't willing to bet money on the odds of that happening tonight.

CHAPTER EIGHT

"No MASON AGAIN?" Lucy asked as soon as Belle and Celia left the parents' waiting room for the studio.

"No."

"The sexy cop have him?"

"Brandon took him out for dinner." She refused to acknowledge the description.

"That's three Wednesdays in a row he's had him. This is becoming a habit. Is he going to start leaving his razor at your place?"

Hannah pressed her lips together in frustration. First Belle, now Lucy. "There's nothing like that between us. And there never will be."

"Then why do you get red and flustered when his name comes up?"

"I don't."

Lucy's eyebrows lifted.

Was she so transparent? Dear heaven, did Brandon know he'd resurrected her hormones? Her face burned hotter, making Lucy chuckle. "I hate having to rely on him when he's the reason Rick's not here."

"Girl, please, be honest. You hate having to

rely on anyone. You even give me a hard time when I try to help. But it's okay to need someone sometimes."

Hannah sighed. She'd relied on her mother and she'd vanished. Then she'd relied on Rick and he'd died. She'd learned the hard way that the only person she could count on was herself.

"Thank you, Dr. Freud. Brandon keeps pushing to search my computer. But you know how careful I am. I can't have Mason thinking I don't trust him."

"If Brandon's really bothering you then tell him to get lost."

"I would if not for…"

"If not for what?"

"Mason has been so good since Brandon came on the scene. No trouble at school. No sneaking out. No foul language. I was starting to hope the tough times were over. Then last night when I knocked on his door I heard him scrambling around before he told me to come in. He was sitting in the bed looking all wide-eyed and innocent, but he was breathing heavy from racing around or whatever."

"At his age he was probably masturbating."

Hannah winced then groaned. "I hadn't considered that."

"Remember, I had brothers. I know these things." Lucy smiled smugly.

"Whatever he was doing, it was something he didn't want me to see."

"Did you ask?"

That seemed like common sense. And for anyone else it probably was. "I don't want him to think I was spying."

Lucky palmed her forehead. "Now I get it. Mason's behavior is resurrecting your mom issues. But Hannah, just because she ran off doesn't mean Mason will."

Lucy was the only one Hannah had ever told about her mom. Not even Rick had known the whole story. "I can't risk it."

"He's a kid. Monitoring what he does is not the same as what your dad did to you and your mom."

"I don't see how it's different. Establishing and nurturing trust is important."

Other parents filed into the bleachers. Hannah and Lucy watched the girls do their warm-up exercises in silence for a few moments. "You never heard from her? Your mom, I mean."

"No. I don't even know if she's alive or dead." But she'd wondered. She'd even questioned whether her father— No. Her father had nothing to do with his wife's disappearance. He couldn't have. She'd never seen him be violent in any way.

"That sucks. I mean, what a shitty thing to do to a kid," Lucy whispered.

"Oh, look. The girls are learning to *jeté*!"

Lucy's level-eyed look said she wasn't fooled

by Hannah's attempt at diversion, but dissecting her abandonment issues wasn't on the calendar tonight. Luckily, the adorable chaos on the dance floor took precedence.

Hannah exhaled slowly, trying to release the tension from her body. Talking about her mother always tied her in knots. Where had she gone and why?

But she was not her mother or her father. She would never abandon or betray her children. All she had to do was figure out why Mason was misbehaving, then get rid of Brandon and get on with her life.

MASON CHARGED PAST Hannah without acknowledging her holding the front door open for him. Dumbfounded, she stared after him stomping up the stairs. His bedroom door slammed shut. Her son was clearly upset.

She turned to the man following him more slowly up the sidewalk. Brandon's carefully neutral expression told her the evening had not gone well. Her protective instincts rose. "What happened?"

"He didn't want to meet the guys."

"The guys?"

"The team meets at the wing place on Wednesdays."

"And you're surprised Mason objected after I told you he didn't want to meet them?"

"You said he didn't want to go to the office." Looking decidedly uncomfortable, Brandon shoved a hand through his hair.

"What aren't you telling me?"

"He threatened to run away if I tried to force him to go inside the restaurant."

Panic nipped at her heels. "It's almost eight. If he refused to eat with you then where have you been for the past two hours?"

"I convinced him to grab a bite elsewhere then took him bowling. I wanted to give him time to calm down, maybe vent his frustration on the ball. It didn't work as well as I'd hoped."

"So you learned nothing about the origin of his behavior?"

"Nothing except he's avoiding cops."

Her stomach churned. "Not necessarily."

"Hannah, last week the idea of meeting the team made him vomit, then today he threatened to run away to avoid time with them. What does that tell you? Something's going on and he doesn't want law enforcement around. And it isn't that he doesn't want to spend time with boring old geezers. If you'd just let me talk to him—"

"No. I've told you before. You're not interrogating him like he's a criminal. I know your pit bull tactics. Rick used to be in awe of them. There's no way Mason's involved in something illegal. I'd know. I watch him too closely."

"Do you know how rich I'd be if I had a dollar for every parent who told me their kid would never break the law?"

She opened her mouth to reply, but he held up a hand.

"That was a rhetorical question. All I wanted tonight was for Mason to hear that his father was a genuinely good guy who was well-liked and respected by all who knew him. The guys were going to tell Mason stories about working with Rick, stories that demonstrated his loyalty, his courage, his ingenuity, his quirky habits and his dedication to his family. That boy needs to know his father would never have left him willingly."

Coming on the heels of her conversation with Lucy, the last phrase hit home. Hannah had faced that uncertainty after her mother left. More than once she'd wondered if she had done something to drive her mom away. Hannah's father had refused to discuss his wife's disappearance. She'd never coupled it to Mason and his father. Did her son have abandonment issues?

But Brandon's impassioned speech also revealed how much he'd missed Rick. She'd been so lost in her own grief that she hadn't considered his.

She'd never asked him the exact details of what happened that day, and he'd never volunteered an explanation. He might have if she'd answered his calls before the funeral. But she hadn't wanted to hear his excuses for failing to protect his partner, the man he'd referred to as "his brother from another mother." All she had was the formal investigative report that stated Brandon had been in another part of the house when the perp had dropped from his place of concealment in the attic and taken Rick's life. It said that when Brandon had encountered the murderer he'd discharged his weapon, firing a single fatal shot. But he'd been too late to save Rick.

She'd been furious with Brandon and then SLED when Brandon hadn't been charged, fired or even demoted for his negligence, and she'd cut all ties with both. She'd blamed the good ol' boy network because they'd obviously valued Brandon's skill in always getting a confession over Rick's life and his less flashy behind-the-scenes computer forensics work.

Now, years later, she realized her thinking was eerily in line with her mother-in-law's venomous, irrational rants. Suddenly, she had a burning desire to know what had transpired.

"What happened that day?"

He stilled, like prey in a predator's sight. The change in him, specifically in his eyes, was so subtle that if she hadn't been looking directly at him she would have missed it. Guarded was the only way she could think of to describe it. "You were given a copy of the report."

At least he didn't pretend he didn't know to

which day she referred. "I need to hear it in your words."

He looked toward the kitchen. "Belle—"

"Is watching her favorite movie in the den. She won't resurface for another thirty minutes. What happened, Brandon? If you loved Rick so much, how did you fail to watch his back?"

He swallowed, his Adam's apple bobbing. His fists clenched by his sides then released, then his chest rose and fell. His eyes remained open, but it was as if he was no longer seeing her or even the here and now.

"The house had been cleared. We—Rick and I—were about to begin gathering the evidence when a call came in reporting that the perp had been spotted at another location. He was armed and dangerous and a threat to society. The rest of the team went searching for him. Rick and I split up to get our job done faster."

"Why? Did you have a hot date that night?" He'd been quite the ladies' man back then. Rick had been amused and maybe a little envious of Brandon's conquests. "Women fall on him like pine needles fall from the trees," Rick had said.

"No. We needed to search the entire premise, including the basement. Rick hated rats, and this house had them down there. We flipped for it. I won the toss and took the basement."

"Because of Rick's phobia." It was a statement, not a question.

"Yes. But I told him it was because the good stuff would be down there."

The sand beneath her anger shifted. If he'd been protecting Rick's ego, how could he have been so negligent with his life? "That wasn't in the report."

"No reason for it to be."

"You were supposed to work together. Side by side. A team."

His gaze returned to hers, and because she knew him so well she saw the pain he tried but failed to mask. He inhaled again, slow and deep, once again drawing her gaze involuntarily to the breadth of his chest.

"Once the house was deemed safe, how we collected the evidence was at our discretion. And splitting it up would move it along faster. We'd been working about forty minutes when I heard a weapon discharge. By the time I reached the bedroom Rick was down and the perp was standing over him."

The official incident report claimed her husband had been shot execution style in the back of the head while on his knees—probably pulling something from beneath the bed. She'd refused to look at the crime scene photos and had requested a closed casket, but she'd pictured that room and Rick's injury hundreds of times in her mind and in her nightmares. Brandon had seen it all.

"So you shot him—the bad guy."

"I had to. He raised his weapon and fired at me. I returned fire. He went down. I called for backup."

The flat recitation sounded as if he were testifying in court. But the lines etching the corners of his eyes and creasing his forehead said more than his words.

Then what he'd said registered. "Wait a minute. The report said you shot the man from a distance of six feet. If he was that close, how did he miss you?"

"He hit the door frame beside my head."

Her eyes went to the tiny scar on his left cheekbone. "The cut you had on your face at the funeral…"

"Was from splintering wood."

Inches. Brandon had been inches from dying with Rick that day. The air left her lungs in a rush.

"And you tried CPR on Rick even though, even though…" She'd been told that from the size of the wound there would have been no chance for survival.

"He was like a brother to me." The creases in his face and the timbre of his voice deepened. "The medical examiner said there was no sign he heard the perp because he hadn't turned toward him. He probably never experienced pain and he didn't suffer. His death was instantaneous."

She wasn't sure who he was trying to convince: her or himself. The emptiness in his voice and eyes reflected her emotions. She'd hated Brandon for so long. But hate took too much energy. All she felt now was numb. Because *maybe* Brandon hadn't been negligent. No. *If* they'd been together, Rick wouldn't have been surprised by the guy.

The air conditioner turned on with a blast of frigid air, making her realize she'd been standing in the threshold keeping him on her front porch for the entire conversation—the same way she'd barred him from their lives since that day.

Politeness decreed she invite him in. But she couldn't. Not tonight. She needed time to process what she'd learned—that losing Rick had hurt Brandon, maybe as much as it had her. It was written all over him, an indelible memory that had left permanent grooves in his skin.

To add to her confusion, the urge to reach out and comfort him, to tell him she was glad he hadn't died that day, too, nearly overwhelmed her. She gripped the doorknob tighter and stepped back. "If you still want to work on the treehouse, come back this weekend. We'll be home."

Then she shut the door in his face and on the past.

She couldn't live in there anymore. She had to focus on the present if she wanted her children to have a future, and that meant accepting that Brandon, with his people-reading skills, might be onto something about Mason's fear of meeting police officers. Her son might have more than behavior issues. He might be in real danger.

HANNAH KNOCKED ON Mason's door. She heard him scrambling around the room before he called for her to enter. She pushed open the panel and found him sitting at his desk with a textbook in front of him. He had a finger on the page as if he was marking his place. But like last time, he was breathing too hard to have been sitting and reading.

Déjà vu. Anxiety prickled through her. "How was bowling?"

"Okay."

"I know how much you love it, and I hate that we don't go more often. Maybe I should try to find you a junior bowling league."

"Bowling teams are for dweebs."

So much for that. "Brandon said you didn't want to meet his friends tonight."

He shrugged and kept his eyes on the book. "I wasn't in the mood for wings."

"You've been begging for wings for a week."

His face reddened with indignation but the eyes he turned toward her were filled with something resembling fear. "He set me up to play darts on a team without asking. I told him you never let me play with Dad's dart set, so I was no good. I didn't want to look like an idiot in front of his friends."

Relief rolled through her. Brandon was wrong.

Mason wasn't afraid of cops. He was avoiding embarrassment. "Did you tell him that?"

He fiddled with a pencil on the desk surface. "Why should I tell him anything? He didn't tell me."

"You should've told him how you felt, because your refusal to meet his coworkers a second time has made him think you have something to hide from police officers."

He paled, swallowed and then returned his attention to the page. "That's crazy! I just don't want to meet a bunch of old, farty, donut-eating cops."

She stepped closer to the desk and knelt down so she could see his averted face. "Are you sure that's all it is, Mason? Because sometimes I feel like I don't know you anymore, and I'm afraid you're into something—"

"I'm not! And I wish you'd stop treating me like a baby."

The attack took her aback. She straightened. "I try to respect your space."

"No, you don't. You never let me go anywhere by myself. I'm ten!"

"Exactly. You're not old enough to go out alone—especially at night, and definitely not to the home of someone I haven't met. That rule is for your protection."

"You can't protect me from everything!" He

slammed the book closed. "I need to take my shower since you make me do that, too."

Bristling with anger, he plowed past her and into the bathroom. The door banged shut. She turned to leave, but then noticed his book bag had overturned and the contents had spilled under the bed. Unlike his sister, Mason never kept his room clean. Huffing with exasperation, Hannah crossed the room and righted the knapsack. Not wanting a crazy last-minute rush to find a lost textbook in the morning, she knelt to retrieve the scattered items.

Once they were all safely back in his bag, she started to rise, but a piece of paper farther under the bed caught her eye. She flattened herself on the floor and stretched to reach it. Her fingers closed around a piece of notebook paper folded into a small triangle similar to the ones boys used to play finger football with when she was in school. She tossed it toward the open backpack and missed. It bounced off the zipper and landed near her foot.

She retrieved it again then hesitated. The paper was worn smooth, the creases frayed as if someone's sweaty and oily hands had folded and unfolded it many times. She glanced toward the door. The shower turned on. Telling herself this would be nothing but a blank page and she was betraying her son's privacy for no good reason,

Hannah nevertheless tucked the triangle into her pocket and headed downstairs.

The credits were rolling on Belle's movie. Hannah bustled her daughter upstairs and gave her a bath in the tub adjacent to Hannah's room. All the while her attention remained fixated on the paper in her pocket. By rote, she bundled Belle off to bed then paused outside Mason's room. No light seeped under the door and she heard no movement. She tapped.

"Good night, Mason. I love you."

No answer.

She covered the tiny lump in her pocket. Should she confront him and ask him about it? No. Why demonstrate distrust when she didn't even know if it was anything of consequence? She descended the stairs and ducked into the kitchen. Guilt weighed heavily on her shoulders and dried her mouth as she carefully unfolded the paper. If it was a note to or from a friend she'd have to refold and return it. She hoped she could remember how.

"Do It Or Else," the messy scrawl said.

It wasn't Mason's handwriting.

Adrenaline pumped through her, quickening her heart rate and making her hands shake. Fear squeezed her throat. Do what? Was this a threat? It sounded like one. But from whom? Would Mason tell her if she asked?

No, she couldn't do that. Picking up his books was one thing. Reading his note was an invasion of privacy. And he'd already threatened to run away tonight. If he felt betrayed by both her and Brandon…the outcome wouldn't be good.

Spying on her children was something she'd sworn she'd never, ever do. But she couldn't let this go. Mason's safety could be at stake.

Brandon. His name flashed into her mind. She immediately rejected it.

Brandon would know what to do, her subconscious whispered again.

Resigned, she pulled out her phone, snapped a picture of the note, then texted it along with an explanation to Brandon.

Found this in Mason's room.

Seconds later her phone chimed, signaling a reply.

Bag it. I'm on my way.

She didn't want him storming in and upsetting Mason any more tonight. She texted back.

No. Meet me for lunch tomorrow.

I'll get a table at Lou's.

Her pulse quickened again. But this time it was more anticipation than fear. Did she want to meet in public where they might be overheard? No. But she didn't want to meet in private, either.

How about the park? she typed.

Roger. I'll bring lunch.

A KICK OF something Brandon refused to name surged through him when Hannah entered the park. The disturbing feeling propelled him to his feet from the picnic table. He took in her slim shape in lemon-yellow scrubs, then the shadows beneath her eyes registered and awareness turned to concern.

He indicated the bench across from him and opened the paper sack from his favorite deli. "Did you get any sleep last night?"

Hannah shot him a wry, censuring look. "Thank you. You look great, too."

He grimaced and set a container of salad in front of her. "I'm sorry, but the worry weighing you down is hard to miss. When you get stressed you look…fragile."

Her eyebrows hiked, making him wish he'd kept his trap shut. That had sounded sentimental— almost as schmaltzy as him remembering which dressing she preferred and that she didn't like boiled eggs on her salad. Damn. He should have brought burgers.

"Do you have the note?" he asked to change the subject.

"I do. But first, you need to know that Mason wasn't refusing to meet your team last night. He didn't want to embarrass himself in front of them by being bad at darts."

"He told you that?"

"Yes."

Sounded plausible, and she'd bought it. He didn't. But there was no reason to raise her defenses. "The note?"

She dug into her tote and extracted a plastic freezer bag containing a sheet of standard, three-hole notebook paper. It had a lot of creases, as if it had been folded into a small package—the kind easily passed off without notice. The black marker used to inscribe the message had a blunted tip, most likely caused by overuse or excessive pressure.

"I found it under his bed folded into one of those triangle football things. It might have spilled out when his backpack tipped over."

Her words confirmed his suspicions. Without removing the page from the baggie, he flipped it to examine both sides. The lab would have a field day getting DNA off this page—in the unlikely event it came to that. Even though he suspected he knew the answer he asked, "What did Mason say about it?"

"Nothing. I didn't ask. He'd already threatened to run away once yesterday."

There was more to Hannah's fear of confronting her son than she'd revealed. He'd have to go there if he wanted to figure out what made her tick. Buying time to think, he passed out the plastic utensils, napkins and bottled water.

"Other than the night you told me about and last night, has Mason tried or threatened to run away before?"

"No."

"Then why are you convinced he will?"

"I just am." She fussed with the plastic wrapper she'd removed from her silverware, folding it in halves then quarters. She didn't have OCD, so this had to be nervousness more than compulsivity.

He reached across the table and covered her hands to get her attention. The combination of her warmth and soft skin shot a comet of fire through him, but he didn't withdraw. He knew better than to give up ground during questioning. Her widened eyes found his, and he had to chase down his train of thought.

"My parents would have been in my face if they'd found anything like this note. And I wouldn't love them any less for it. Hannah, I need you to level with me. Why are you so afraid to be a parent?"

"I'm not. I have rules and I enforce them."

"You are a good mom, but…" He sought the

right words to explain what he meant. "It's almost as if you're afraid of pissing off Mason. But that's part of the parenting job description. Kids do and want stupid stuff and parents must set limits. If he threatens to run away every time you get in his grill, making you back off, then he holds the power in your relationship. Make me understand why you're so cautious with him."

She snatched her hands away and ducked her head then grabbed her water bottle and twisted off the top. She stalled even longer by taking a sip. Watching her swallow drew his gaze to the pulse fluttering too fast in her throat.

"My mom ran off when I was sixteen. Because my dad spied on her." The words rapped out like two separate barrages of gunfire then her eyes narrowed and her lips flattened in regret. She plucked at the bottle's label.

He wrapped both hands around his cold bottle, trying to extinguish the fire still burning in his palms from touching her. What in the hell was wrong with him? "Rick never mentioned your mom taking off."

"He didn't know the details. He only knew she wasn't part of my life."

That took him aback. She and Rick had been the perfect couple. He would have sworn they knew everything about each other. "Tell me what happened. Back then."

She picked her label until it tore free. As she

had with the utensil wrapper, she folded it repeatedly. "Dad was deployed *a lot*. He'd volunteer for missions every chance he could—for combat pay, he'd say. Mom claimed it was because he was an adrenaline junkie. She and I were used to going about our business while he was away. She was only eighteen years older than me. We were close, more like sisters than mother/daughter.

"Whenever Dad came home things were... different. He'd monitor every step we took, every person to whom we spoke. It wasn't unusual to hear the phone click as if someone had picked up the other extension to listen to my conversations. And sometimes my things would be moved around as if my drawers had been searched while I was at school. I always suspected Dad because Mom was at work during the day, and I never believed she would do anything like that.

"At the time I thought it was because I'd discovered boys and Dad wanted to know who the guys were and if I was sexually active. It was... weird, but I didn't have anything to hide, so I didn't confront him about it. Plus, Dad had...a bit of a temper.

"One morning I caught him eavesdropping outside their bedroom. I knew Mom was on the phone because I could hear her voice through the closed door. I realized then that he must have been spying on her, too. Before I could ask him why, she opened the door and caught him. They had a huge argument and didn't even see me standing there. I had to catch the school bus. The last thing I heard her yell before I left that day was, 'If you loved me, you'd trust me.' When I came home she wasn't there. I asked Dad where she was and he said, 'Gone.' That's all I could get out of him. He refused to discuss it. She never came back, and I never heard from her again."

"Was she cheating on him?"

"Statistically, I know that's the most likely scenario. But I never saw any sign of another man, and Dad never asked me if I had. She didn't even leave me a note."

Poor kid. Pain reverberated in her voice and reflected from her eyes. Even though the incident had occurred more than a decade ago, she was still marked by it. "Did he file a missing person report?"

"Not that I know of."

"Did you?"

"I tried, but we were living in base housing. The people there listened to my concerns but then did nothing."

"Do you think your father had something to do with her disappearance?"

Her hesitation spoke volumes. "I don't think so."

"And you're afraid that if you question Mason too closely he'll take off like your mother did."

"Yes."

"Hannah, you can't let fear keep you from having the difficult conversations."

"That's easy for you to say. You're not afraid of losing your child."

He pulled out a pad of paper. "What was your mother's name?"

"Janine. Why?"

"Maiden name and birthdate?"

"Brandon, what does it matter?"

"I can look into her disappearance. It'll only take a few minutes. Humor me."

"Wilson. April tenth, 1968. But you're wasting your time. I've done internet searches and found nothing." She checked her watch. "I'm running out of time. What do you make of the note?"

"Probably just from a schoolyard bully. But with social media being what it is these days, you can't ignore that threat."

"Mason isn't on social media."

"He might have an account that you don't know about. I didn't think to check when I looked at your computer. Other kids his age have accounts. You need to ask him about the note, social media and if he's having trouble with a bully."

He unwrapped his Philly cheesesteak sandwich and his mouth salivated. Hannah didn't appear to be having the same reaction to her salad. Her brow remained puckered with worry. Her fist clenched beside her plate. After a moment she shook her head.

"If I ask about a bully he'll know I read his note."

At least now he understood her fear. But she was going to have to get over that before Mason hit his teenage years—if not sooner. "Then talk to the school and find out if they know of any bullying issues."

"I can try that. I don't like the idea of him being bullied."

"Neither do I." His stomach churned with hunger and concern. "Eat, Hannah."

"I don't think I can. But go ahead."

"No can do. My momma taught me to always wait for the lady at the table."

She blinked. "That's old-fashioned."

He shrugged. "That's my family. Good ol' Southern stock."

Reluctantly, she popped the clear plastic lid from her takeout container. The spicy aroma filled the air.

"It's a Cajun chicken salad. Hope you still like spicy food."

"I do. Thank you." She stabbed a piece of meat with her fork and slipped it between her lips. The simple process of eating shouldn't be fascinating, but she had his attention. "I'm eating. That means you should, too."

"Right." He pried his gaze away from her mouth and took a bite, trying to focus on something he could have rather than something he couldn't.

"Thank you for bringing lunch. Next time's on me."

He liked the sound of that. Too much. "You can cook Saturday. I'm coming over to work on the treehouse. I'll also talk to Mason about bullies."

Once again, he held up a hand when her lips parted to protest. "A couple of weeks ago I promised him I'd teach him some self-defense moves. This will be follow-up. He won't suspect a thing. And if I'm good, I'll even get a description of the kid—if there is one—at the same time."

CHAPTER NINE

"No wonder you called dibs," Lucy said over Hannah's shoulder as they both looked out the kitchen window into the backyard Saturday morning.

"I did no such thing! I only said he wasn't your type." Hannah flushed and turned away, but the sight of Brandon, stripped down to his jeans and work boots, with sweat rivulets rolling down his tanned skin to dampen his waistband, was tattooed on her retinas.

"Wrong!" Lucy fanned her face with her hand. "He's hot. And girl, I don't mean because it's pushing ninety degrees today." She took the position Hannah had vacated and leaned closer to the glass. "Is that a six-pack or an eight-pack? I wish he'd turn this way so I could see better. Lordy, I would love to lick that slice of pale skin between his jeans and his tan line."

Hannah bit her tongue on the unexpected need to tell Lucy to keep her bawdy comments to herself. If she said anything it would only reinforce the idea that she had a more-than-friendly interest in Brandon. And she didn't. Never would.

She fisted her hands, and her engagement diamond bit into her palm. She turned it around and the sun caught the stone and flashed, reminding her of Rick, the one who'd put it on her finger. Fast on the heels of that memory, she recalled her husband telling her that Brandon had helped him pick out her wedding set and loaned him the money to buy it.

Guilt settled heavily on her chest. Why couldn't she have a simple thought about her husband without his former partner tainting it? Even if she had none of Lucy's desire to test-drive Brandon in bed, she had no business being so preoccupied with his physique.

She rolled her shoulders, trying to loosen the kinks, and directed her attention to her friend. "You always did like a guy in a tool belt."

"It's not the tool. It's whether or not he knows how to use it. If you know what I mean." Lucy waggled her eyebrows, making Hannah's face burn hotter. She'd heard similar comments from Lucy before, and they'd never bothered her the way they did now. But knowing the subject of Lucy's lust changed everything. She hated for Brandon to be discussed like a bar pickup.

"He has the confident swagger of a guy who knows how to please a woman." Then Lucy's expression sobered. "My rampant hormones aside, he seems to be good with Mason, and very patient teaching him to use the power tools. I wish my ex would show half as much interest in his girls."

Hannah remained silent even though she was tempted to spur Lucy on to another rant about her deadbeat ex rather than listen to her discuss Brandon.

"And Brandon has common sense—a rare quality these days," Lucy continued, making Hannah wish she'd spoken up. "He put up the slide first so the girls would stay out of his hair while he worked on the rope. I just about melted when he let each of them screw in a bolt. I might go down the slide a time or two myself. Just to show my appreciation."

"You do that." But Lucy was right. Brandon was surrounded by children, and he interacted with them comfortably. She didn't know many single guys who could do that. He'd done the same at his family's cookout when the kids had climbed all over him. Like a train car connected to the engine, the memory of how she'd practically crawled into his pocket in the barn followed.

She derailed that unwelcome thought by remembering Rick, who'd been natured differently. Her husband had preferred to tackle projects alone and without interruption. Brandon, on the other hand, included those around him, and he taught as he worked, talking the kids through unfamiliar deeds repeatedly, if necessary—the same way he had with Rick.

And there she went again, making unfair comparisons.

Lucy pushed away from the counter. "He looks

thirsty from all that hard work. I think he could use some lemonade. Wasn't it smart of me to have made a gallon?"

"Brilliant." Hannah tried and failed to keep the sarcasm from her voice.

Lucy and the girls had shown up unexpectedly with cookies, lemonade and a sack full of hot dogs to grill thirty minutes ago. Hannah wished she'd never mentioned Brandon was coming over. And while she was grateful to her friend for providing lunch, it meant the double batch of chicken tetrazzini Hannah had made this morning would have to wait until tomorrow, and because she and the kids couldn't finish it, she'd be carrying it for lunch every day next week. Carb overload.

Lucy grabbed the pitcher from the refrigerator and headed for the back door, carrying only one cup.

"Lucy, what about Mason and the girls? I'm sure they're hot and thirsty, too."

"Oh, right. Why don't you bring some extra cups? After we cool 'em off then maybe we'll both test Brandon's skills." She paused. "Wipe that look off your face, Hannah. I meant test the slide he installed." Then the door shut behind her precocious friend.

Hannah shook her head. Had she made a face? She'd have to be more careful with her expressions. And because she really didn't know if she could trust Lucy not to put the moves on Brandon, she quickly piled the cups, along with a bucket of ice, on a tray and headed outside. The girls came galloping toward them, but Hannah's gaze locked on Brandon. He stood with his back to her and his hands on his hips, staring up at the rope he'd draped over the giant oak tree branch twenty-five feet above his head. He had swimmer's shoulders. Her gaze drifted from his deltoids and trapezii to the thin, pale strip of flesh above his waistband. Darn Lucy for mentioning it.

Brandon turned. She yanked her gaze north. But not before the thin, dark line of hair descending from his navel to behind his fly snagged her attention. Rather than drift any further into forbidden territory, she averted her gaze to her son, who stood beside him.

"It's up, Mom." Excitement sparkled in Mason's eyes, revealing no sign of worry over the note she'd found in his room. Maybe it was an old one. Or a joke. Or something he'd picked up in the hall to play finger football with and never unfolded. Maybe it wasn't his and he had no idea what it said.

"All set?" she asked. It was more of a struggle than it should have been to keep her gaze fixed on Brandon's face and not his flat nipples or the defined rectus abdominals Lucy had pointed out.

"Almost. I want to make sure it's safe before anyone else climbs it." Brandon reached up to grip the rope and tugged, making his impressive back and upper arm muscles flex. He had to work out hard and regularly to get that kind of definition.

"Hannah?" Brandon's rough voice forced her gaze from the curve of his pectorals and biceps to his eyes. The awareness reflected back at her made her stomach swoop. He'd caught her looking. Again. Her face overheated. Ogling him was taboo. She forced air into her empty lungs and set the tray on the table before she dropped it.

"Think you'll be able to reach the top?" he asked.

She blinked. "Me?"

White teeth flashed and his hazel eyes twinkled. "Mason and I are taking bets as to whether you can make it. He says no."

His grin weakened her knees. She turned to a safer subject—her traitorous son. "Really? You have so little confidence in me?"

"You're a girl and you're old," Mason stated baldly.

Ouch. "I'm only thirty. And as for being a girl—you should never underestimate us. Just for that, smarty pants, I might have to prove you wrong." She turned back to Brandon. "Do I even want to know how you voted?"

"Wheee!" Lucy cried out as she emerged from the corkscrew slide before he could answer. Her momentum carried her forward. She stumbled several steps, landing conveniently against Brandon's broad chest. He caught her. Then she looked up at him and said breathlessly, "The slide is great, Brandon."

Hannah's nerves jangled anew and a sour taste filled her mouth. Lucy's obvious bid for Brandon's attention disturbed her on multiple levels she didn't want to explore.

He steadied Lucy and released her. "Glad you and the girls like it. Better yet that you just showed me where we need to dump mulch for the kids' landing zone."

Then he turned to Mason and clapped a hand on his shoulder. "So, you ready to learn to climb?"

Hannah saw the stunned look on her friend's face. Lucy was pretty—so pretty that guys rarely turned down her overtures. But Brandon had acted as if he hadn't even noticed her flirtatious pitch.

"Uh…" Mason dug his sneaker toe into the dirt.

"Come on, man, you were excited about the rope earlier."

"I um…don't know how to climb. I kinda… suck at it actually."

"No problem. I'll teach you. Watch my technique. Focus on my feet. How you trap the rope between your arches is as important as your handhold. Your upper body strength is something you'll have to work on and build up. That takes time. But there are several ways to climb. I'll show you one today that uses your legs more than your arms."

Then Brandon jumped, grasping the rope as high as he could. He curled his lower body, lifting his knees and revealing the eight-pack Lucy had mentioned and widening that sliver of pale skin. After clamping the rope again with his feet at waist level, he straightened and repeated the process, inch-worming his way upward in a rippling, mesmerizing display of physical power.

She tried to tell herself her appreciation of his physique was purely professional because she worked with a lot of athletes. But her dry mouth and erratic pulse gave away the lie. And she wasn't the only one watching his ascent. Lucy seemed equally awestruck.

At the top, he clung precariously with his feet while he bounced to test the stability of the limb and tree. Fear clogged Hannah's throat. What if he fell? He was pretty high. Broken bones would be inevitable.

Finally, he descended. Once his boots hit the ground air gushed from her lungs. Only then did she realize she'd been holding her breath.

"You're pretty good. For an old guy," Mason jibed.

Brandon mock-punched his shoulder. "Knucklehead," he said with a smile on his face that made Mason beam. "Ready to try?"

Mason shook his head.

"Then who's next? Hannah? You going to show your boy how it's done?"

She gulped and prayed Brandon had no idea of the excitement that watching him climb had stirred in her veins. Good grief, she was almost as bad as Lucy. Apparently, avoiding dark places with him wasn't going to be enough to keep her unwanted hormones in check.

Lucy squeezed between them. "I take a pole dancing exercise class, and I have excellent upper body strength. I'll bet I can climb it. Could you give me a boost?"

She flipped Brandon a look from under her lashes, but he stepped back, shaking his head. "I won't be here to help you later. You need to get started by yourself."

As far as rejections went, it was a gentle one. And Lucy took it well. Looking determined, she jumped at the rope, grasped it and hung for several seconds. She climbed a yard, but her arms weren't strong enough without the proper foot grip and she soon slipped to the ground. "My hands must be slick with suntan lotion."

Brandon swung his attention to Hannah. One corner of his mouth lifted and his hazel eyes sparkled in a challenge. He caught the thick rope and pushed it toward her. "Come on. Show me what you've got. I have five bucks riding on you reaching the branch."

He had bet on her. Exhilaration raced through her. Did he know one of her clients owned a CrossFit gym, and that Hannah often worked out with him? She'd climbed enough to know she should be able to do this. But trying and failing in front of Brandon was different than having a bad day at the gym. Talk about pressure. Then she saw Mason, Belle, Celia and Ella standing by with rapt expressions.

"Come on, Mommy. You can do it," Belle cheered.

"Put up or shut up, Mom," Mason said with a smirk.

She couldn't refuse. Hannah stepped to the rope. Impressing Brandon was not her goal. Really, it wasn't. She deliberately turned her back on him and took a deep breath, psyching herself up for the climb, then she leaped into action and locked her fingers and feet around the thick hemp. Nervousness made the first couple of yards difficult. Her muscles quivered. Then she blocked out everyone on the ground and focused on reaching the branch above her.

Hand over hand and one foot grab after the other, she worked her way to the top. Her arms and thighs protested the effort. She could hear the girls cheering then the bark of the neighbor's dog, but she didn't dare look down with the branch only a yard away. The girls' screams intensified as she reached the top and touched the limb. Pride surged through her. Then the rope went sideways and Hannah almost lost her grip. Panicked, she clamped her arms and legs around it and looked down.

Rocky, the neighbor's new oversize mutt had the end of the rope in his mouth like a giant chew toy. The kids chased him, trying to get it away, but Rocky took that as an invitation to play and ran in circles with the rope tip. Brandon caught the dog by the collar with one hand and anchored the rope with the other, stabilizing it. If she hadn't nearly fallen, the circus below her would have been funny. Heart racing, she descended. About a yard from the bottom she released the rope, intending to drop the last few feet.

Brandon caught her around the waist and snatched her tight against him. With her back to his bare chest she slid down, her buttocks gliding over his groin. The moment her feet touched the ground he spun her to face him. "Are you all right?"

His pallor surprised her, but the heat of his body so close to hers made it impossible to process words. His hands branded her just below her bra band. They must have slipped beneath her loose tank top when he grabbed her. The skin-to-skin contact stole her breath.

"I'm fine."

He searched her face as if he didn't believe her, and his hands tightened. She could feel the hard, fast thump of his heart beneath her palm. The urge to stroke and soothe him coursed through her. Then suddenly, her surroundings penetrated. Lucy and the children were all watching.

She broke the connection, twisted free and knelt to scratch the panting, tail-wagging pup at her feet while she struggled to regain her equilibrium. "Are you looking for a playmate, big guy?"

"The damn dog almost made you fall. You could have been hurt."

"But he didn't. And I wasn't." Brandon had been afraid for her. She heard the concern in his voice, but she couldn't look at him. She focused on the pooch. "Rocky, does your momma know you've dug out of your yard again?"

"He's a hazard," Brandon insisted.

"He's a puppy. And the kids adore him."

Mason bounded forward. "He wasn't trying to hurt her. I'll take him home." Leading Rocky, he headed toward the fence but paused to look over his shoulder. "That was pretty cool, Mom."

Then her son continued on his way. Hannah's heart swelled with love. Mason was a good boy. Whatever the cause of this rough patch, she'd get him through it.

"It's not safe to use the rope with that dog out."

"He's just an overgrown puppy who likes to play." She risked looking at Brandon. His scowl deepened and she added, "I'll talk to my neighbor and see what we can do to keep Rocky in the fence."

"Who's ready to cook some hot dogs?" Lucy asked in an overly bright tone.

The girls all squealed, "Me, me, me."

Brandon shifted his attention to the girls. His tight grin was clearly forced. "I'd better light the grill."

He strode toward the patio like the Pied Piper, with Belle, Celia and Ella skipping behind him. She wasn't disappointed when he stopped to pick up and don his shirt. When she peeled her gaze away, she caught Lucy staring at her. Embarrassed, she didn't know what to say.

Her friend threw up her hands. "Forget it. He's yours. I know when I'm beaten."

"He is not mine," Hannah protested.

"Oh, please. You two are circling each other like boxers in the ring. You can fight the attraction all you want. But girl, you are going down. And if you're smart, you'll stop fighting it, and write yourself a prescription for some therapy with him. You need it. And from the way he looks at you, he does, too."

"I can't write prescriptions."

Lucy rolled her eyes. "You know what I mean. You swear you'll never marry again, and a fling with him could never be more than a temporary scratch to your itch because of his job. So screw his brains out, for pity's sake, and relieve some of that tension before you pop an aneurysm. Then give me all the juicy details."

She strolled after the others, leaving Hannah dumbfounded. Lucy was wrong. She and Brandon weren't going to have an intimate relationship. They just had the unfortunate spark of bottled-up chemistry between them. But that could be controlled.

BRANDON'S SISTERS HAD always predicted that one day his need to be a hero would bite him in the ass. Today was that day.

Hannah's near-fall and his instinctive dive to catch her had left him with a hunger that he hadn't been able to soothe throughout cooking and consuming lunch. He'd been stung by that same bee in the barn at the orchard and in her stairwell during the storm. You'd think he'd have enough sense to avoid the nest.

But he'd made a promise and the job here wasn't finished.

He sprung to his feet after the meal. "Mason, let's head to the front yard, and I'll teach you some self-defense moves."

Mason scanned the squealing, talkative girls and jumped up. "I'm in."

Brandon intended to cover a few basic strategies and slip an interrogation into the process. They rounded the house. Brandon found an area with thick grass and kicked a few pinecones out of the way. "This is a good spot."

Mason looked eager and focused as Brandon faced him. "Remember, your goal is to escape."

"Yeah, yeah. I know. Fighting's a last resort. So what do I do? Kick the guy in the nuts?"

"Try it."

Mason looked at him like he was crazy then kicked. Brandon caught the boy's heel and held it. Off balance, Mason jumped on one leg, flailing his arms to keep from falling.

"This is why going for the groin is not the best starting point. Everyone expects it. All I'd have to do is yank your foot out from under you, and you'd be flat on your back and at my mercy." He released his hold and Mason regained his balance.

"That's not good."

"No. Now, picture your opponent." He gave the boy a moment. "How big is he?"

"About your size," Mason replied without hesitation.

"Age?"

Mason's eyes narrowed with suspicion. "Why?"

He'd anticipated the question. "Age determines experience and often strength and ability. You don't have to be exact. Ten? Fifteen? Twenty? Fifty? Ninety? Is an old man going to whip you with his cane?"

Mason snorted a laugh, distracted, just as Brandon had hoped. "Um…fourteen."

He made a mental note. "Is this attacker a bully who's a pain in the ass or someone threatening your life?"

Mason's feet planted. His gaze lowered to his shoes. "Um… I don't know."

Brandon kept circling him, trying to keep Mason focused on actions rather than the questions. "C'mon, kid. It's important. The level of threat determines how you respond and what I need to teach you. If the guy's just a nuisance who harasses you in gym class then you don't want to cause permanent damage by say, gouging his eyes out or slamming the heel of your hand into his nose and driving bone fragments into his brain."

He demonstrated each action as he spoke with quick jabbing movements that stopped short of Mason's face but captured his attention. "That could possibly kill him. If he's after your life, then all bets are off. You do what you have to do."

"I uh… I don't think I'll need to kill anybody."

Two questions answered. "Good. Physical threats aren't the only ones. These days with social media, you have to worry about cyber threats. Do you have any accounts?"

Mason lowered his arms to his sides, his body language going tight. "I'm thirsty."

Filing the evasion away, Brandon reached out and grabbed Mason's wrist to prevent him from returning to the house. "See if you can escape."

Mason squirmed and twisted, but Brandon held fast. "Stop. Now rotate your wrist so that your thumb points upward." He waited until the boy complied. "Snap your elbow as quickly as you can, bringing your fist to your shoulder."

Mason did, successfully breaking the hold. "Cool."

"See how easy that was? You're using physics to find and break the weakest point. And if that doesn't work you can twist and break loose. Grab my arm and I'll show you how." Mason did and Brandon quickly freed himself with a circular sweeping motion. "Same thing works if someone grabs both arms. You use their own body against them. Try it."

He caught a glimpse of movement at the dining room window. Hannah. His heart thumped and his brain emptied. His flesh burned anew at the memory of touching her soft skin and the slick slide of her bare back against his abdomen when her shirt had ridden up when he'd caught her.

He wanted her. And she knew it. But that didn't make it any less wrong.

Willing himself to focus because he was gaining ground with Mason, he quickly broke Mason's grip then circled the kid again, turning his back on the window.

"Regardless of the threat level, a good slap to the ear hurts like hell. Make sure your palm is flat. Like this." He demonstrated the technique without making contact.

"Slapping's for girls."

"Not when it ruptures an eardrum. Now turn

around. I'm going to grab you from behind in a bear hug." He followed through. "If someone gets you in this position, you drop to a squat, pivot and step away. It works well when the attacker is bigger than you, but you need to react fast—before they can lift your feet off the ground. Try it."

Mason did, then straightened. His gaze flicked to the house. "Mom's watching."

"I know. Try to block her out and concentrate," he ordered himself as much as his sparring partner. But how could he forget Hannah's strength as she'd climbed the rope or the triumphant gleam in her eyes when she'd reached the top seconds before that damned mutt had endangered her life? Brandon's visceral reaction to *Rick's wife* was almost enough to derail his strategy with Mason.

"Let's do it again and this time we'll add an additional level of defense. As you escape, fight. Either throw an elbow back into your attacker's groin as you go down or turn and punch his nads as you come up."

"I'm not touching another guy's junk!"

Another clue. "If you're in danger you will do whatever it takes. Try it but without contact. I want to be able to walk to my truck later."

Mason snickered, getting on with the lesson as Brandon had intended. He tried the turn and punch maneuver.

"Good. Now we'll try a variation on that. Drop, turn and follow up with a kick to the kneecap instead of the groin using your instep. You'll drop 'em fast. It hyperextends the leg, and causes serious and usually permanent damage. Only use it in a potentially lethal attack."

"You keep saying that."

"Keeping my job depends on me reading the threat level accurately and reacting appropriately. It's a skill I didn't pick up until I was much older than you. I used to fight at the slightest provocation. Got me into after-school detention more times than I care to admit."

"What did you fight about?"

"Not what. Who. Your dad."

"You fought my dad? Why?"

He shook his head and grabbed both of Mason's wrists this time. "I fought *for* your dad. He was an egghead. That seemed to draw bullies like roadkill draws buzzards. Know what I mean? Try to escape."

Mason broke Brandon's hold with the skills he'd just learned and then rounded his shoulders. "Yeah. I know."

"Being a brainiac is like being a star athlete. Everybody wants to be you, but they can't. So some will try to take you down out of spite." Brandon circled him and grabbed the boy from behind, practicing the moves he'd taught him moments ago and trying to keep Mason engrossed in the physical rather than the mental part of this exercise.

"I'm a farm boy," he said into Mason's ear. "You don't mess with me, my family or my friends. If someone was bothering you, your mom or Belle, I'd be battle-ready in the blink of an eye."

Mason hesitated, giving Brandon time to lift his feet off the ground. "See how helpless you are now? You need to react faster. But if you get caught like this become a deadweight. Your captor expects you to fight not go limp. It's likely to throw him off balance, and if it does, it gives you another shot at getting free."

He set Mason down. "Try again."

Mason dropped as soon as Brandon grabbed him then turned. "Now practice the kick but don't bust my knee."

The boy grinned and followed through.

"Good. There's all kinds of intimidation. We covered bodily threats, but we haven't hit on verbal or written ones yet. You have to figure out how to respond to those. Sometimes, the best way is to ignore them, too. Other times the only solution is to ask for help."

Mason stiffened, his lips pinching tight. Brandon pretended not to notice and kept circling him like a boxer in the ring.

"When someone wants to control you verbally, they'll try to cut off your escape routes with threats against you or your family. In every kidnap movie you've ever seen the bad guys always say, 'Don't contact the police,' because they know that's exactly what you should do. If you don't, they maintain control."

He clamped a hand on Mason's shoulder. The kid's muscles were rigid. His fight or flight instincts had kicked in. Brandon was on to something. He had to narrow it down.

"If someone grabs you like this, come around and strike their face with the heel of your hand. It's almost like swinging a baseball bat. Try it."

Mason complied, then Brandon repeated the procedure, this time holding tighter—just long enough to say into Mason's ear, "You know you could talk to me if you had a problem."

Mason twisted away and backed several steps out of Brandon's reach. "Why does everybody keep saying that?"

Defense. Damn.

"Because you're about to enter your teen years. I'm not going to lie, Mason. Parts of being a teenager suck rotten eggs. Your body will do things you can't control, and you'll be put in situations that are uncomfortable. Middle school is a training ground for juvenile delinquents and future felons. If you haven't encountered any of those yet, you will. You need to know how to handle them. It helps to have someone who won't judge you but will listen and give advice. Your dad's not here to do that, but I am. I've seen just about everything."

"No! You haven't. Not you or my mom," Mason exploded, rocking Brandon back on his heels.

"My world is completely different than yours was at my age. You have no clue! So don't tell me you understand. You don't!" Then Mason pivoted and raced toward the house. He bolted through the front door, slamming it behind him.

Brandon watched him go. The over-the-top reaction was telling, albeit circumstantial, evidence. He'd need something concrete to move forward with the investigation. But Hannah stood between him and the facts.

UNABLE TO BEGIN the task she'd been avoiding for five years, Hannah perched on the edge of the bed she'd shared with Rick and stared at the dresser. Rick's dresser.

His spare change still filled the beer mug in front of the mirror. His broken sunglasses—the ones he'd kept meaning to repair, but hadn't— were hooked over the glass rim by the remaining earpiece. Beside the mug lay an unopened Chapstick, two peppermints and a money clip he'd been given as a gift but never used.

The line of his personal items stood like sentinels, guarding the contents of his drawers. The bedroom still smelled like him. That was the main reason she never entered this room except for a rush dust job and vacuuming once a month.

When she'd answered the phone last night she'd still been shaken up over the close encounter with Brandon. More specific, she'd been rattled to the core by her response to him. The church's be-reavement coordinator had asked a favor. Hannah had agreed without thinking about how hard—how paralyzing and gut-wrenching—the simple act of giving could be.

She wasn't ready. And now she had to find the nerve to call the coordinator back and renege on her promise.

The clank of the backyard gate jarred her. She checked on Belle, but her baby was sleeping on the sofa. Mason's youth pastor had picked him up and taken him to church. Who could it be? Surely Mason hadn't run away from church?

She hurried to the French doors overlooking the yard. Brandon, pushing a wheelbarrow, crossed her lawn. Her heart thumped against her ster-num like a bass drum as she watched him dump his load beneath the slide. Mulch. He turned and headed back out the gate.

Anger stirred in her chest. She couldn't afford more of his "help." She'd be repaying him for the next decade. She shoved open the door and marched outside. "What are you doing?"

He stopped, glanced back to the master bed-room door she'd exited, then his gaze returned to her. "Why aren't you at church?"

"Belle has the stomach flu. I asked you not to spend any more money on us, Brandon. And yet you sneak in here while you think I'm away?"

"I got the mulch free from a day care center

that's closing. I figured I'd install it and reinforce the fence between you and your neighbor's dog while you were out."

She crossed the lawn, halting a yard from him. He wore jeans and a gray T-shirt, which already sported sweat-dampened armpits. The shirt also happened to accentuate his pectorals and biceps. He hadn't shaved. The stubble made him look— She squashed her appreciation and focused on her anger.

"You figured, huh? Without asking. While I was out. Because you knew it was wrong."

He parked his leather-gloved hands on his hips. "Would you have agreed?"

"No."

"But you want the kids to be safe using the equipment, right? And the rope isn't safe without cushioning underneath."

He had her. "You swear the mulch was free?"

"To anyone willing to haul it away. Just let me finish. I'll stay out of your way."

"Fine." Distance would be for the best. She turned to go back inside.

"Hannah?" She paused. "Have you moved back into the downstairs bedroom?"

If anyone could understand the difficulty of the task ahead, Brandon would. She slowly pivoted. "No. One of our church members lost everything in a fire Friday night. He needs clothes—clothes he can't afford to buy because he wasn't insured.

He's Rick's size—tall and thin. One of the church ladies asked if I'd donate Rick's stuff."

He dragged a hand across his face and whistled. "You still have everything?"

"Yes. I couldn't… I haven't…" She met his somber gaze and sucked in a shuddering breath. "I don't think I can do this, Brandon. It hurts too much."

"Yes, you can. I'll help." He peeled off his gloves and tossed them into the wheelbarrow. "Rick would be the first guy to give someone the shirt off his back. He'd want you to do this, Hannah."

Her eyes and throat burned. "You're right."

"Let's get it done. Do you have boxes?"

She nodded because she couldn't speak. He put his arm around her shoulders and steered her back to the house. The first shock of contact rippled through her. She ordered herself to relax. Brandon was only offering comfort—comfort she desperately needed to get through the job ahead. That was all it was. All it could be. Nothing more. That meant leaning into him and soaking up his surety was a no-no.

Inside the bedroom he paused and slowly scanned the room. His arm dropped to his side and his fists clenched. His jaw muscles bunched and grief invaded his features, carving lines across his forehead, at the corners of his eyes and bracketing his mouth. Then he directed pain-filled eyes her way. He obviously wasn't any more eager to do this than she was.

"I'll take the closet if you'll take the drawers." Without waiting for her reply, he set off like a man on a mission.

Forcing herself into action, she started with socks. There were no memories attached to those. She dumped them into the box then surveyed the rest of the drawers. Underwear was next. Rick had been a tighty-whitey guy. No nostalgia in those. But then in the back corner she found a set of satin boxers covered in kisses that she'd given him as a gag gift one Valentine's.

The strength left her knees. She sank onto the bed. He'd only worn them the one time. The night Belle had been conceived. She hugged them close. She couldn't give these away. The scrape of hangers across the rod jarred her. She sprang to her feet and shoved the boxers back into the drawer seconds before Brandon exited the closet with an armload of clothing.

He took one look at her face and stopped. "You okay?"

The smile hurt her cheeks. "Yes."

His skeptical expression told her he knew better. But he deposited his load and returned to his task.

She let her shoulders relax, then tackled a pile of white undershirts. Then she had nothing left but the T-shirt drawer. She dreaded that. Rick had loved to collect shirts from places they visited or products he used. Each one would have a memory attached. Parting with them would be hard. So she'd do it quickly, like ripping off a bandage.

She grabbed an armload, pivoted and dumped them into the box. One snagged the cardboard. She reached out to pluck it free and froze. Her fingers clenched the worn fabric. She bowed her head and fought the urge to bury her face in it.

"Hannah?"

She hadn't heard him return. The lump in her throat refused to dislodge. Her lips quivered and tears pooled in her eyes. She blinked furiously, determined not to cry in front of him. "This is the shirt he was wearing when we met."

Brandon dumped his load on the bed and took her into his arms, tucking her face against his shoulder. He stroked her back. "It's okay to keep it. No one is asking you to forget him, Hannah."

"Everyone says I need to move on."

"Remembering Rick is important. For your sake and for Mason's and Belle's." She felt his chest rise and fall beneath her cheek, and his jaw tense against the top of her head, then for a brief moment, his arms tightened. "For mine."

The cadence of his strokes along her spine changed, slowing, the pressure lightening. A shiver ripped through her. Ashamed, because she knew he only meant to comfort her, and against her will, her body was interpreting his actions as something else. She stiffened. His scent filled her lungs and his body heat seeped into hers, settling in the pit of her stomach. Her heart and respiratory rates picked up.

She pushed away, putting needed inches between them, and prayed he hadn't noticed. She tried to brush it off. "You're very good with crying women."

"Years of practice." His words were clipped, his eyes unreadable.

Her mouth was dry, her tongue thick. "Your sisters."

"I learned to get them past the meltdown. Then I put the fear of God in the jerk who'd hurt them."

"You're protective." He had been of Rick, now he was of her and her family. Whether she liked it or not.

"Comes with the territory."

She studied his strong face. He was a man who'd go to battle for his loved ones.

Rick had been a good man, a great husband and a fantastic father. But he'd been a peacemaker, not a fighter. He preferred to avoid conflict. She'd always thought that a contradiction to his choice to go into law enforcement.

"I'll carry all this to my truck then deliver it for you after I finish with the mulch."

"Thank you."

Two men with the same job and very different personalities.

She'd loved Rick, everything about him. So why now was her body responding to his polar opposite?

CHAPTER TEN

HANNAH'S PHONE VIBRATED in her pocket Wednesday evening. Normally, she would disregard it during Belle's dance class, but since it was her birthday, and ignoring anyone who called with good wishes was rude, she dug out her phone and checked the screen. *Brandon*. Her pulse blipped.

Sunday had been…unsettling. He'd been too easy to lean on. And then she'd wanted more. And more was impossible.

She debated ignoring his text, but curiosity got the better of her and she swiped the screen and looked at the message.

I know what happened to your mother.

Her heart plunged to her belly then galloped back up her throat. She glanced around the parent waiting area, but all of the other mothers were too engrossed in their cell phones or conversations to notice her. And Lucy was watching the girls.

What? she typed back.

Meet me at Giuseppe's after dance class. I'll tell you over garlic knots.

Her fingers flashed over the screen.

Coercion? Seriously?

2 much 2 text.

She glanced at Mason, who was immersed in a book, then Belle, then Lucy. They were supposed to go to the chicken restaurant after dance. The girls wanted to play on the indoor playground.

But he knew.

As badly as she wanted answers, she needed to keep her distance and her promise to the kids. She typed,

Can't. Have prior plans.

Change them, came the quick reply.

"That was adorab—Hannah!" Lucy stared at her as if she'd grown another head. "You're missing the girls' new dance routine. What is wrong with you? You never play on your phone at practice."

She shoved it back into her pocket. "Sorry."

He knew.

"Who's texting you? Did your father remember it's your birthday?"

"Dad called early this morning, smarty pants. It's Brandon."

"Wishing you a happy, happy?"

"He says he knows what happened to my mother, and he'll tell me if I meet him after practice. I told him we had other plans."

"Are you kidding me? You could solve the great mystery? Meet him where?"

"Giuseppe's."

"Ooh. That yummy Italian bistro? Let's eat there instead of the chicken place."

"I love Giuseppe's," Mason chimed in. "And Mom, you ate all the garlic knots last time."

"You had your share before I got mine," she reminded him. "The girls wanted to play in the ball crawl at Clucky's."

Lucy shook her head. "They're getting all the exercise they need here. And that ball pit is smelly and nasty. I always wonder what kind of germs are in it. I'd rather have pizza than chicken bites. How about you, Mason?"

"Absolutely," her traitorous son affirmed. "Their pizza's the best! You could get garlic knots and that Caesar salad thing you like, Mom. Please, *please*?"

Hannah's heart pounded. She wanted the information. But she didn't want to see Brandon. Dreams about his touch had given her a couple of restless nights. Nonetheless, she pulled out her phone and texted.

We have Lucy and the girls, too.

I'll get a big table, he replied.

She couldn't believe she was even considering giving in to his ridiculous request. Excitement and trepidation warred in her chest. Where was her mother now? And why hadn't she contacted her in fifteen years? She could finally get answers. But what if she didn't like them?

Be there in 20.

It seemed to take forever for the class to finish, to get the girls changed out of their leotards and load the tribe into their respective vehicles. And though the restaurant was only five minutes away, the drive felt like five hours. They caught every red light and had to stop at every crosswalk.

He knew. And soon, she would, too. That was the only reason she was excited. Her rapid pulse had nothing to do with Brandon.

By the time the bistro came into view Hannah was a rat's nest of nerves. She saw Brandon's truck in the parking lot immediately, but the place was packed. She had to drive around a few times to find a spot for herself. If it was this crowded inside, they'd never get a table for seven.

A pretty college-age hostess greeted them. Hannah scanned the dining room. The place hadn't changed since she and Rick had eaten here. Nostalgia squeezed her throat.

Lucy pushed forward. "We're meeting a good-looking dark-haired cop for dinner. Brandon Martin?"

The hostess smiled. "I put him in the back room. He said you'd have kids to corral, so I thought that would work best."

"That'll be great," Lucy answered.

"Mom, I gotta pee," Mason volunteered with embarrassing frankness and volume.

"I'll take the girls back, Hannah. You wait for him," Lucy volunteered.

"Okay."

Mason headed to the restrooms nearby, and the girls followed the hostess to the back. Hannah suddenly felt every one of her thirty-one years. It seemed like only yesterday that she'd taken her son into the ladies' room with her instead of standing guard outside the men's room door.

She surveyed the other diners. From the number of cars in the lot, she would have expected every red-and-white-checkered table to be full, but several were empty. Then she checked her watch. Mason seemed to be taking longer than usual. She vacillated between worry that he was having problems and impatience for answers. Then finally, the bathroom door opened and Mason exited, holding up his hands. "Yes, I washed them."

"Good." They walked side by side to the back

room then Mason jumped in front of her and opened the wooden door. Pleased by the show of manners—something he must have picked up from Brandon—Hannah stepped forward.

"Surprise!" a group of thirty or so party-hat-wearing people shouted, startling her backward.

Lucy and the girls stood front and center, surrounded by Hannah's coworkers, friends from church and a few of the other dance moms and kids. Brandon stood by the back table. His cocky grin numbed her knees, and he somehow managed to look sexy even with the pointy hat on his head. Wait, no. Not sexy.

Who was she kidding? Definitely sexy.

The group launched into the birthday song. Emotion choked her up. She blinked and diverted her attention to the flowers and confetti on every table, the pink and purple balloons and streamers bunched in each corner and the "Happy thirty-first birthday, Hannah" banner stretched across the back wall. Someone had expended a lot of time and effort.

Hannah laughed when the song ended and addressed the group. "Thank you. This is… overwhelming. I had no idea."

"Pretty cool, huh?" Mason said beside her.

"I…yes. Very cool. Were you in on this?"

He beamed. "Yep."

"And you kept it secret?"

"Yep."

"Did Belle know?"

Mason snorted. "Are you kidding me? She'd have blabbed everything."

Belle skipped forward carrying an elaborate tiara. "You have to wear your birthday crown, Mommy."

Hannah knelt for Belle to put it on her head then she straightened. Lucy draped a sash over Hannah's head. "Birthday Queen," it read. Then Belle and Celia took her hands and led her to a balloon-decorated chair at the back table and seated her behind a three-tier pink and white cake with a smaller tiara on top.

"Isn't the cake bootiful, Mommy? Uncle Brandon let me pick it out," Belle gushed. "He said I can keep the crown so I can be a princess, too."

So Brandon was the culprit behind the party. She'd suspected as much. Him or Lucy, but her friend had never done anything this extravagant, and Lucy was on a tight budget, too.

Birthdays had never been a big deal in her family. Before her mom left it had usually just been the two of them having a special dinner, then...

Her mother! Brandon wouldn't be able to tell her what he'd learned with all these people around. She sought him out and found his hazel gaze locked on her. He lifted his water glass in a silent toast and mouthed, "Happy birthday."

Warmth filled her chest then doubt doused it.

Did he really have information about her mother or had the text been a ruse to get her here?

Before she could go and ask him, guests surrounded her, offering hugs and felicitations. Then the servers paraded in with platters of food.

Over the next hour she interacted with each guest—except Brandon, who somehow managed to always be on the opposite side of the room from her. Someone had set up a game of pin the tutu on the ballerina on one wall and a rubber-tip dartboard on the other. After the meal the children took turns between one and the other. Mason, she noted, seemed quite proficient at darts. That set up another worry that maybe he hadn't been as afraid of embarrassing himself at dinner with Brandon's friends as he'd claimed. She pushed that aside. Of course a child would fear competing against adults.

As wonderful as the party was, it seemed to last forever. When people began to leave, she rose, determined to corner Brandon.

Lucy intercepted her, grabbing her by both shoulders and looking her in the eye. "If you don't nab him you're an idiot. Love you. Happy birthday." She hugged Hannah and hustled her girls out the door.

Finally, only Brandon, Mason and Belle remained. "Brandon, do you really know what happened to my mother or was your text a trick to get me here?"

"I know. Take the kids home. Get them to bed. I'll deal with this then stop by."

Her heart tripped faster. Had he been the only party organizer? She eyed the bedraggled room. "We should help clean up."

"It's a school night. Go. Good night, kids. Thanks for your help."

Belle rushed forward and threw her arms around his hips in a big hug. "I love you, Uncle Brandon."

Horrified, Hannah watched him hug her back. Belle didn't seem to notice Brandon's silence, but Hannah did. As soon as Belle released him Mason sidled over and gave Brandon a fist-bump. The almost hero-worship on her son's face filled her with even more concern. Letting Brandon into their lives had been a mistake. Her children would pay the price.

Lucy had put the remnants of the cake into a box. Brandon shoved it into Hannah's hands. "I'll be there in about an hour."

She nodded and urged the kids out the door, knowing that for her children's sakes and hers she had to cut ties with Brandon tonight.

HANNAH PACED THE FOYER. After the excitement of the party, the children had been difficult to settle. Her anxiety over Brandon's pending visit probably hadn't helped.

Mason had chattered like the sweet boy he'd

been before the trouble had started. And Belle…
Belle had asked again why Brandon couldn't be
her daddy. Hannah didn't know how to explain
to them that Brandon was the reason their father
hadn't been here tonight. And even if Brandon
wasn't responsible, he was still a cop—which was
a very high-risk job. She couldn't afford for any
of them to depend on him and then have him
ripped away.

Finally, headlights cut through the darkness of
her front yard. Her heart rose to her throat. She
opened the door, letting in the warm, humid night
air even before Brandon parked his truck. The
full moon hung over her head. A lover's moon.
She'd spent many a night like this by the fire pit
with Rick, planning their future projects for this
big, old house.

She tucked the memory back into its safe
place and focused on the man retrieving something from his back seat. Impatience made her
dance in place. Then Brandon turned toward the
house. His arms were overloaded with two pizza
boxes, a sack holding something and dozens of
balloons. She vaulted into action, meeting him
halfway down the sidewalk.

"I brought the leftovers. Mason can have pizza
for his lunch for a few days, and you'll have garlic knots. And there was no point in leaving the
flowers behind. The restaurant would throw them
out." He offered the balloons and the bag con-

taining the flower arrangements. Their fingers brushed as she took the strings. The sparks of awareness dancing up her arm almost shocked her into releasing the balloons. Her involuntary reaction only reinforced her decision to tell Brandon goodbye tonight—once he shared what he'd learned about her mother.

"Did you plan all this?" she blurted, trying to derail her wayward reaction.

He shrugged. "It was a group effort."

The master interrogator was a master deflector.

"Instigated by you?" she pressed as she retraced her path to the house with him by her side.

One corner of his mouth lifted. "Actually, it was Belle's idea. She wanted you to have a princess cake. She drew a picture of it and Mason scanned it and emailed it to me. I promised her I'd get it. We didn't tell her we were expanding on her idea. Mason and Lucy helped pull it together."

Rick had never thrown her a party. Continuing her mother's tradition, they'd usually had a quiet dinner for two somewhere. Splurging on a sitter had been a big deal budget-wise. "Well, thank you. It was a wonderful surprise and the children enjoyed it."

"Did you?"

"I…yes."

"Then you're welcome."

"But Brandon, you have to quit spending money on me, on us."

"Hannah, I'm not keeping a tab. What I give, I give freely with no strings or expectations of recompense. I'll put the pizza in the fridge while you figure out what to do with the flowers and balloons." He headed for the kitchen.

She hated being beholden to anyone. With fingers that didn't want to cooperate, she tied the ribbons to the banister then joined him in the kitchen and extracted the vases from the bag. The heady fragrance of stargazer lilies filled the air, but it was nervousness, anticipation and dread that clogged her throat.

"What did you find out about my mom?"

He pointed to a chair. She sat at the table, mainly because her knees were shaking. The guarded look in his eyes increased her anxiety. Then she bounced back up again. "Do you need a drink or anything?"

"No. Are you sure you want to know? Sometimes truth is hard—"

"Tell me!"

He studied her for interminable seconds, as if judging whether she could handle what he knew. "Your mother was killed in a car crash three days after leaving you and your father."

The bald statement stole her breath and her strength. She sank back onto her seat. Then a confusing tangle of relief and loss engulfed her. Hannah would never have answers to the multitude of questions that had come up over the years. "How?"

"She was leaving town with her lover. A car crossed the center line and hit them head-on. She was probably killed on impact."

She focused on the first part and rejected it. "I never saw signs of an affair."

"She worked with the guy. He was a civilian contractor on base. Apparently, they held their assignations over their lunch hours. Sometimes meeting at your house. Sometimes his."

Shock kept her mute. She sifted through her memories for any man who might have been a frequent visitor or one whose name her mother might have mentioned, but she came up with none. She made a "continue" movement with her hand.

"She was pregnant. When your father found out, he realized that because of the timing of his deployment, there was no way it was his. He ordered her to get out."

The story was almost too much to comprehend. She didn't want to believe it. "Dad told her to leave? Did he tell you that?"

"After I confronted him with the facts, yes."

"Where did you get your facts?"

"I started with a news article about a vehicular fatality in a town near the base. It stated the man, a woman and her unborn child had been killed. Once I had that, I tracked down a coworker quoted in the article. She gave me the details.

She also said the rumor mill had been active and she suspected your father knew about the affair. That's when I called him. He verified that he'd heard the rumors while deployed, but had refused to believe what his friends were saying until your mother confirmed the information."

"So that's why he spied on us. Why didn't he tell me?"

"You'll have to ask him. But you should also know that he did tell me she'd insisted she was coming back for you as soon as she and her lover got situated, and he told her, quote, 'Over his cold ashes,' end quote."

Her mother hadn't abandoned her. And her father hadn't been willing to let her go. She'd often wondered if he loved her or just kept her out of a sense of duty. He'd never been the demonstrative sort. She rolled the discoveries around in her head and tried to make sense of them. The knowledge changed her view on so many things. Maybe Rick and her children weren't the only ones who loved her.

"Thank you for investigating and telling me. I don't know how you uncovered all this when I did multiple internet searches and turned up nothing."

"Digging up the hidden truth is what I do, and I'm used to searching for obscure details. I'm sorry I don't have better news." He reached out, as if to cover her hands, then stopped and sat back in his chair.

She was grateful for his restraint. As shaken as she was, and as much as she needed to be held, she had no idea how she'd handle his unsettling touch. The sympathy in his eyes tightened her chest with guilt, especially given what she was about to do.

"Would it have been better to learn she'd abandoned me without second thoughts?"

"Guess not." He rose. "Are you okay?"

"Yes. It will take a while to...digest."

"I'll let you get to be—I'll say good-night."

To bed, is what he'd almost said, but hadn't. Why did that hit her like a double espresso? She rose on shaky legs and walked him to the front door while she struggled to find the courage to say what would no doubt seem ungrateful under the circumstances.

"Brandon, thank you for tonight. I've never had a birthday party before."

"Then it's time you, Mason and Belle start some new traditions."

He stood there in the foyer for an awkward moment. In the past, before Rick's death, he'd have hugged her good-night. She'd been the one to stop that five years ago. And given her crazy reaction to his touch now, it wasn't a practice she'd resume. She definitely would not be taking Lucy's advice and "nabbing him."

"Brandon... I think it would be best if you didn't come around anymore." A line formed between his eyebrows. She opened the door and when he didn't take the hint to leave, she stepped onto the porch and waited for him to follow then closed the panel behind them.

"What about Mason?"

"He's behaving now. Maybe he was only going through a phase."

"And the note?"

"Maybe it wasn't his."

"That's a lot of maybes, Hannah."

"Belle already loves you. She keeps asking for you to be her daddy. Mason is getting attached. It's going to hurt them when you disappear. Lingering will only make it worse."

"Who says I'll disappear?"

"Me. I appreciate all you've done, but I can't forget...the past or how dangerous your job is."

His jaw and shoulder muscles bunched. "I promised Rick I'd look out for you."

"I'm relieving you of that promise."

He inhaled, long and slow, filling his chest and making it seem even broader. Then he dipped his chin once, sharply. "Take care of yourself, Hannah."

He pivoted and walked away. Seconds later his truck engine started. Tension drained from her, but it didn't leave her feeling relaxed. It left her empty. Instead of watching his taillights, she walked back inside and locked the door. The engaging dead bolt sounded like a loud gunshot echoing off the foyer walls. Cutting Brandon from their lives was the right thing to do. For her sake and her children's.

HANNAH WANTED HIM GONE.

Brandon climbed into his truck and drove through the darkness. He'd tried to fulfill his promise to Rick, but to do so he'd have to keep fighting Hannah. He already had a lot on his plate between work, his dad and his rental houses, and given the way his neglected hormones reacted to Hannah's proximity, it was best for both of them if he cut a wide berth from Rick's widow.

He should feel relieved to be released from the burden of watching over the Leith family. Instead, he was frustrated, irritated and, damn it, hollow. He worried about the kids. And he worried about Hannah.

She'd looked so shattered tonight when he'd told her that her mother was dead, he'd been compelled to take her into his arms. Thank God he'd nixed the gesture. It hadn't been easy. But he couldn't risk comfort turning to desire the way it had when they'd packed up Rick's clothes. He'd almost kissed her. Right there in the bedroom she'd shared with her husband. His best friend. What kind of bastard did that make him?

He hadn't intended to get attached to her or Mason or Belle. But how could he not? Hannah's surprise and delight over the party had made everything that went into the event worth it. Mason's excitement on being included in the plot had been a bonus. And it had taught Brandon just how adept the boy was with a computer. He'd scanned Belle's drawing and created and sent the invitations—both online and via US Mail.

Mason was geeky enough to need someone to help him navigate the difficult teen years ahead. And the kid might be in serious trouble, no matter what Hannah thought. There was too much evidence to clear that possibility with wishful maybes.

When Belle had hugged him tonight and told him she loved him, he hadn't responded. Not because he hadn't wanted to, but because he'd been so choked up he hadn't been able to. He'd felt as if he'd had a ten-ton hazmat truck parked on his heart with its bumper blocking his throat. She should be saying those words to her father. And she never would.

He turned into his driveway, killed the engine and sat in the dark cab. Hannah had asked him to leave her and her family alone. Again. Could he abide by her wishes and forget about her, Mason and Belle and his promise to Rick? No. Setbacks in investigations were commonplace, but they'd never stopped him from pursuing the desired outcome.

He'd give Hannah some space. But she hadn't seen the last of him. Whether she liked it or not.

HANNAH TURNED AWAY from the door.

"Why did you do that?" Mason bellowed from the upstairs landing.

Startled, Hannah looked up. Mason and Belle stood by the railing. Her son looked furious. Her daughter was crying.

"Why did I do what?" she asked, wondering exactly what they'd overheard.

"You told Brandon to stay away. He and I made a deal. And now you've screwed it up!"

"What kind of deal?" she asked, not sure she wanted to know.

"When I helped him with your birthday party he promised to teach me how to run the lawn mower so you won't have to pay the yard guy anymore, and then this summer I can start earning money mowing grass. And he talked to Mrs. Cohen. She's gonna let us borrow Rocky so we can both learn dog obedience. Rocky and me, I mean. Brandon already knows. Then I can make even more money walking the neighbors' dogs or taking care of 'em when they're on vacation. If I make enough money from my jobs then I want to get my own dog. But you've screwed up everything!"

Flabbergasted, she gaped at him. While part of her was proud of him for making a goal and plotting a way to achieve it, the other part was incensed that Brandon had made these plans without consulting her.

Mason working? While in theory it was a good idea, she wasn't sure he was old enough for that much responsibility. Lawn mowers and strange dogs were dangerous.

"I think it's great that you want to earn money and save it, but I never promised you could have a dog, Mason."

"You never let me have anything. Maybe I ought to go to boarding school. It couldn't be worse than here."

The comment stole her breath. "You don't mean that."

"Brandon's cool. He teaches me stuff. And he doesn't treat me like a dumb kid. I like him. And he likes me."

"I like him, too," Belle whimpered with big, fat tears streaking down her cheeks. "I don't want Uncle Brandon to go away."

Hannah's heart ached. She climbed the stairs. "Guys, Brandon has a very dangerous job. And—"

"Then shouldn't we try to take extra special care of him?" Belle asked.

Out of the mouths of babes… Hannah stared at her son and daughter. Was she making a mistake? No. She was protecting her children. "There are grown-up things you're not old enough to understand."

"See! There you go again treating me like a baby. I hate you!" Mason shouted then stomped into his room and slammed the door.

Belle's lips quivered. "I don't hate you, Mommy, but I'm not very happy with you right now. You ruined your birthday day."

Then she returned to her room and quietly shut the door. Hannah stared at the closed doors. She wanted to comfort her children, but she had no idea what to say.

What she'd feared had come to pass. But Brandon hadn't broken her children's hearts. She had.

CHAPTER ELEVEN

HANNAH LOWERED HER phone and tried to ward off panic Friday afternoon.

"Are you okay?" her coworker Seth asked.

"Mason didn't get off the bus at after-school care." It was nearly impossible to force the words through the terror constricting her throat.

"Have you called his school?"

"Yes. That was them just now. They said he was in his last class. They don't know where he went after the final bell rang."

"I'm done for the day. I can take your last client. Go look for Mason."

"Thank you. I… I don't even know where to start."

"The police?"

She shook her head, fear curdling her stomach. What would the Leiths make of this? Would they try to use it against her as proof she couldn't control her children?

"Not if I can avoid it. South Carolina has runaway laws. He'd end up in legal trouble."

She'd looked that up after the first incident.

"Do you think he ran away?" Seth pressed.

"I hope not. But he's…not happy with me right now." Mason hadn't forgiven her for sending Brandon away, but other than a slight coolness, he'd been behaving normally. He hadn't taken anything to school with him other than his book bag today. Suddenly, Brandon's chastisement haunted her. She hadn't searched the contents. It still felt like an invasion of privacy. If she'd missed an important clue to his whereabouts, she had no one but herself to blame.

She brushed her hair back with a shaky hand. She hadn't texted Brandon to tell him about the incident with Mason and Belle. The idea of calling him now made her insides jumpy, and inviting him back into their lives was the last thing she wanted to do. But who else could help her? No one. She was back where she'd started when she'd contacted him the first time.

"I'll call Brandon."

"The cop from the party? He seems like a nice guy. He'll help. Go. I've got you covered. And if for some crazy reason Mason turns up here, I'll call you."

"Thanks." Hannah grabbed her bag and raced out the door, dialing Brandon as she climbed into her car.

"Brandon Martin," he answered.

The sound of his deep voice rumbled through her. "Mason didn't get off the bus at after-school care. The school doesn't know where he is, but he was in his last class. He may simply have missed the bus or…or something."

"If he missed the bus wouldn't he have gone to a teacher?"

She wished he wouldn't be so calm and logical. "I guess. Should I file a report?"

"Let's look for him first. I'm five minutes from the school. I'll take the most likely route from there to your house and see if I spot him."

"My office is near the after-school place. I'll take the road from there to the school."

"We'll meet at your house."

"If you get there before him or me, I keep a spare key in a pocket inside the red pillow on the swing."

"Hannah, don't panic. He's been missing less than an hour. We'll find him. Now hang up the phone and drive carefully." He disconnected the call.

She headed straight to the after-school facility, but neither his teacher nor the administrator had seen him and had no clue where he might be. She raced back to her car and headed for the school, driving slowly and searching each road and between businesses. No sign of Mason. She regretted every lost opportunity to ask him about the note.

When she reached the school she drove around the building, hoping to see him hanging out with some of the students still waiting for their rides or staying for athletic practice. There were plenty of loitering kids, but none of them were hers and the ones she asked hadn't seen Mason. Most didn't even know who he was. She parked and went straight to the principal's office. The woman was at the front desk talking to Mason's homeroom teacher.

"Does he have a friend that he might have gone home with?" Hannah asked them.

The homeroom teacher shook his head. "I'm sorry, Ms. Leith. I don't know of anyone with whom Mason pals around. He's a bit of a loner."

Nauseated from nerves, she returned to her car and headed home. "Lord, you took Rick. Please don't take Mason. Please, help me find him. And please, please let it just be that he missed the bus and was too embarrassed to ask a teacher to call me."

But she knew deep in her heart that he hadn't missed his ride. Something was troubling her son. Maybe he was angry with her for sending Brandon away. Or maybe the old problem was still a factor. As much as she wished otherwise, she would have to rely on Brandon once again.

WHEN BRANDON DIDN'T pass Mason on the road he headed to Hannah's house, retrieved the hidden key and let himself in. He conducted a quick search of the residence, even checking the kitchen because that had always been the first place he'd headed after school as a kid. But he found no sign of Mason and no dirty dishes or crumbs to indicate that he'd been in for a snack.

On his way to the backyard Brandon passed the laptop on the coffee table and fingered the thumb drive in his pocket. He'd been carrying it since soon after Hannah had first contacted him. If he didn't find Mason he would have to look for signs of foul play. And he'd start with that computer. He'd promised Hannah he wouldn't install tracking software unless Mason was in danger. This qualified.

The yard and treehouse were empty. He scanned the area, searching for signs of disturbance. There were none. Had the kid gotten into a fight? Had overconfidence after one self-defense lesson led him to confront the bully? If there was one. Brandon mentally kicked himself for not stressing that the moves required enough practice to make them autonomic.

Was Mason hurt and lying somewhere? Or worse? Had he been kidnapped? Statistically, the latter was unlikely. Columbia, South Carolina, didn't have much of that kind of crime. But Mason was into something. Most likely something online. And if the kid was involved in chatrooms or private networks, that upped the risk factor substantially.

Brandon's job dealt with the sordid side of reality. He couldn't prevent the routine checklist from clicking through his mind. Time was always a factor in a missing person case, and he tried to tell himself that was the only reason for the urgency pounding through him. But it was more than that. Mason was more than just another potential victim. He liked the kid. If this became a true investigation, then ethically he should recuse himself. He wasn't sure he could do that.

He returned to the den, booted up the computer and installed the software. While it ran he scanned Mason's visible documents and the computer's hidden files. Nada. No emails. No chatrooms. No social media. The search history was as clean as before. He would have to take the laptop to the lab to run a deeper examination for erased data or dark web activity. He hoped like hell Mason hadn't been lured into the invisible internet. The dark web was full of nothing but trouble.

Using his cell phone, he took a picture of the school photograph of Mason that Hannah kept on a table. Then he texted it to a few of his fellow officers with a message that it was an unofficial BOLO. Each texted back, promising to keep an eye out while on patrol.

The program finished loading. He withdrew the memory drive, stuck it back in his pocket and shut down the device. Then he headed upstairs to give Mason's room a more thorough search. The drawers yielded nothing unusual. Neither did the closet or bathroom.

The front door clicked open. Brandon hustled to the landing. But Hannah, not Mason, entered the foyer below. Looking pale and rattled, she surveyed the area.

"He's not here," he said.

Startled, she glanced up. He'd seen that fearful, devastated expression countless times before, and it had never hit him as hard as it did now. Because this time, it was personal. This time it was Hannah and not a stranger.

"I was hoping…"

"I'm searching his room."

She stiffened. Her face filled with rebuttal. "Brandon—"

"Hannah, you can respect his privacy and possibly never see him again. Or you can take action and help me look for clues." He hated the horror on her face that his bluntness caused, but she needed to face facts. "Come up and let's go through his drawers and closet together. You're his mother. You have knowledge that I don't. You might see something out of place that I missed. You'll know if there are clothes missing."

After a moment's hesitation, she climbed the stairs and followed Brandon into Mason's room. "I have to find him."

Slowly, methodically, she went through each drawer then turned to the closet. She withdrew a shoebox from the back corner. Brandon knew from his earlier examination that it contained the usual boy trinkets, including the pocket knife Brandon's father had given Rick for his thirteenth birthday. Brandon had one identical to it.

He noted Hannah had carefully returned each item precisely to its place. With her shoulders rounded in defeat, she rose, looking so fragile he had to fight an urge to take her in his arms. "Nothing is missing. And he'd never voluntarily leave behind his pocket knife. It was Rick's. I gave it to Mason on his tenth birthday. He carries it everywhere except to school."

Together, they lifted the mattress and the box spring and looked between each. When they found nothing, Hannah sank onto the bed. Her hands shook as she brushed back her hair—a habit she employed when nervous or agitated.

"He and Belle overheard me Wednesday night telling you not to come back. He's angry with me. But I didn't think he'd run away. I can't lose him, Brandon."

Mason hadn't run away. But Brandon didn't voice the words. A vise closed around his chest. The strong, confident woman who'd climbed the rope just days ago was nowhere in sight. Hannah was hurting and afraid, and it was his job to help her. For her sake. For Mason's. For Rick's.

"We'll do everything in our power to find him." He'd repeated the phrase hundreds of times to other families of victims, but until now he hadn't understood how empty and uninspiring the words were.

"I've tried so hard to be both mother and father to Belle and Mason. But I'm failing, Brandon. My son is in trouble and now he's missing, and I don't know why. And this house—" Her voice broke. She blinked rapidly, fighting back tears. He had sisters and was no stranger to their emotional meltdowns. But this was different. He felt helpless and wired simultaneously.

He sat on the bed beside her and lifted an arm to put it around her shoulders, but caught himself and lowered his fist to the bed behind her instead. Even that was risky. She was close. Too close. The heady combination of her flowery shampoo and her lemon-scented hand lotion ignited a spark of something he didn't want to claim. Then she fell into his chest and he had no choice but to enfold her.

She was scared and needed comfort. That was all this was, and he could offer that. But as he'd learned Sunday, holding Hannah wasn't remotely similar to holding his sisters. Her left breast seared his pectoral like a hot coal, and a shower of sparks rained across his torso to settle unnervingly in his groin.

"The place is a money pit. It's falling apart and I can't keep up the maintenance," she whimpered, her breath steaming his collarbone with every word. "But it's all they have left of Rick and the dream he and I had for them, for us. There aren't enough dollars in the bank or hours in the day to get everything done and to also be there for Mason and Belle as often as they need me."

He fought his way out of the smoke circling his brain. "I can help with the house. I'm part of the reason you have it. And you do an amazing job with the kids, Hannah. Rick would be proud of them and of you."

She lifted her face. The tears she fought to keep from falling hit him ten times harder than an all-out cryfest. "Do you really think so? Because it feels like I'm not…enough. No matter what I do, I always feel inadequate. And now, Mason…"

Couldn't she see how strong she was? "You're a great mom."

She bit her lip, and the action riveted him. Damn it. He rerouted his attention to safer territory, but when he stared into her eyes he saw something budding there—something curious and sensual that expanded her pupils and flushed her cheeks. She stilled, and the atmosphere in the room changed. The awareness he'd experienced that night on the landing and again in her bedroom came whooshing back like a brushfire breaching a firebreak. He tried to ignore the force propelling him toward her. Tried. And failed. Against his will, his head lowered, but he caught himself and stopped.

Her sigh whispered across his lips then she lifted up to meet him. He lost the battle and sank into the softness of her mouth, into discovering the taste and sweetness of her. An ember of sanity floated to the surface and he tried to retreat, but then her fingers curled into his shirt and down he went, deep under her spell. Her tongue torched a quick path across his bottom lip. The hot, wet contact jolted him like a Taser, stalling his heart.

Her mouth was slick and hot. Hunger raged in him. He'd never reacted this fast or this intensely to anyone before. Head reeling, he grasped her upper arms, like a drowning man would a passing log, in a last-ditch effort to save himself from drowning in her. Hannah splayed her palms across his chest and his skin burned as if she'd branded him. Then she cradled his face and the soft touch of her hands incinerated his good intentions.

He tunneled his fingers into her silky hair and devoured her mouth, then greedily mapped the satiny skin of her cheeks, her neck, her shoulders, and her rib cage. He slid his hand between them to cup the soft mound searing his chest. A beaded nipple branded his palm. She gasped, sucking every last atom of oxygen from his brain, deflating his lungs and inflating his groin. Hunger engulfed him in a flash fire.

Her arms encircled him, her short fingernails kneading his back like a cat. The nipple beneath his thumb hardened even more, and a quiet rumble, not unlike a purr, erupted from her.

A click and thump penetrated his concentration. Peeling his mouth from Hannah's, he dragged himself from the mental flood and put a few inches between himself and oblivion. She blinked at him, her desire-filled eyes questioning. He gulped sobering breaths. Muffled steps ascended the stairs. A different kind of adrenaline surged through him. He shot to his feet, stepping in front of Hannah to shield her, seconds before Mason appeared in the doorway.

"What are you doing in my room?"

Relief and remorse and self-disgust cycloned through Brandon. What had he just done? He'd betrayed Rick. He turned his anger outward. Damnation! He'd kissed Hannah. And he wanted to again.

"Where in the hell have you been?" he barked at the boy.

Mason paled then his face took on a defiant expression. "Walking home. You said avoid a fight if I could. So I did."

Mason's logical answer doused Brandon's irritation with the kid. His anger toward himself, however, still burned. He should have had better control. But his worry over Mason had impaired his judgment.

Cursing his weakness, he stepped aside so that

Hannah could see her son was in one piece. At least one thing had gone right today. Mason was safe.

HANNAH SHOOK OFF her stupor and launched herself at Mason. Relieved to have him home safe, she hugged him tight enough that he squirmed. "Jeez, Mom, you're suffocating me."

In an effort to pull her shattered nerves together, she took a shuddery breath, but the aroma filling her nostrils wasn't the sweet scent of a little boy. Instead, Mason smelled like a sweaty preteen on the brink of puberty who'd walked almost four miles on a hot day. It was an unwelcome reminder that his hurts couldn't be solved with Band-Aids and get-well kisses anymore.

She pulled back, grasped him by the shoulders and inspected him from head to toe. She found nothing swollen, broken or bleeding. "A fight with whom?"

He shrugged off her touch. "A kid. Nobody important."

"If he's bullying you then I need to talk to his parents."

His eyes rounded with horror. "Don't! Please! If the guys thought I went running to my mommy everybody would laugh at me. It's nothing. Really. I got this."

"You didn't skip the bus because I asked Brandon to stay away, did you?"

"No. Didn't you hear me? I was doing what he told me and avoiding trouble."

"Why didn't you call me if you were going to miss the bus?"

"Cuz you have to work."

A sharp sliver of guilt slipped under her skin. "Your safety is more important."

"Well, I couldn't call. I don't have a cell phone."

Another jagged splinter hit home. Some of the middle-schoolers had phones. She couldn't afford one for Mason, and even if she could she doubted she would get one. She was a lousy parent. *Brandon doesn't think so.*

She risked looking at the man who'd held her, kissed her and turned her inside out with desire and saw regret in his eyes. A wave of mortification swamped her. She wanted to crawl under Mason's bed and hide. He'd offered comfort and she'd thrown herself at him.

"You could have used the school's office phone," Brandon pointed out. "I was minutes from issuing an official BOLO."

"If I'd gone to the office they'd have made me get on the bus."

"Apologize," Brandon commanded in what she suspected was his cop voice.

"For what?"

"For scaring your mother."

"But—" Mason caved under Brandon's stern stare then ducked his head and stubbed his toe into the carpet. "I'm sorry, Mom. I didn't know what else to do except hide in the bathroom till the bus left then walk home."

Before she could respond Brandon stepped forward and hugged Mason so tightly her son's eyes rounded, then he released him. "I'm glad you're okay. And I'm proud of you for avoiding the fight. But next time you pull a stunt like this without calling me or your mom, you'll have an even bigger problem with me. Are we clear?"

"Yes, sir."

Brandon held up his fist. Mason bumped it with his much smaller hand. "We need to practice those self-defense moves before you test them in a real situation."

"Got it."

Then Brandon's hazel gaze pinned Hannah to the carpet and her breath locked in her lungs. "I need to call off the guys."

Alarmed, she inhaled a sharp breath. "You have people looking for him?"

"Relax. It was unofficial. No paper trail."

Good. That meant the Leiths wouldn't hear of it. "Thanks. I know you need to get back to work. Could you show yourself out?"

His lips tightened at her less than subtle hint. "We'll talk later."

She couldn't speak for the dread clogging her throat, so she jerked a nod. Then he left, his soft tread descending her stairs. The door opened then clicked shut. She heard the clank of the dead bolt turning. He must have used the spare key.

Tension drained, leaving her suddenly exhausted. She did not want to talk to Brandon later. She wanted to forget the entire afternoon, especially the part where she'd hurled herself at him. At least she'd been spared that embarrassment of blubbering her eyes out. But that she'd kissed him—or had he kissed her? It didn't matter who'd initiated it. She'd wanted it. Every cell in her body had come to life, and for precious seconds she'd forgotten all the trials currently plaguing her.

Remorse settled heavily over her. How could she have been so disloyal to Rick? And with Brandon of all people?

She looked at her son. "You're grounded."

"For how long?" he whined.

"Probably until you go away to college." Then she sighed. Her heart swelled with love. "I don't know, Mason. I'm thankful you're home and proud of you for avoiding a fight. I'm also really angry. You scared me."

"You're the one who always says we have to take care of ourselves and not depend on other people."

Another guilt shard pierced her. Her need for self-reliance had put her son in jeopardy.

"There's a difference between being independent and being inconsiderate. You should have let someone know your plan."

He slumped. "I didn't think you'd find out I skipped after-school care."

"They called me the minute you didn't get off the bus. That's why I chose that place. They're the best. And if they hadn't called, what would have happened when I arrived to pick you up this afternoon?"

"I was going to call you from the house phone when I got here, but you and Brandon were already here…"

"He took off work to help look for you."

"Does that mean you apologized for telling him to get lost?"

"No." She hadn't, and he'd helped anyway.

"You should 'admit when you've made a mistake, and apologize.'" Mason quoted her own words back at her. "So do it, Mom. I'm starving."

He thundered down the stairs, leaving Hannah staring after him. Apparently, her lessons hadn't fallen on deaf ears even though it often felt like it. And if they were talking about anyone but Brandon she would agree with Mason. But she couldn't afford to have Brandon around.

Ever since Rick's death, she'd believed she couldn't trust Brandon. But after today, she knew the one she really couldn't trust was herself.

HANNAH SHOULDN'T HAVE been surprised to find Brandon waiting outside her office when she broke for lunch Monday. The bottom dropped out of her stomach, a sensation similar to plunging over the highest roller coaster hill.

He held a small cooler in his left hand and had a look of determination on his face that told her she wasn't going to escape. The meant discussing something she'd rather forget. But she couldn't. She recalled the persuasive pressure of his mouth and every caress of his hands. Her nipples beaded in memory and her heart pounded like a stampeding herd.

"Let's go to the park," he stated.

Maybe she could avoid this awkward conversation by tackling another one first. She'd been meaning to reprimand him for filling Mason's head with job ideas without consulting her. Either way, she didn't want to argue right in front of her coworkers. At least the park was a public location where she wouldn't do anything stupid like hurl herself at him again. Her skin burned at the memory.

She matched his brisk pace down the sidewalk. Once they'd passed through the arch he headed for their usual table. A college kid on a skateboard took it before they could get there. After a second's hesitation Brandon diverted to the only other vacant table—one secluded from the rest of the park by the trunk of a fat oak tree. Privacy. Not what she needed.

Without speaking, he unloaded the meal: thick sandwiches wrapped in paper bearing a nearby deli's logo, dill pickles, big brownies and two bottles of sweet tea.

His silence only increased her discomfort. She decided to dive right in and get this confrontation over with. "Mason isn't old enough for the responsibility of mowing yards or walking neighborhood dogs. You should have spoken to me before filling his head with ideas."

"I had several jobs around the orchard when I was his age. So did Rick. My dad made sure of it. He always said, 'Busy boys don't have time to find trouble.'"

He was missing the point. "He thinks he's going to be able to buy a dog once he's saved enough. And then I'll have to be the bad guy and tell him he can't."

"Hannah, credit me with some sense. Rocky is an ill-mannered mutt that needs to learn some manners before he hurts someone. The best way to make sure he does is to teach him myself. Mrs. Cohen is too frail to do it. I spent some time with Rocky. He's not the brightest pup in the pack. Mason will have a hard time getting him to listen and behave, and every walk will include picking up dog cra—poop. See how much he enjoys the reality of having a dog."

She hadn't thought of that. "What if that doesn't kill his enthusiasm?"

"Then maybe you'll need to rethink your objection to letting him pet sit."

Brandon unwrapped his sandwich and patiently waited, reminding her of his Southern manners. He wouldn't eat until she did. Although she had no appetite, Hannah removed the paper and discovered three layers thick of turkey, ham, bacon and at least two cheeses along with the lettuce and tomato. She'd be lucky if she could finish half.

She took a bite and he mirrored the action. The moment his mouth opened over the sandwich, she remembered his taste and the hot sweep of his tongue against hers. The errant and unwelcome thought made her choke. Brandon shot to his feet as if to render aid. She waved him off, chewed and gulped and then washed the lump down with tea.

He met her gaze across the table. "Hannah, I apologize for crossing the line Friday. It won't happen again."

And she didn't want it to. So why did his apology evoke a sinking sense of disappointment? The agony darkening his eyes told her he blamed himself. But she was honest enough to admit the kiss hadn't been entirely his fault. *Admit your mistake*, Mason had said. "I kind of threw myself at you. I was scared and panicking and I… I'm sorry."

"You were vulnerable and I took advantage. It's been a while since you've been with someone. Feeling desire is a normal biological need."

Could this get any more uncomfortable? "You're having the sex talk with me? Like I'm one of your sisters?"

His face went ruddy but he didn't look away. "All I'm saying is, I should have known better. Don't beat yourself up. You're young, smart and attractive. You have a lot to offer the right guy. One of these days you'll be ready for another relationship."

The muscles that had turned to mush over his compliments clenched in denial. "No, I won't."

"You will. Rick wouldn't want you to be alone. And he'd want you to have someone to help you look out for Belle and Mason." He covered her fist on the table. Then jerked his hand back. Had he experienced the same zap of electricity shooting up his arm that sizzled through her veins? "But I'm not the man you need. I'm not a forever kind of guy. And that's what you should look for."

Yes, apparently it could get more uncomfortable, she answered her own question. "Brandon, I'm not interested in a relationship with you or anyone else."

He held up a hand. "Hear me out. I'm attracted to you. And I hate that. It's disloyal to Rick and a betrayal of the trust he placed in me. But I'm not a kid. I can control myself. And I will from here on out."

Sliding beneath the table looked pretty good right now.

Determined to end this awkward conversation as quickly as possible, she stiffened her spine. "This…incident has reinforced my decision. Belle and Mason overheard me telling you not to come around, and they were very upset with me. But I stand by what I said. They already love you and their attachment will only grow stronger if you keep showing up. So please…let's make this a clean break. They'll be hurt less in the long run."

He shook his head. "That's why I wanted to meet you here away from their ears. I've thought about what you said, and the answer is no, I won't go back to sneaking around behind your back to help. I respected your need for space and time to heal, but I promised Rick I'd look out for you and the kids, and I will."

"I don't want your help."

"But you're going to get it. I'm Mason's godfather and thus far I've done a piss-poor job of fulfilling that duty. Mason's into something. You can't 'maybe' your way out of it.

"*And* your house is an ongoing project. The only reason Rick agreed to buy it was because I promised to help with the work it required. I can teach Mason basic home maintenance along with life skills—the way my dad did with Rick and me.

"Get used to the idea of having me around, Hannah. Because I'm going to be there whether you like it or not."

CHAPTER TWELVE

WHEN HANNAH FAILED to reply to Brandon's text, he arrived at the usual time Wednesday night to hang out with Mason during Belle's dance lesson. He wasn't going to let her shut him out.

The guys were giving him hell about missing another week of darts and wings, but he needed to get his hands on Hannah's computer and uninstall the tracking program before she discovered it. He believed it needed to be there, but he would respect Hannah's wishes—in that matter at least.

An unfamiliar car sat in her driveway. A Lexus. He slowed. She had company. He'd believed she hadn't answered his text because she wanted him to go away. But was another man the real reason? Had she found some guy with whom she could test out her newly rediscovered libido? A guy who made a hell of a lot more money than a cop, if the car was an indicator.

The question sent an ugly sensation spiraling through him. He punched it down and forced his clenched jaw to relax. If she had, he'd wish her well. But only after running a thorough background check on the man. He owed Rick that much.

Brandon parked and headed for the front door. It flew open before he reached the steps and Belle, decked out in a white leotard, tights and a sparkly tutu, bounced out onto the porch. "Uncle Brandon! Are you coming to my 'cital, too?"

Cital? Before he could translate Hannah appeared behind her, also wearing white and with the same flowery headband in her hair. In Hannah's case, the white outfit included slim-fitting pants and a silky tank top with a scarf of the same silky fabric fluttering around her narrow waist. She looked good. Good enough for a date except for the tightness of her lips and the vertical line between her eyebrows. Acid burned the back of his throat.

"Hello, princess. Hannah." He nodded and battled an urge to tuck an escaped lock into her headband.

Hannah's tension in no way resembled Belle's excitement or foretold of an evening of bliss. Her troubled gaze met his. "Belle has her first recital tonight, and we have company."

A not so subtle hint to get lost.

He clamped his molars together. He hadn't been invited to Belle's big night. But some other clown had. Why did that irritate him like a canker sore?

"I made arrangements with Mrs. Cohen for Rocky to have his first obedience lesson tonight. Can Mason help or does he need to go with you?"

"Please let me stay to help with Rocky, Mom,"

Mason begged from behind Hannah. "I don't want to watch a bunch of girls trip all over each other."

"They don't trip. They dance very well for their age. And you need to spend time with your grandparents. They've driven a long way."

Grandparents? "The Leiths are here?"

Mason rolled his eyes. "Yes. Grandmother Leith put spit in my hair."

Brandon grinned. "She used to flatten your dad's cowlick the same way. He hated it, too."

"Tell Mom you need me. *Please*, Brandon."

"I didn't know they were coming until this morning," Hannah admitted. "It was a surprise."

"Some surprise," Mason groused. "I'd rather have Ebola."

Hannah shot him a chiding look. "That's not nice."

"Can I please stay and play with—*work* with Rocky?"

"Hannah, you're letting out the air-conditioning," harped someone from inside the house. Brandon recognized Rick's mother's voice instantly even though he hadn't spoken to Margaret Leith in four years. "I feel the hot draft all the way in here."

"I should probably say hello." Not that he wanted to.

"You're volunteering to face the dragon?" Mason wailed. "Are you crazy?"

"Mason Leith!" Hannah scolded.

Brandon climbed the stairs and squeezed the kid's shoulder. "It's the right thing to do."

Hannah stood her ground with her eyes shooting angry sparks. She blocked the door for a full ten seconds, then with a huff of irritation, turned and led the way inside, leaving a trace of her scent behind. His pulse thumped harder as he followed her into the den despite her clear-as-glass message that she didn't want him here.

Walter and Margaret sat on opposite ends of the sofa with arms folded and familiar sour expressions on their faces. A walker stood on the floor beside Rick's father—a walker the man hadn't had last time Brandon had seen him. And judging by the unevenness of his scowl, he might have had a stroke. Rick's dad looked every one of his eighty years, whereas Margaret was still fighting not to look her age. She'd been forty-five when Rick was born. That made her seventy-seven. She probably still kept regular visits with her plastic surgeon and personal trainer.

Margaret stiffened the second she saw him then addressed Hannah. "What is he doing here?"

Some things never changed.

"Hello, Mrs. Leith. I'm keeping an eye on Hannah and the kids the way Rick asked me to," he replied before Hannah could. He nodded to Dr. Leith. "Sir."

"I hope you won't let him ruin your son the way he did mine," Mrs. Leith sniped, still addressing

Hannah. "Is he going to the recital? Because if he is, I'll stay here."

For a moment Hannah looked dumbfounded by her mother-in-law's rudeness, then her jaw went rigid.

"No, ma'am. Brandon is staying here with Mason," she squeezed out through clenched teeth. He'd backed her into a corner and she wasn't happy about it.

"Yesss!" The boy cheered his mother's words with a leap and a fist pump, earning him a squinty-eyed look from both grandparents.

"Then Walter will stay, too. Someone needs to supervise. And it's difficult for him to get into and out of the car and up and down the stairs anyway."

Mason's excitement deflated. He directed an anguished look toward Brandon. Brandon shared the sentiment. He couldn't get to the computer with Walter here.

"We're giving the dog next door obedience lessons. Walter's welcome to watch."

Mason, bug-eyed, mouthed silently, "Are you crazy?"

Brandon winked.

"I'm allergic to dogs, as you well know," Walter announced in a crotchety tone. Until he'd retired ten years ago, the man had been a gifted surgeon with the stereotypical God complex and lousy bedside manner.

"Then perhaps we can help you onto the porch

where you can observe from a distance," Brandon offered. The comment earned him another aghast look from Mason.

"Why in the hell would I want to sit outside in this heat? I'll stay here in the air-conditioning and watch the news—if I can find a decent channel. Hannah doesn't have cable."

Brandon kissed his plans with the computer goodbye for the night.

"We need to go," Hannah said.

Margaret rose and snatched up her purse. "Hannah, before we leave you need to put on some rouge. White makes you look insipid. And that headband is inappropriate for someone your age. Leave it here and comb your hair. Why you wear it in that flyaway style, I'll never know. A nice bob would be much neater and more professional."

Rick's mother was still a mean-hearted bitch. How she'd succeeded in a people-oriented business like banking was hard to imagine. As if to confirm his thoughts, she continued, "We'll take my car. It's much more comfortable than that old thing you drive. Fix your face and hair and meet Belle and me outside."

Then she stalked to the front door. Hannah's spine looked tense enough to snap. Wearing an expression similar to the ones officers wore when entering a nasty murder scene, she followed her mother-in-law toward the door.

Brandon had to bite his tongue against the

urge to tell Margaret that Hannah was pale because both Leiths were pains in the ass, and she'd dressed in white to match Belle because Belle liked it. Funny that he knew that but the child's grandmother didn't. Brandon snagged Hannah's elbow as she passed—a mistake. He knew it the moment her soft skin scorched his palm. But he held fast.

"You look great. Ignore her."

The color that had been lacking bloomed in Hannah's cheeks. "Thank you. I...needed that." Then she leaned closer, close enough for her scent to envelop him. "Please, whatever you do, don't mention Friday's excitement."

She was still paranoid about the Leiths taking her kids. "Are you sure you don't want me to go with you and run interference?"

Hannah shook her head. "We'll survive it." Then she straightened and turned her attention to Mason. "Be good."

"Belle, knock 'em dead, princess," Brandon called out and the little girl beamed. Then the door closed behind the females.

He turned to Walter. "Can we get you anything before we head outside, sir?"

"Find a decent news channel."

"Yes, sir." Brandon did then left the remote and a bottle of water on the table beside the doctor and headed outside.

"Why are you nice to him?" Mason asked as

they crossed the lawn. "He's mean. Both of them are. I don't know how Dad could stand them."

Brandon debated telling Mason the truth—that Rick had stayed as far away from his always-critical parents as he could. But he wouldn't do that.

"The best way to handle difficult people is to kill 'em with kindness. No matter how ugly they get, smile and be polite. Rude people get their kicks by getting a rise out of you. Don't give them the satisfaction or the power."

Mason rolled his eyes. "Huh. Easy for you to say."

"I never said it was easy. But look at it this way. When they push your buttons and you react by being as nasty as they are, they've won. It's a mind game, kid. Don't let someone else control your behavior."

Mason's eyes narrowed. "A mind game, huh? I like that."

Brandon stepped onto Mrs. Cohen's porch and rang the bell. Inside, Rocky sounded the alarm. Brandon took a good look at the boy beside him. If he ever had a kid he'd want him to be like Mason. But he would never have a family of his own. That was a luxury he couldn't afford.

HANNAH WANTED OUT of the car. The sooner, the better. And not just because she was driving a strange vehicle and she didn't know where the controls were in the dark.

Her mother-in-law had been in fine form tonight, beginning with the drop-dead look she'd delivered when she'd realized Hannah had ignored her instructions to put on makeup and remove the headband. Throughout the recital, she'd criticized the dancers, the teachers and the facility.

She had insisted that the programs and schools near her were far superior to the ones in which Belle and Mason were enrolled, and that if Hannah had any love for her children at all, she'd move closer to them, or in with them, and enroll them there. Hannah was, she maintained, denying her grandchildren the opportunity to reach their full potential, and if they lived near the Leiths they'd learn manners, implying that Hannah hadn't taught them any.

Hannah had bitten her tongue so frequently tonight it was a wonder she hadn't tasted blood. She always came away from their encounters feeling like a failure as a mother, and she had to keep reminding herself that the Leiths loved their grandchildren in their own unique way. They sent birthday cards and gifts and sometimes, like tonight, they showed up for special functions. Many of her children's contemporaries didn't have that. Hannah certainly never had. Her mother's family had disowned their daughter when she'd run away to marry a soldier the day after graduating high school. Her father's parents had been too distant from wherever her father was stationed to visit, and he'd rarely made the effort to go to them. Sadly, they were all gone now.

As unappealing as the prospect might be, Hannah took uneasy comfort in knowing the Leiths would take care of her children if something happened to her. Her father on the other hand...well, she didn't know what he'd do or even in which country he'd be living. He'd probably send Mason and Belle to boarding school.

But the hours of unrelenting criticism made it difficult to be grateful that Rick's parents cared enough to make the drive for their granddaughter's first recital. The only positive was that Belle hadn't heard the diatribe. The program had run long, and she'd fallen asleep within minutes of climbing into the leather back seat.

Hannah heaved a sigh of relief when she turned the sedan onto her street. Would Brandon still be at the house? Or had he had an earful of Dr. Leith and left Mason to fend for himself? She wouldn't blame him if he'd bailed. She'd wanted to several times tonight. If the studio instructors hadn't kept all the dancers backstage during the event, she would have gathered her daughter and left immediately after Belle's performance.

She said a quick prayer that the Leiths would go to bed early, and then immediately felt guilty for being so selfish. But she desperately needed some downtime before turning in. Otherwise, as overwound as she was, she'd never sleep.

She spotted Brandon's pickup in her driveway, and like one of Pavlov's dogs, she reacted as if she'd knocked back a double espresso. Her pulse quickened. Her palms dampened. And her whole body caught a case of the jitters.

The front door opened, and the light framed his broad shoulders for a moment before he descended the stairs and opened the driver-side door. His eyebrows hiked when he saw her behind the wheel.

"Driving Miss Daisy?" he murmured in a low rumble and with a half smile that made it difficult to recall where she was and what she was supposed to be doing.

She caught herself smiling at the movie reference then blinked back to the present and reminded herself he was forcing himself where he didn't belong. "Mrs. Leith doesn't like to drive after dark."

He offered his hand, and she put hers in it without thought. As soon as their palms met, her stomach did a little loop de loop. It threw her so off balance that she stumbled when he pulled her from the car. He steadied her then released her quickly before circling to the passenger side to assist Mrs. Leith. Hannah scrubbed her hand against her hip, trying to erase the tingling. His old-fashioned manners were…kind of nice. She definitely wasn't used to them. Not that Rick hadn't been polite. He'd just accepted her independent streak.

"What are you still doing here?" the older woman sniped as he assisted her from the car.

"Helping Dr. Leith with Mason," he replied evenly, as if he hadn't noticed her nasty tone. Then he met Hannah's gaze over the roof. "The princess is out cold. Want me to carry her upstairs?"

The gesture surprised her. "If you would, then I won't have to wake her. Once she's asleep, she usually stays that way till morning."

He opened the back door, unbuckled Belle's seat belt then lifted and maneuvered her from the vehicle. He did it with such ease she knew he'd done it before. He must be a very involved uncle.

Hannah trailed him inside. "I'll follow you up and get her out of her costume."

"We're going to bed," her mother-in-law announced loudly.

"See you in the morning," Hannah replied quietly, hoping her relief wasn't obvious, then she raced upstairs to pull back her daughter's bedcovers.

"Tough night?" His voice was so low she barely heard him as he laid Belle in her bed.

"Probably no worse than yours," she whispered back.

He chuckled, a deep sound that reverberated through her. "Mason and I managed pretty well by using the techniques I learned from Rick. He finished his homework, had his shower and brushed his teeth. He went down for the count about twenty minutes ago."

"Early?"

"The dog wore him out. Told you the mutt's slow."

She wasn't used to having help. She liked coming home and feeling as if she had someone on her side. But she couldn't get accustomed to it. "Thank you."

Brandon paused by the bedroom door with one hand on the jamb. "I found a couple of beers in the pantry and stuck them in the freezer. Meet me at the fire pit when you're done here."

He was gone before she had time to protest that she didn't need one of Lucy's leftover beers or his company. What she needed was time to unwind, and the fire pit was her favorite place to do it. No matter which season. But not with Brandon.

Sitting in the spot she and Rick had built always reminded her of him and the nights they'd carried the baby monitor outside to share a few quiet moments at the end of their day. More than once they'd made love in a blanket he'd spread on the nearby grass. The fire pit was *their* spot.

Ten minutes later she had tucked Belle in and checked on Mason. She passed by the short hall to the old master suite on her way to meet Brandon. One of the Leiths was snoring loud enough for her to hear through the closed door. She stepped out into the balmy June night, took a cleansing breath and smelled smoke. The fire pit flickered in the distance. She made her way to the dark shadow sitting beside the flames.

Brandon reached beside his chair, twisted the cap off a bottle and offered it to her. "I lit her up to keep the bugs away."

She ought to be irritated with him for infringing on her space and the ritual she and Rick had shared. She ought to send him home. But because he was probably the only other person who understood how difficult Rick's parents could be, and he'd earned a beer and a minute of peace after an evening of dealing with Walter, she didn't. His presence made her feel as if she had someone on her team, and having Brandon on her side was not a circumstance she would have ever anticipated.

She took the beer and lowered into the chair beside him then sipped from the bottle. The cold brew slid down her throat. Mrs. Leith hadn't wanted to stay for the reception after the recital. No reception meant no punch. And after two hours of cheering and clapping and nervousness, on Belle's behalf, Hannah was parched. "I thought I was out of wood."

"Mason and I gathered some. The fire pit and chairs need sanding and painting. He and I will do that next week."

She sighed. "Brandon, I appreciate what you're trying to do—"

"Then don't waste your breath arguing. I promised Mason and I keep my promises."

"You didn't five years ago." The words were out before she could stop them.

He stiffened. "Which one?"

"To keep Rick safe for me."

"You're right. I failed to keep that one."

Then because the question had been eating at her for five years, she asked, "Why, Brandon? Why did you leave him alone in that room? You were supposed to work as a team."

Brandon said nothing for several moments. The sounds of crickets, the crackling fire and the occasional night bird filled the air. "He asked me to."

Sure she'd misheard his quiet statement, she swiveled his way. "What?"

"He claimed you'd bitten off more than you could chew with the party of the century and needed him to help set up. But we couldn't leave until we'd processed the scene. He insisted that if we split up we could finish faster."

The party of the century. The words hit her like an echo from the past and brought a fresh pang of grief. That had been Rick's phrase for describing Hannah's elaborate plan for Belle's first birthday. "Why didn't you tell me that when I attacked you at the funeral, or even the last time I asked?"

She couldn't see his eyes in the dark, but she

could see the lines of anguish carved in his face. He sat with his legs stretched out and his head tilted back against the chair. The pose looked relaxed, but she knew him too well to buy his pretense. A muscle ticked beside his upper lip. The cords in his neck stood out, and his knuckles were white on the chair arm and around the bottle.

"Does knowing bring him back?" he asked in a flat tone.

"No."

"Then what good would it have done? You needed someone to take the brunt of your anger, and I was as good a target as any. *And* because I knew that if I hadn't agreed to break protocol and work separately there's a good chance he'd still be here."

"Or you might both be dead." Overwhelmed, she looked up to see what had captured Brandon's attention and saw a thick blanket of stars scattered against the black velvet background. She took a few moments to let the information sink in.

Rick hadn't been so lost in his work that he'd forgotten his family—something she'd accused him of doing more than once. He'd wanted to be here. A knot of anger she hadn't realized she'd still been carrying toward her husband unraveled.

She turned her head to look at the man sitting stiffly beside her, the man blaming himself for Rick's death. Brandon hadn't been responsible. The enmity she'd carried inside her for so long drained away, leaving a big ravine of emptiness. Where did that leave them now?

Her children wanted and needed him in their lives. But even if she didn't dislike and distrust him anymore, he still had a dangerous job—the same one that had taken her husband.

Could she and Brandon be friends for her children's sake even at the risk of losing him later?

For whatever reason, he was the one who'd awakened her body from slumber, and she couldn't trust herself around him. Was her physical reaction to him only a phase, like Mason's bad behavior? She would never know if she didn't find the courage to work it out. She hoped she didn't regret her decision.

"What techniques did Rick teach you for dealing with Margaret and Walter?" she asked without lifting her head. "Because he never taught me any. We rarely saw them when he was alive."

"He let his parents—or anyone that irritated him—talk or preach until they ran out of gas. He never argued or called them on their BS, and he never let their opinions change the course he'd set for himself or allow them to get a rise out of him."

The description pulled a chuckle from her. "He did the same with me. Whenever I lost my temper, he'd let me vent until I ran out of words. I had no idea he was 'working' me."

"I learned a lot from watching him handle peo-

ple. I hope I imparted some of that wisdom to
Mason tonight."

"Did Walter test you?"

"No more than usual." He finished his beer then
set down the bottle. "How bad was his stroke?"

She couldn't help being impressed that he'd not
only noticed but that he also cared. "Pretty bad.
He was in rehab for months. When he got out he
took up building model trains. Mrs. Leith credits
that for the continued recovery of his fine motor
skills."

"Mason told me he had a train set in their basement. Is it Rick's? He had one down there years
ago."

She nodded. "Dr. Leith started with Rick's old
set. He's added on to it since. It's about four times
the original's size. He's an avid collector now and
belongs to several clubs. In fact, he made arrangements for the kids to go with him to a train collector convention and told them all about it—of
course, without asking me first. I don't know
whether to let them go or not. I'm inclined to
say no, but Mason and Belle are already excited.
They'd get to ride a train out there then fly home.
They've never done either."

It was the kind of invitation she'd never had
from her grandparents. And it was an experience
she couldn't afford to give Mason and Belle. But
the fact that the Leiths had made plans without
her approval bothered her.

"What about you? Why aren't you going?"

"I wasn't invited. And even if I had been, I can't take off work. One of the other therapists is going to be out of state that entire week for her sister's wedding."

"The Leiths will keep the kids safe, if that's what you're worrying about. If anything they'll be over-protective."

"I know, but…" How could she explain that as much as she'd wanted her children to have involved grandparents, she hadn't considered quite what that might involve?

"But what?"

He'd probably think she was crazy not to want a break. Lucy did. "Mason and Belle have never been away from me before. I don't know if *I* can handle them being gone for four days."

His mouth tilted in that half smile that did stupid things to her vital signs. "It'll suck. But you'll do okay."

"The Leiths are so critical with the kids. I wouldn't be there to act as a buffer."

"I think you need a happy distraction." He pulled his phone from his pants pocket, punched a couple of buttons and offered it to her. "Mason's good with Rocky. I'm not sure who was more worn out after our lesson. Check out the video."

She took the phone. It was still warm from being pressed against Brandon's thigh. The buzz in her palm combined with the heat from the fire merged low in her belly to create a flutter of awareness that was wrong—doubly so because this was her and Rick's spot.

She hit Play and the screen filled with Mason trying to teach an exuberant young dog tricks. Her son's wide smile and laugh were balm to her soul. This was the boy she remembered, the one who'd morphed into a tense, argumentative pre-teen a few months back. Brandon's presence had changed that. When the video ended, she stared at the blank screen, wanting to play it again and again. Mason's silly antics were the perfect antidote to her difficult evening.

Reluctantly, she extended the device to Brandon. "Thank you. I needed that."

His hands remained in his lap. "Email it to yourself so you can watch it again later."

How had he read her mind? Rick had been one of those men who took whatever you said at face value. It wasn't that he was stupid. Far from it. But he'd never picked up on subtleties. Rick had envied Brandon's uncanny ability to read people, and claimed that skill was what made him so good at getting confessions. More than once she'd gotten the impression Brandon ignored what she said and heard what she didn't say.

She forwarded the video then passed back his phone. Their fingers brushed and the now-familiar sparks erupted, betraying Rick's memory again. She wrapped her hand around the sweating bottle, trying to dampen the sensation. She had to get a handle on her reaction to Brandon because it looked like he was going to be a fixture in their lives for a while.

"Hannah, the Leiths mean well. But like I explained to Mason, by the time Rick came along his grandparents were already leaders in their fields. Barking orders was routine, and they never adjusted that skill set to accommodate their son or anyone else. They definitely have a hard time interacting with children. But they're trying. And kids need all the love they can get. Part of my job is dealing with what happens when they look for it elsewhere."

He rose, then towered over her. "There's a bucket of water to your left. Douse the fire before you go inside and call me if you need me. Good night, Hannah."

She opened her mouth on the sudden urge to ask him to stay then closed it. What was she thinking? That wouldn't be smart—not given how she was reacting to him these days. How did he simultaneously get her to let her guard down and put her senses on high alert? The effect was...disturbing.

She leaned back in her seat, gripped the arms of her chair and stared into the dancing flames. Friendship with Brandon. Did she dare risk it?

Had he given her a choice?

THE GUY WAS lying through his teeth. Frustrated, irritated and becoming majorly pissed off, Brandon sat back in the uncomfortable chair and fought to maintain his cool with the subject across the table. He had better things to do with his Friday night than sit here with someone feeding him a crock of crap.

No. He didn't. Another Friday night and he had no date. He might as well be working. *What was Hannah doing*? He squelched the thought.

His phone vibrated in his pocket. He didn't have time for interruptions now. The suspect was getting tired and hungry. His stomach had been growling for the past hour. The likelihood that he'd slip up soon simply because of those factors was high.

"Let me make sure I have all the details right. Tell me again when you first suspected something was wrong with the accounts, and then I'll order us a pizza."

The guy considered it, then said, "I want a lawyer."

Shit. "Fine."

Brandon rose and strode from the room, relayed the news and headed back toward his office to finish some paperwork. Then he remembered his phone, pulled it out and checked the message. He stopped in his tracks. Mason's computer had alerted him, indicating the boy had visited a porn site.

Double shit.

He had to call Hannah. But how could he do

that without telling her he'd downloaded the program? He stepped into his office and tapped her contact.

"Hello?"

He could barely hear her over the noise in the background, but that didn't stop his heart from jolting at the sound of her voice. Leaving her Wednesday night had been harder than it should have been. The strain on her face after the recital had put him on a "fix it" mission. The best way he knew to unwind was with sex. Not an option with Hannah.

Then she'd blindsided him with the questions about the day Rick had been murdered. He almost hadn't told her. But he'd grown weary of her thinking he'd let Rick down for selfish reasons. She'd seemed to take comfort in knowing Rick had wanted to be with her.

A screech in the background hurt his eardrum. "Sounds like you have half the school at your place."

"I'm not at home. I'm at a birthday party for one of Belle's friends."

The hair on the back of his neck prickled. "Is Mason with you?"

"No. I left him at home with Kim, our sitter. Why?"

Could the babysitter be on the website? He'd have to go to Hannah's house to find out, but he didn't want Hannah giving Kim or Mason a heads-up or they'd log off. He knew for a fact that Mason knew how to cover his tracks. That meant he couldn't tell Hannah his plan. He'd just gotten rid of the one secret between them. And now he was starting another. But it was necessary if he wanted to get to the bottom of Mason's issues.

"I need to talk to him about our next obedience lesson, but it's not urgent. I'll catch him later. Have fun with the kiddos."

"Okay…have a good night, Brandon."

"You, too." He disconnected, grabbed his gear and rushed to Hannah's house as fast as the speed limit would allow. He debated knocking. But again, that could tip off whoever was on the computer. However, entering without permission wasn't kosher, either. But this wasn't a crime scene. He didn't need a search warrant.

He grabbed the spare key and let himself in. Following the sound of the TV to the den, he discovered a teenage girl parked on the sofa. She was totally engrossed in her phone and ignoring the blaring television. She was also oblivious to his entry. Not good. He surveyed the room. He didn't see Mason and the computer wasn't on the desk where it should be. If the sitter wasn't on the computer then Mason was.

He moved closer to the couch, stopping two yards from the teen. "Hello, Kim."

The girl jumped up, dropped her phone and turned. "Who are you?"

He'd scared her. Good. She might be more cautious next time. "Brandon. A friend of Hannah's. She told me you'd be here. Where's Mason?"

"Oh. He's upstairs. Want me to get him?"

"No. I'll run up and see him."

"Okay." She picked up her phone and flopped back on the sofa.

Wrong. On so many accounts. She hadn't asked for ID or questioned how he'd gotten into the house. She'd turned her back on a stranger and made too many other mistakes to list. But he had more urgent issues to deal with than warning her about how her carelessness could get her raped or killed. For Mason's, Belle's and Kim's safety, he'd speak to her before he left and hit her with a few hard statistics.

He jogged up the steps as quietly as possible. After a quick tap on Mason's door, he pushed it open without waiting for a reply. Mason was on the bed with the computer in his lap. His eyes went wide, his mouth opened. "What are you doing here? Um... I mean, hi."

He tried to shut the laptop, but Brandon sprung forward and grabbed the screen before he could, then snatched away the device. "I'm here to check on you."

"Hey! Gimme that back. You can't take my computer. You have no right!"

He couldn't tell him about the software notification. But the boy's frantic tone told him he'd found the culprit. "You're not allowed to have the computer in your room." He turned the screen and saw a porn video. Oral sex, to be exact. He closed the page. "For exactly that reason."

Mason ducked his tomato-red face.

"Talk to me, Mason. Why are you watching this stuff?"

"Don't you?"

"No. Answer my question. Why?"

The boy examined his fingernails as if he'd never seen them before, then he shrugged. "I'm just curious. About how stuff works."

The reasoning rang true for a ten-year-old, but something in the delivery didn't feel right. Brandon couldn't put his finger on what. The kid's eyes looked earnest. Too earnest? "Your mom says she had the sex talk with you and that you had a class at school."

That garnered him one of the boy's famous eye rolls. "Right. Like you're going to get real information about sex from your mother or a teacher. All they say is don't do it."

"True. And it's hard to ask questions in front of your classmates. I get that." He sat on the edge of the bed. "My dad told me what I needed to know. It was still embarrassing, but less painful than talking to my mom would have been. I can answer your questions, if you want."

Mason said nothing.

"Do you have a girlfriend?"

"No."

"A guy friend?"

"*Jeez!* No!"

"Some middle school kids experiment with sex."

Mason slouched and mumbled, "Oh, brother."

"But it's not worth the risk of being a parent at ten or twelve. It happens. Our state ranks eleventh in the nation for teen pregnancy. Did you know that? You need to get your facts straight. Other kids often don't."

Mason's expression turned even more pained. "Are we done yet?"

The kid couldn't be half as uncomfortable as Brandon. Brandon had never had to have this discussion with anyone other than Rick, whose parents had handed him a book on the topic. But the dry medical manual hadn't been half as interesting as the old dusty box of men's magazines in the neighbor's barn. So Brandon understood curiosity and sneaking around to satisfy it. Those magazines had been eye-opening, to say the least.

And if this was only curiosity, as Mason claimed, then Brandon would respect the boy's confidence. "If you promise me you'll stay off the porn sites and come to me if you need information or have questions, then I won't report this to your mom."

"Do I have a choice?"

"Yes. You do. You can give me your word, and

I'll give you mine. Or I take this to your mom."
He stuck out his hand.

Mason, after a noticeable hesitation, put his in
it. "Okay. Yeah."

"Your mom told me she had installed parental controls to keep you off unauthorized sites. I
knew you were pretty good with a computer, but
how did you get around those?"

The boy blanched instead of boasting of his
prowess as Brandon had expected. "I don't know.
I just clicked on a link, and…it came up."

"Where'd you find the link?" Silence. "In a
SPAM email?" The kid remained mute. "Did
someone send it to you?" Brandon caught a tiny
twitch. "Who?"

Mason jumped off the bed. "I don't remember."

"Do you still have it?"

"No. I deleted it. A long time ago. I gotta take a
shower before Mom gets home." Then he hustled
out and shut the bathroom door. The lock clicked.

Brandon wanted to believe the kid was simply curious. But something about the whole encounter bugged him. He checked the computer's
drop-down URL history. As expected, it had
been erased. He hesitated before checking Mason's mail folder. But to keep the kid safe, the in-
trusion was justified.

Mason didn't have many emails, and none of
those had links. They were all recent and his deleted file had been cleared. Nothing dated back

several months to the time when Hannah said the behavior issues had started.

Without the software to search for erased material he had no leads. But if he took the computer in for forensics work, he'd have to explain his action to Hannah and his supervisor. He didn't like keeping secrets from Hannah, and if this was simply boyhood inquisitiveness, then he didn't need to worry her. She had enough on her plate. But if it was something else...

He shook his head, shut down the device and carried it downstairs. Telling her about tonight's adventures meant having to admit he'd installed the software. Against his better judgment, he was going to give Mason the benefit of the doubt *this time*. But if it happened again, all bets were off.

One thing was certain. He wasn't uninstalling the program tonight. In the meantime, he would have to be more vigilant. If Hannah thought he'd hung around too much before, she'd definitely object to how much he was planning on being around in the future.

CHAPTER THIRTEEN

HANNAH'S HEART BOUNDED like a jackrabbit when she spotted Brandon's truck in her driveway. A beehive of emotions whirled in her abdomen. Despite the decision to let him into their lives, she wasn't ready to see him again.

"Uncle Brandon's here! Hurry, Mommy. Hurry."

Belle bounced in her seat until Hannah stopped the minivan in the garage then she threw off her seat belt, bounded from the vehicle and ran into the kitchen. Hannah followed more slowly.

"Uncle Brandon!" Belle streaked to Brandon's side and hurled herself at him. Hannah caught a glimpse of his fierce expression before it melted into a smile for her daughter. He scooped up Belle and gave her a hug. "Hello, princess."

The tension in the room was palpable. Kim sat on the couch with arms wrapped around her folded knees. Her eyes were wide and her face was the color of vellum. Brandon stood by the fireplace. His hazel gaze met Hannah's over her daughter's head as he set Belle down. He nodded but something about him looked…intimidating despite the smile stretching his lips. "Hannah."

The flash of white teeth looked forced. Concern twined through her. "What's wrong? Where's Mason?"

"He's fine and in the shower," Brandon answered.

She searched the faces, one pale and pinched, one stern with a slight crease between his eyebrows. "Then what's going on?"

"I was entertaining Kim with stories about some of the cases I've worked."

Hannah knew from the wariness chasing across the girl's face that wasn't the whole truth as sure as she knew her own name.

Kim jumped up and stuffed her feet into her sandals. "I guess I'd better get going." Her uneasy gaze flitted to Brandon. "If that's all, sir?"

Brandon inclined his head. "Be careful."

"Yes, sir."

Hannah escorted the sitter to the front door and paid her. "Kim, is everything okay?"

Kim's eyes widened—too wide. "Umm…yes, ma'am. Mason behaved and did his homework. Bye, Mrs. Leith." Then she sprinted to her car and drove away.

Something about her chipper attitude didn't ring true. Hannah returned to the den. Brandon stood with his elbow on the mantel and his ankles crossed while Belle chattered excitedly about the party, the cake and the boy who threw up in the bounce house. His pose looked relaxed, but like the other night, she saw too many contradictory signs to believe it. Tension tightened his jaw and shoulders.

"Belle, get ready for bed," she said when her daughter paused for air.

"But Mommy, I wanted to tell Uncle Brandon about the creepy clown."

"You can tell him another time. Go on. Get into your pajamas and pick out your book."

"What about my bath?"

"It's late. It will have to wait until morning. I'll be up in a minute."

Belle wilted like a flower then slinked out of the room. Hannah waited until she heard footsteps reach the upstairs landing then turned to the man in question. "Why did Kim take off like a scalded cat?"

"She didn't ask for ID before letting me go upstairs to see Mason. So I just gave her a few examples of why she needed to be more cautious in the future."

Rick had never discussed cases with her. He'd insisted that he dealt with ugliness all day, and he didn't want to drag it into his house. She couldn't imagine the stories Brandon must have told to put that look on the girl's face.

He was wearing the standard black polo and tactical pants with his badge still clipped to his belt. He must have come straight from work, but other than the shadow darkening his jaw, he looked sharp. "You're in uniform. Maybe that's why she..."

"Plenty of bad guys masquerade as law enforcement."

True. "I hope you didn't scare her so badly that she won't sit for me again. The kids love her and she's dependable."

"You don't want her here if she puts them at risk." His protective tone sounded more like a father than a friend. Then his lips twitched. "Did you enjoy the cake?"

Then she recalled how she'd looked when she'd caught a glimpse of herself in the restroom mirror before leaving the party. She'd had bright blue icing in her hair and smeared on her shirt. "All the icing I am now wearing is a perk of helping with twenty-five cupcake-eating children. I didn't know you were coming over."

"I wanted to talk to Mason."

"About?"

"I'll need his help with a project for Belle's room."

Had she imagined a hesitation before he answered? "What kind of project?"

"I want to build a rotating dress-up stand for all of Belle's costumes. My sisters had something similar when they were small."

Why couldn't he get the message that she hated being in his debt? "Like I've said before, please stop spending money on us."

"I'm using salvaged materials. One of my tenants left behind a narrow wooden bookcase and a back-of-the-door mirror. I have some casters we can mount on the base. Once Mason and I put it all together then Belle can paint it with leftover pink from her room."

Hannah stifled her objections. Belle would love it, and Mason would enjoy the construction. "Okay. We'll work out a time to do it."

"Sunday afternoon."

Her breath caught. She didn't know how to do this friendship thing with someone who made her nervous and jittery. He took up a lot of space and a lot of oxygen. "Sure. Sunday. If that's all, I need to get Mason and Belle to bed."

He didn't take the hint to leave. "Leah's taking the twins to our parents' to pick strawberries tomorrow morning. She wants you, Belle and Mason to join them. Then the farrier is coming after lunch. Mom thought Belle might like to see how horses get new shoes."

That was how normal families operated. A sense of yearning filled Hannah. Other than her marriage to Rick, she'd never lived what most would consider a normal life, and she wanted that for her children. But Brandon's family wasn't hers, and she couldn't be sure how long this would last.

"It's a long way to drive for berries."

"The kids will get to ride the horses after lunch."

Belle would be over the moon with excitement. How could she deny her that opportunity? "Will you be there?"

Her pulse fluttered irregularly at the prospect.

He shook his head. "Doubtful. I'm in the middle of something."

Work, she suspected. Rick had often had to work weekends. The sinking feeling wasn't disappointment. It was fear. Brandon still did the job that had taken Rick from her. It was a sobering reminder that he was off-limits no matter what her hormones did when he was around, and so was his family, but... "Belle and Mason would love to spend the morning with Eva and Evan at the orchard."

"I'll tell Mom to expect you around ten." He pushed off the mantel and headed toward the front door. "Good night, Hannah."

Then he was gone, and the house fell silent. Solitude was what she wanted, wasn't it? So why, after years of being contented, did she suddenly feel like something was missing? She shook it off and headed upstairs. She had her children, and that was all she needed. And tomorrow they'd get to experience the kind of family outing Hannah had dreamed about as a child—even if it wasn't their family.

"WHEN ARE YOU going to realize that Hannah is not Rick's girl anymore?" Brandon's father asked

EMILIE ROSE 287

from the passenger seat of the pickup as they headed back to the orchard Saturday.

"What? Of course she is."

"Rick's gone, son, and you want Hannah for your own."

Brandon glanced at his dad to see if he was joking, but his expression was dead serious. "That's crazy."

"Her name has come up in every conversation we've had since the beginning of April and some before that, too, when you sneaked over to her place to do work. You have spent every moment of your free time with her for the past month or more, and this morning we drove all over two counties searching for things for Hannah's house."

Words of denial careened in Brandon's skull, but before he could organize them and get them out, his father held up a hand. "That's not a complaint. I like Hannah. Always have. I'm just holding the flashlight on your actions so you can see what you're doing. You can't fix something if you can't see it."

"Hannah and I don't have that kind of relationship."

"But you want to. So maybe you need to quit thinking of her as Rick's girl and treat her like the one you want to be with and start courting her."

His dad was interpreting clues completely wrong. Brandon debated keeping his trap shut. But this was his father. Anything he told him wouldn't go further. "Hannah's son's having some trouble, and she called me to help figure out what it is. It turns out it's bigger than I expected and than she'll admit."

"What kind of trouble?"

"In school. Behavior, not academics. She said he's on the verge of getting expelled. And I think the bad behavior is linked to something on the internet."

"You sure about that?"

He'd asked himself that a hundred times. "The evidence I have is pretty strong."

"Then you need to help in any way you can. But son, you also need to open your eyes. You're interested in Hannah, and you're crazy about her children. I hear it in your voice each time you talk about them. Once you figure out what's going on with the boy, you'll need to decide whether fixing the problem is going to do more harm than good."

"What does that mean?"

"You'll know when it happens."

After that cryptic comment, his father leaned forward and turned up the volume on the radio. Ever since Hannah had introduced music therapy, his father kept the tunes playing anywhere he happened to be.

His father was wrong about Hannah. Brandon didn't want her for himself. Sure, he found her attractive, smart, capable and a great mom. And he couldn't deny she had his neglected hormones in an uproar. But that didn't mean he wanted to take Rick's place. Nobody could do that.

One day Hannah would find a nice guy who'd be good to her and Mason and Belle. They'd build a new life. But she needed security. His job and the unpredictable illness slowly destroying the man seated beside him meant that that guy wasn't him.

But a nagging voice reminded him that his father was the smartest man he'd ever known. And Brandon couldn't remember the last time Thomas Martin had been wrong about anything.

AFTER THE BERRY PICKING, Rebecca Martin herded the children into the house and through washing up with an ease Hannah could only envy.

"Your years as a teacher are showing," Hannah told Rebecca and earned a wistful smile from her hostess.

"When you love what you do, it's always a joy. I miss my students, but God had bigger plans for me. Use soap, Evan," she called out without missing a beat. "When everyone is finished we'll have strawberries with our lunch."

Hannah brought up the rear of the line as the children paraded down the hall. "Can I help with anything?"

"No, dear. Everything's ready. All I have to do is peel back the plastic wrap. Have a seat."

Hannah, Leah and the children sat around the

large kitchen island. Leah leaned closer to Hannah and whispered conspiratorially, "Wait till you see what she whips up."

Mrs. Martin returned with a tray and set a plate in front of each child. The sandwiches had cute faces on them with the eyes, noses and mouths made from blueberries, kiwis and strawberries. The ears were tangelo segments. The "curly" hair atop the bread was made from sliced grapes, and she'd cut bananas into hair bows for the girls' sandwiches and bow ties for the boys'. They were adorable, and nothing like Hannah's mother had ever done, but she braced herself for Belle to refuse to eat.

Rebecca took the last stool. "Eva, it's your turn to say grace, sweetheart."

The four-year-old endearingly blessed the food in a sing-song verse then everyone—including Belle—dug in. Hannah's surprise must have shown on her face because Brandon's sister winked and whispered, "Mom has a way of getting even picky eaters to try new things. Me, I never have this kind of luck. But then, my sandwiches don't look like this, either."

"Mine, either." Hannah soaked it all in as she ate: the companionship, the chattering children and the happy faces. This is what having a grandmother was supposed to be like, or so she'd always thought. But she'd never had that experience for herself, and Mason and Belle didn't have it with Mrs. Leith.

Rebecca touched Hannah's hand to get her attention. "Thank you for referring us to your friend. Thomas not only enjoys physical therapy now, he's also made great progress in only three weeks."

"I'm glad I could help. Where is Mr. Martin now?"

"He and Brandon went scrounging for some big project. They won't come home until the truck is full or they've run out of places to hunt."

Hannah's pulse skipped. "I thought Brandon was working."

"Not today, although he often works weekends. But you know all about that."

"Yes, I do. I love your kitchen," she blurted to change the subject away from the man she'd spent too much time thinking about lately. "This is very similar to what I want to do with mine."

The woman beamed. "Thomas and Brandon did all of the renovations, and trust me, dear, there have been a lot of those in this hundred-year-old house. Luckily, I don't think there's anything those two can't build or refinish."

"Did Brandon pick up his carpentry skills from his father?"

She nodded. "And his grandfather. For a while we were certain he'd become a builder after high school, but then he and Rick became interested in law enforcement, and that was the end of that."

The twins became noticeably droopy as their tummies got full. Hannah, on the other hand, became antsier with each minute that passed as she dreaded Brandon turning up.

"Thank you for including us today."

"You're more than welcome. I enjoy having young ones underfoot." She directed her attention to Hannah's children. "Mason and Belle, I have some photo albums on the coffee table for you to look at while we wait for the farrier. Your father is in many of the pictures. See if you can find him."

Belle scampered off but Mason hung back. "Why do you have pictures of my dad?"

"Because he spent much of his childhood here, starting when he was a little younger than you. He was here so often it was almost like having twin sons. He followed Brandon everywhere."

"Dad called them Pete and Re-Pete," Leah added. "They were always taking things apart to see how they worked."

"I…umm do that, too," Mason admitted.

"Then we know where you inherited the trait, don't we? Brandon did it because he liked to build. Your father did it because he wanted to know how things worked," Rebecca replied with a smile then shooed everyone from the kitchen.

Hannah found Belle poring over one of the

photo albums. Belle looked up. "I found Mason, but I can't find Daddy. How come Mrs. Martin has pictures of Mason and not of me, Mommy?"

Hannah looked at the boys on the page. "That's your father when he was Mason's age."

"I look like him," Mason stated quietly.

"Yes, you do. And you're very good at problem-solving like he was, too." For several minutes she watched her children flip the pages and drink in the pictures of their father. Her heart ached a little and she suddenly felt selfish. She'd put away so many reminders of Rick after the funeral, because she couldn't bear looking at them.

"Oh, my. I remember that day," Rebecca exclaimed as she joined them. "That's when your father was learning to paddle a kayak."

"If he was in a boat then why is he all wet?" Belle asked.

"Because he tipped it over so many times," Rebecca replied. "But by the end of the day, he was almost an expert. You see, failing is okay as long as you don't get discouraged and quit trying."

"I wish everybody felt that way," Mason mumbled. Hannah put a hand on his shoulder in sympathy. He shrugged it off, and that hurt.

The rumble of a truck engine penetrated the windows. Rebecca crossed to look outside. "The farrier is here, and Brandon and Thomas are right behind him."

Hannah's breath caught and her heart clanked

like a bad grocery cart wheel. She fought for calm. She could handle this new "friends" status. All she had to do was, as Rebecca said, keep trying until she got the hang of it.

Hannah, Mason and Belle followed Mrs. Martin onto the back porch. The farrier parked near the barn. Brandon, with the bed of his truck piled high with something under a blue tarp, stopped beside him. Mr. Martin carefully climbed from the cab of his son's truck, then Brandon drove into one of the barns.

Belle bounced with excitement. "Are the horses going to get new shoes now?"

"Yes, they are. You may go out and watch if you stay right beside Mr. Thomas and do what he says," Brandon's mother said.

Belle dashed across the yard. Mason followed more slowly. Rebecca patted her shoulder. "They'll be fine, dear. Thomas will watch them and doing so will make him feel needed. Come back inside where it's cool and rest a bit."

Hannah lingered by the rail. She didn't need to hear Belle to see that she'd begun peppering the farrier and Mr. Martin with questions the moment she reached them—questions that were being answered patiently. Why couldn't the Leiths be this kind to her children?

"What is it, dear?"

Hannah met her hostess's gaze, but she was reluctant to share her uncharitable thought. "I was just thinking how idyllic it must have been to raise your children here."

"Idyllic?" Rebecca chuckled. "Hardly. Life on any kind of farm is full of pitfalls. Frost can wipe out an entire year's crop overnight, so income is, to say the least, unpredictable. And who knows what the coming years will bring with Thomas's diagnosis, but I intend to count my blessings instead of my troubles. The rest will fall into place."

Hannah wished she shared the woman's positive attitude. Then Brandon strode out of the barn. Hannah's heart *clip-clopped* faster than the pony galloping around the pasture.

Belle launched herself at him, getting her hug, but Mason held back. That was odd. Brandon approached him and said a few words. Mason, instead of gazing at Brandon with his usual hero-worship, kept his head low. Where was Mason's cheerful fist-bump greeting for his hero? Had he and Brandon had a disagreement? If so, what about and why had neither of them said anything?

As much as Hannah had longed to avoid Brandon before, now she wanted to talk to him—very much. He glanced up at the house and waved. A swarm of excitement buzzed in her abdomen then shot to her extremities. Before she could summon a response and lift her hand to return his greeting, he stiffened, pulled out his phone from his pocket and spoke into it briefly. Then he lowered the device and said something to his father.

Mr. Martin handed him a set of keys. Brandon hustled to another pickup truck parked near the barn, started the engine and drove off the property without stopping.

"It looks like Brandon has been called into work," Rebecca said from behind Hannah.

Finding out what was causing the tension between him and Mason would have to wait.

BRANDON HAD TO get to Hannah's fast. And not, as his dad insisted, because he wanted to see her, but because he needed to add additional software to her computer.

Mason had been too on edge Saturday for someone who'd just been caught looking at naked people. The kid had refused to make eye contact. That act had nagged Brandon throughout working the case that had wrapped up at four this morning. If not simply porn, then what was Mason into? He had to find out.

That was what had him restless. It had nothing to do with the conversation he'd shared with his father during Saturday's scavenger hunt. Nothing whatsoever. His father was wrong. End of story.

On his way home to catch a few hours' sleep, Brandon had checked in with his mother as he always did after a stretch of being incommunicado. She'd told him about Belle and Mason's upcoming trip with their grandparents. Since he and his father had acquired everything needed for Hannah's kitchen reno, pushing forward with that project seemed to be his golden ticket to laptop access.

He pressed her doorbell Thursday evening. After a moment he heard feet pounding down the stairs then Hannah yanked open the door. The look of concern on her face morphed into one of surprise. Unwelcome surprise. He probably should have taken time to shave. Five days' beard growth darkened his cheeks and chin.

"Just off a case?" Her breathless voice was sex—no, just breathless. That was it. Nothing more.

"Yeah. Hello, Hannah." He took in her rubber gloves, worn-thin T-shirt and frayed shorts. And leg. *A lot of leg.* He yanked his gaze north to her flushed cheeks and wary eyes.

"The kids aren't here," she blurted. "They're gone for the weekend. With the Leiths. To the model train convention." Then she bit her bottom lip and took a deep breath that tested the threadbare cotton stretching across her breasts.

Damn. *Eyes up, buddy.* "You decided to let them go."

"Yes. I thought you were them—the Leiths. That they'd forgotten something or, more likely, that Belle had started crying and begged to come home." Her rapid-fire delivery revealed her nervousness.

He didn't want her to be on edge around him.

He wanted her to be as relaxed as she'd been out by the fire pit. "Did I interrupt something?"

She grimaced then wiggled her bare toes. The move was sex—*cute*. "I was scrubbing tubs and toilets. Cleaning distracts me from worrying about whether or not I made the right decision."

"And your conclusion?"

That earned a big sigh and droopy shoulders. "Rick's parents will never be as loving and supportive as yours. But they're all Mason and Belle have. My dad…" She shrugged. "He's just not interested in spending time with them."

"If you're that ambivalent about letting the Leiths be around your kids, then why do you?"

"Because as a mother, I can't deny Margaret access to the only link she has to the son she buried."

Hannah was a good mom and a caring person. He wasn't sure he'd be as generous. "If you say so. And I'm sure they'll be fine. On the bright side, we'll get more done without their help."

Her brow puckered in confusion. "More of what done? What are you talking about, Brandon?"

"Renovations." He stepped aside and jerked a thumb, indicating the truck he'd backed up to her porch.

"What's under the tarp?" she asked.

"A granite countertop and a few boards. We're redoing your kitchen this weekend."

Her lips parted and her eyes widened with excitement that quickly faded, then she shook her head. "Brandon, I can't afford—"

He wanted to bring the excitement back, and he could, but he hated that he'd come here with an ulterior motive. "Dad and I found everything you need. All of it free or close enough."

"The scrounging your mother mentioned?"

"It's something he and I have always done together. Their house, like yours, has been a bit of a money pit, and I get a lot of supplies for my rentals that way, too."

Still, she hesitated. He pulled the engineer's report from his back pocket and stepped forward, deliberately crowding her out of the way. She scrambled backward. Then he strode into her kitchen. The door shut behind him and her footsteps followed. She stopped two yards from him and tugged at the hem of her shorts. Didn't help. They were still eye-catchingly short, and she had the legs to make them work.

"I looked over the structural engineer's report. The packet included a rough sketch of what you wanted to do. We can do it."

"It's a big job. I don't think we can handle this alone."

He'd expected resistance. "You underestimate yourself. I saw those muscles when you climbed the rope. Other than lowering the upper cabinets from the wall, there won't be any heavy lifting, and there's only one outlet to relocate. I can do that."

He spread the papers across the table. "Isn't this your drawing?"

She inched a yard closer and leaned. "Yes."

He caught a whiff of her scent and wanted more. Crushing the thought, he redirected his attention to the sketch. "We'll use the base cabinets as the foundation for your kitchen island. The countertop is one that the granite guy cut wrong for a custom order. It's been sitting at his place collecting dust for almost a year. He hasn't been able to sell it. We can make it work. We only need to take down the top half of this wall for you to have your dream kitchen."

The excitement returned to her eyes, but indecision and then doubt chased it away. "I'm not sure that's a good idea."

"We'll be finished before the kids get back Sunday."

She was tempted. He could see it. She did the lip-biting thing. The pencil snapped in his fingers, and he was clenching his jaw so hard it's a wonder his molars didn't crumble.

"Brandon, I have to work tomorrow, and I'm covering the nursery at church Sunday morning. I can't be here."

Even better access to the computer than he'd hoped. "I'm off tomorrow and Sunday. I can work alone until you return."

She dithered a little more, then her eyebrows dipped. "What's going on between you and Mason?"

He fought to conceal his surprise at the shift in topic. "What do you mean?"

"I saw you talking to him at the orchard. He was very reserved."

And she was very observant. But then he'd never doubted Hannah's intelligence. "I don't know what to say. I barely spoke to him before I got called in on a case."

"Did you have an argument?"

"No." Truth. Diversion needed.

"Let's get started emptying the cabinets." He opened the first one and started lowering the contents onto the countertop. He half expected Hannah to press him for details or tell him to get the hell out. He prompted, "Trust me, this will be a quick and easy job. Do you have any boxes?"

"I think there are some in the attic." And then she left.

He eased out a breath. Close call. He had to get to the point of no return in a hurry if he wanted computer time. He pulled a pry bar from his toolbox and yanked down the trim wood before she returned. When she did, she carried an armload of collapsed cardboard. Her eyes rounded when she saw the strips of wood and the old, ugly paint now showing. Uncertainty returned to her face.

"You'll want to keep the kids' baby dishes," he suggested.

She slowly moved forward. "Yes, but—"

"Your dream kitchen, Hannah, for nothing but sweat. The kids will love being able to sit at the bar while you cook."

With a shake of her head, she started packing. For half an hour they emptied cabinets and filled boxes. It was close work in the narrow kitchen. Hannah bumped into the counter a couple of times to avoid touching him, and he had to fight harder than he wanted to admit to keep his eyes off her legs and the sliver of bare waist that showed each time she reached for a high cabinet. The atmosphere was similar to that night on the landing, but on steroids. By the time they finished it was almost seven o'clock, and he was ready to take a sledgehammer to something. But that was the kind of crap they did for show on TV. It wasn't necessary to make all that mess, and it could cause more damage than good.

"Have you eaten dinner?" he asked.

"No."

"Carry that box to the garage. I'll be right behind you." He waited until she left the room then dialed the Chinese restaurant nearby and placed an order. Then he grabbed the biggest box and met her head-on in the washroom. She twisted sideways to give him room to pass, flattening her back against the wall. He misjudged the width of the box. His forearm brushed across her breasts as he passed, sending a current of electricity straight to his groin. Holy mother of—

"'Scuse me." He squeezed through the noose cinching his throat.

In the garage he took a moment to regain control of his overheated body. He needed to get laid in the worst kind of way. But not by Hannah. What was wrong with him? He'd never had thoughts like this about her when Rick was alive. Hannah was Rick's girl.

Rick's gone.

He ignored the voice in his subconscious—a remnant of the conversation with his father—and returned to the kitchen. Hannah wouldn't meet his gaze and he couldn't blame her. His out-of-control libido was embarrassing for both of them. But her awareness was equally plain from her darting glances and quickened breaths. He grabbed the last box and marched out.

When he returned she pushed a glass of ice water toward him. He reached for it and noticed her nipples tenting her shirt. Fire burned through him like a lit fuse. He faced the wall and guzzled half the water, willing his brain to rise out of his shorts. This reno was going to be hell. And not because of the work required.

The doorbell rang. She jumped and her eyes filled with panic—probably thinking it was the Leiths returning her children. She started for the door. He grabbed her arm. Mistake. Her skin was soft, warm, and the urge to stroke her was almost impossible to resist.

"It's dinner," he ground out and headed for the foyer, putting some much-needed distance between them. He paid the delivery guy and carried the bag to the kitchen to feed the appetite he *could* satisfy. "Are Subgum Wonton and Vegetable Lo Mein still your favorites?"

Her expression softened. "Yes. I can't believe you remembered. I'll get plates."

He couldn't even remember his sisters' favorite foods. But he remembered Hannah's. Why?

At the table in the breakfast nook they passed cartons. He made damn sure their fingers didn't touch. Crazy, but he was as nervous as a teen on a first date.

He shoved food in his mouth and dutifully ate despite a lack of appetite *for food*. Tomorrow he'd have his shit together. But tonight…tonight he was going to need to jack off then take a long, cold shower when he got home.

"Thank you for dinner," she said.

"Least I can do since I sprung this on you. We'll remove the upper cabinets after we eat, then we'll call it a night."

She looked up from her plate. He eyes were deep and dark, and he couldn't look away. "As long as we're done by nine. I need time to upload some files to my laptop before work tomorrow."

The statement sank his gut like a brick. He lowered his fork. "You use your personal computer at work?"

"Not for patient files. But when I have new exercises I want to try with a client, I take it in."

Damn. The program download would have to wait until Sunday.

CHAPTER FOURTEEN

"TWO SCREWS LEFT," Brandon said behind Hannah, "and your last cabinet will be down."

With one big hand on the stepladder and the other supporting the bottom of the cabinet, his muscle-corded arms bracketed her on her perch three rungs from the top. If she moved an inch left or right her bare legs would brush his biceps. His body radiated heat, and if she twisted on the ladder, his face would be…in an intimate position.

Her stomach fluttered—for the umpteenth time in the past ninety minutes, and once again she regretted insisting he teach her how to do each step of the demolition. But given the number of projects left on her list she'd thought she might use these skills in the future. One day, she might appreciate what he'd taught her, but right now she was so distracted by her physical awareness of him she was ready to scream.

Screw his brains out. Lucy's crazy suggestion floated through Hannah's mind. She banished it.

Using the battery-operated drill he'd brought, she lined up the bit then squeezed the button. The screw slowly backed out, then suddenly the cabinet fell. She scrambled to catch it and lost her footing on the ladder. One moment she was falling, then Brandon swung her out of the way as the upper cabinet slammed onto the countertop and the ladder clattered to the floor with a resounding crash.

His arms banded around her, trapping her against his torso, then he slowly lowered her to the ground. Her breasts slid down his chest, creating an arousing friction that permeated every cell in her body. *Déjà vu*. Only face-to-face this time. And this time, she knew how he tasted, how his hands felt on her skin. She couldn't forget though, dear God, she'd tried.

His gaze found hers. "Are you all right?"

The huskiness of his voice and the warmth of his breath sweeping across her mouth did crazy things to her equilibrium. She forced a nod. "The last screw didn't hold. I wasn't expecting the cabinet to fall."

"It shouldn't have. Bad attachment." His lips barely moved.

She tested the ground beneath her toes. The movement increased the friction against his fly—his *distended* fly. He inhaled sharply and stepped back, but not before the burn in her belly ignited. He was turned on. By her. She hadn't felt wanted like that in a long time. Except by him.

He did a quick survey, patting her down like he would a suspect. Each brief press of his hands on her legs sent shockwaves through her. He knelt with his hand branding the base of her calf. "You have a scrape here." A fingertip grazed the skin across the front of her ankle. "Did you twist your knee or ankle?"

"No. I'm…okay," she croaked out and glanced down to see the red mark. Funny, she hadn't even felt it. She'd been too aware of Brandon.

He rose. His pupils nearly eclipsed his irises. His lips parted, and his chest expanded. Her attention returned to his mouth. The temptation to close the scant inches separating them swelled within her until she couldn't draw a breath.

Therapy. It would be good for both of you. She shushed Lucy's voice once again.

He cupped her shoulders, his grip sure and warm. Her eyes fluttered closed. She didn't dare meet his gaze lest he see how badly she needed to be held. Kissed. Touched. Desire raged inside her—desire she couldn't deny or suppress. Desire for Brandon.

"Hannah." Low and insistent, his voice rumbled through her, then a knuckle lifted her chin. "Look at me."

She forced heavy lids to rise. The hunger in his eyes multiplied hers. She sucked in much-needed oxygen. He took the drill and set it on the counter, then his palm settled on her waist. Holding and yet not holding. The unspoken message was clear. She could step away if she wanted to. Did she want to?

No, she didn't. Couldn't. The whole night of dancing around each other in her tiny kitchen, of bumping and dodging, had been leading to this. She'd only been fooling herself when she'd tried to tell herself otherwise.

Lucy was right. Hannah needed this physical release. And so did Brandon. Why not share the physical act with someone she liked and trusted? She and Brandon were friends now. Why couldn't they be friends with benefits? She would never let herself love again, and because of his job, she would never have to worry about loving Brandon. And he had stated he would never expect forever from anyone, either. A temporary, mutually beneficial relationship between them could work.

As soon as she made the decision, anticipation flowed through her, making her heart hammer with near-deafening force. She leaned infinitesimally closer to him. He met her halfway, lowering his head and brushing his lips across hers. Her world centered on his mouth, on the tickle of his unfamiliar beard and mustache. Then his hands tightened and the heat of his tongue found hers.

She wrapped her arms around his neck, rising on tiptoe to meet his hungry kiss. His palms skimmed down her back, grasping her hips and pulling her closer, close enough to feel the imprint of every ridge of chest muscle and the thickness of his erection. Her feminine parts awakened from a long slumber, like the sun peeking over the horizon and sending shafts of light radiating out.

His hands skimmed upward, sweeping beneath the hem of her T-shirt. The calluses on his palms lightly abraded her skin, acting like fuel to the fire he'd started inside her and making it spread. Then his thumbs edged beneath the elastic band of her bra and stroked the hypersensitive crease below her breasts.

Want rose inside her, traveling up her throat and through her lips to emerge in a needy cry. Struggling to regain control of the sensations rapidly overcoming her, she lowered her arms, slowly bumping her fingertips across his clavicles, his pectorals, the tiny, tight beads of his nipples. He groaned then tore his mouth from hers and pushed her back a few inches.

His hunger-filled gaze found hers. "Hannah, be sure about this. Be very sure."

Doubts wavered like heat off the asphalt. She'd never had a purely physical encounter before. But Brandon made her feel alive in places that had been dead for a long time. Having an intimate relationship with no prospect of a future might be wrong, but it felt right. In that moment she couldn't imagine walking away.

She stroked his jaw, testing his beard and finding it somewhere between bristly and soft. His facial hair was definitely attractive and the tickle-prickle on her palms aroused her in ways she hadn't known possible. She swept a thumb across his mustache, then over the unexpectedly soft flesh of his lips. His tongue slipped out and teased the pad of her thumb. She felt the erotic curl deep inside and the want expanded to an excruciating pressure. Her doubts evaporated.

"I'm sure." She coasted the sensitive pads of her fingers down the length of his powerful arms and threaded her fingers through his. When she turned to lead him upstairs, she heard his breath whistle between his teeth. On the landing outside her bedroom, reservations assailed her again, slowing her steps.

Lucy did this all the time and with men she didn't know half as well as Hannah knew Brandon. Her resolve kicked in. Their chemistry had been brewing since the rope climb and the kiss in Mason's bedroom. It wasn't going to go away until she filled the empty well.

She entered her room and, without turning on the lights, crossed to the bed, then pivoted to face him and released his hand. With only the light from the quarter moon streaming through the windows, she couldn't see his eyes, but she could make out the hunger stamped in the lines of his face. She took a deep breath for courage then lifted the hem of her top and whisked it over her head. Cool, sobering air brushed her skin. Before she could change her mind, she reached for the button at her waistband.

Brandon gently nudged her hands away. "Let me."

But instead of removing her shorts, he feathered his thumbs across her belly, sketching her ribs, outlining her navel. Her muscles contracted involuntarily. Each sweeping pass wound something tighter deep in her core. Then he traced her bra straps, starting on her shoulders then descending down the cups to the valley between her breasts. Her nipples puckered, aching to be touched, tasted.

As if he'd read her mind, he bent forward and brushed his lips across one swell then the other. Then he peeled down the straps so slowly she wanted to rip off the garment. One swollen tip popped free. He caught it in his mouth. The hot, wet heat shocked a gasp from her. The tickle of his facial hair only magnified the sensation. Then he suckled and her knees weakened. She grasped his shoulders for support. When the second breast sprung from its lace cage he transferred his attention to it, and covered the wet tip he'd abandoned with his fingertips. He tweaked one nipple and laved the other, sending pleasure pulsing through her.

The emptiness inside her expanded, aching to be filled. She grasped his shirt and pulled. He resisted long enough to release the back hooks of her bra. After whisking it away he tossed off his shirt and pulled her back into his arms. His skin melded to hers.

Brandon took her mouth in a ravenous kiss, devouring her with a passion just shy of pain. His loss of restraint only magnified her response. She wound her arms around him. His chest hair teased her breasts. Impatient, she skated her nails down his back and tucked her fingers behind the waistband of his jeans. In her mind's eye she could see the pale line that had haunted her dreams. She traced it to the front, pausing behind the brass button. With trembling fingers, she plucked open his fly then tugged down his zipper. The thickness of his erection filled the void, tenting his briefs. She covered it, testing the length and breadth. Eagerness made her shift her thighs.

With a hiss, he moved out of reach and unfastened her shorts. Hot palms skimmed them along with her panties over her hips. They fell to her ankles. She kicked them aside then shoved his jeans over the firm globes of his butt and wrapped her hand around his thickness. He hissed a breath again as she stroked him.

She'd had sex before. It shouldn't feel different. But it did—in ways she didn't want to probe right now. Urgency overcame her, but before she could kneel to remove his boots he backed toward the bed, towing her with him. After he sat, he urged her forward and captured her breasts, nipping, suckling and plucking, teasing, tasting, until all she could do was surrender to the knots of desire forming in her womb.

"Brandon, please, I—I need you."

Upon hearing her plea, he combed his fingers through her curls then dipped between her lower lips. He bumped across her center and shockwaves rocked her, making her jerk, making her cry out. Then he stroked, each slick pass pushing her closer and closer to the edge. Her legs quivered. She dug her fingers into his shoulders then fisted them in his hair. Sounds she couldn't contain escaped her mouth.

"Open for me, Hannah," he said against her breast. And she eased her feet apart.

Then he clasped her buttocks and bent, replacing his fingers with his mouth. He lapped and swirled, building a whirlpool of sensation until an orgasm roared through her. She cried out as wave after wave cascaded over her like water tumbling through a broken dam. If not for his hands cupping her buttocks she'd have fallen to the floor.

After the waves ebbed, he kissed a damp trail up her belly to her breast, then he rose and covered her mouth. She tasted herself on his lips and felt the hammer of his heart beneath her palms. Then he lifted his head and stepped back. Air cooled her sweat-dampened body as she tried to make sense of his retreat.

He scooped up his pants, retrieved his wallet

and extracted a condom. The condom gave her pause, but before she could process the reason behind her hesitation, he donned the protection, snaked an arm around her waist and slipped his fingers back into her damp curls.

His kiss was even hotter than before. Within seconds he'd rekindled the fire and obliterated whatever notion she'd been chasing. Teetering on the verge of release, she kneaded his shoulders, then she raked her fingers through his hair and broke the kiss to inhale a deep pre-orgasmic breath. Then he stopped. She wanted to howl in frustration.

"Come here," he commanded, backing to the bed and sitting. "Straddle me." He tugged her forward. She did as instructed, then he pulled her down onto his shaft and surged upward simultaneously, filling her deep, oh, so deep. She gripped his shoulders, rising and lowering to meet the rapid thrusts propelling her toward the climax he'd left pending. When it hit, a champagne shower of tingles rained from her head clear to the tips of her toes. He rode her through the swells buffeting her body, then he groaned as he found his own satisfaction.

Weak and breathless, Hannah melted against him, resting her face in the warmth of his neck. He smelled good. She nuzzled her cheek against his beard then tasted his salty skin. He shuddered and banded his arms tighter around her middle.

His damp chest pressed hers, rising and falling at the same feverish tempo. His grip on her buttocks loosened, and his head dipped to her shoulder. The heat of his breath scalded her breast, making her nipple rise to attention.

Brandon lay back on the bed, pulling her with him. She lay atop him, her ear pressed to his chest above his pounding heart. Satiation left her limp, her limbs heavy, her mind numb. But then her brain reengaged and along with it, doubt.

Sex. That was all it had been, she assured herself. Very satisfying sex. But it was purely physical. She'd been without a man for a very long time. It was only natural that her body respond more enthusiastically than it had before. Not that making love with Rick hadn't been great. It had. But this—she staunched the thought. To think of her husband while intimately linked to another was...wrong.

Uncomfortable, she shifted, breaking free of the arms he had loosely wrapped around her, and sat up. She felt Brandon move inside her and her lungs stalled. The urge to rock on him and rekindle the euphoria hit hard and fast. Shocked by her behavior, she stared at the man in front of her as her damp body cooled and reason slowly encroached. What was wrong with her? Thinking of Rick and wanting to ride Brandon simultaneously?

"Where are your rings?"

She'd been so tangled in her thoughts she hadn't noticed Brandon lifting her left hand. *Her wedding rings*. At least she hadn't dishonored Rick with the symbols of his love still on her finger.

"I left them by the sink. I don't wear them when I'm cleaning." She tugged her hand free and scrambled off him. She tried to ignore the vacant feeling. The need to escape swelled within her. She grabbed her shirt and pulled it over her head then donned her shorts. Covered, albeit without her undergarments, she took a shaky breath and dredged up the courage to meet his gaze.

"Hannah—"

"Thank you," she said to ward off whatever he'd been about to say. She wasn't ready for a post mortem. Not until she processed what had just happened and figured out how she felt about it.

He blinked and sat up, his brow furrowing. "Thank you?"

"I obviously needed that. And I think you did, too. As you said, neither of us has been with anyone for a long time, and we were both in need of a little…relief."

"You're treating what happened like a therapy session?" He didn't sound pleased.

"Can't we just be f—"

"Don't denigrate what we just shared with a four-letter word." He stood and hiked up his pants then crossed to her bathroom.

She knew the phrase he meant. Lucy had used

it a time or two. "I was going to say 'friends with benefits,'" she said when he returned.

"Friends. With benefits." His flat tone made her stomach sink. He wasn't taking this as well as she'd hoped.

"It can't be more. You said so yourself. Because of your father. And your job. And I can't… I can't let myself care about another cop."

He bent and snatched up his shirt then shrugged it over his head. She shouldn't be mesmerized by the play of his muscles, but she couldn't tear her eyes away. "Right. I'll be back in the morning to work on the island."

Then he turned and stalked out. Hannah remained motionless. From his dark expression, she didn't think he appreciated her *not* making demands on him. She heard the front door shut then the roar of Brandon's truck engine.

She'd had incredible sex and thoroughly satisfying orgasms. Why did she feel more tense and unsettled than she had before?

BRANDON DROVE TOWARD Hannah's Friday morning, rehashing the argument he'd had with himself since leaving her bedroom last night.

His dad was right. He wanted more from Hannah than friendship. He hadn't realized it until she'd described what they'd shared as nothing but a good f— No. He couldn't go there. But *more*, as she'd reminded him when she'd thrown his words back in his face, was something he couldn't have. Because of his job. Because of his father's disease. Because she was Rick's girl.

So where did that leave them?

As fuck buddies? No. Hell, no. No matter how many ways he looked at it, the idea repelled him. He still desired Hannah, but he couldn't disrespect Rick by treating his wife as a convenience. And now that he knew how Hannah tasted and the sexy sounds she made when she melted all over him, there wasn't a snowball's chance in hell that they could return to their prior status. No matter what she hoped.

Walking away after he resolved Mason's issue wasn't an option, either.

So where did they go from here? He still had no answer to the question that had kept him awake most of the night when he turned into her driveway. The best he could do was focus on the tasks ahead—finishing Hannah's kitchen and figuring out Mason's issues—and work out the details as the need arose.

He knocked. When she didn't answer he used the spare key and let himself into the house. The silence told him Hannah had already left for work. Deliberately timing his arrival to avoid her had worked. So why did that leave him feeling…out of sorts? Surveying his surroundings was a habit his sisters claimed he did wherever he went. He did so now, making a cursory sweep of the premises, beginning with the garage. Yep, her mini-van was gone.

On his pass through the den he spotted Hannah's computer on the desk and stopped in his tracks. Had she forgotten it? He checked his watch. She should be with a patient by now. That meant she was unlikely to return for it before lunchtime at the earliest. Her absence gave him an opportunity to search for the cause of Mason's problems. The kitchen could wait.

Heart thumping, he jogged back to his truck, retrieved his laptop bag. He experienced a twinge of guilt as he linked their machines. Hannah wouldn't like what he was doing. But he was certain Mason's safety was at stake. Within minutes he was combing through her computer's hard drive. Finding the TOR browser tucked away in an innocuously named file set alarm bells clanging in his subconscious.

Occasionally, an average citizen who was paranoid about online tracking and identity theft used the browser. Hannah didn't strike him as that kind of end user. The software didn't come preinstalled on computers. A user had to download it.

There was no legitimate reason for Mason to have installed the software, which had been developed by the US Navy and was often used by the military, law enforcement and journalists who wanted to provide anonymity for informants. More than likely, Mason was caught up in the dark net with criminals who used the TOR because it allowed anonymous web surfing via encryption and server-hopping. In general, paths couldn't be traced. But Brandon had been trained to break that anonymity.

"Aw, hell, Mason, what are you into?"

Brandon hit a few keys and fought impatience while the program ran. He lost track of time as he tried one command after another until the computer's browser history appeared. Not erased, just buried. Deep.

He clicked a URL. Porn images and video links popped up. No surprise there. Mason had admitted to looking. Each successive click took him to the same page. Someone, most likely Mason, had visited this page often.

Clicking on Menu brought up a collection of thumbnail photos. The "actors" looked young. He zoomed the images. On closer inspection, they didn't just appear underage, they were. The boys' peach-fuzzed faces gave it away. Some appeared younger than Mason.

The fine hairs on Brandon stood on end. Raking his hands across his head, he sat back in his chair and whistled out a breath. Because of his job he saw similar web pages on a regular basis. But this wasn't your average porn site. This was a crime scene because of the ages of the participants. Busting this site could be the biggest bust of his career to date.

He turned on the sound and endured a few videos, repulsed. On a pad of paper, he made notes as he searched, counting the kids involved and looking for clues to location by their settings. The crude language used explained where Mason had picked up the terms that had landed him in trouble at school.

Then it hit him. Could Mason be more than a voyeur? Was he a victim? The laptop had a camera at the top of the screen. As smart as the boy was with computers, he would know how to use it. Brandon fast-forwarded through the rest, keeping a close eye on the faces. Only when he reached the last screen without seeing Mason in any of the images, did his muscles relax slightly.

But the discovery of the illegal page combined with the browser raised questions. Why was Mason surfing the dark web? Was his browsing history linked to his troubling behavior and the note? Did he visit this page just for kicks, as he'd claimed? Or was he connected in another more dangerous way?

As a cop Brandon had taken an oath to report any wrongdoing. He'd always been a black or white guy. Breaking the law a little was like being a little bit pregnant. You were still breaking the law. Could he have a chat with Mason, warn him of the perils and drop it? No. There were too many other kids being victimized on the site.

If Mason was part of the site in any way he

would be no less guilty of committing a crime than the others involved. The warning prickle traveled along Brandon's nape. He had to find the sick bastard in charge and shut down the operation. But doing so could implicate Rick and Hannah's son. If that happened, the legal fallout would irrevocably change the boy's, Hannah's and Belle's lives.

And she'd hold him responsible. The same way she had for Rick's death.

CHAPTER FIFTEEN

"WHAT DO YOU mean you can't go out?" Lucy protested from her seat in front of Hannah's desk. "You're done for the day and you don't have the kids. You promised we'd get drinks tonight. I have a sitter."

Focusing on closing out the file in front of her, Hannah kept her eyes on her laptop and replied, "I'm sorry I forgot to call you. Brandon showed up at my house last night unexpectedly. He should be there now remodeling my kitchen."

"He spent the night?" Lucy asked in a shocked whisper.

"*No.* He...probably came back this morning. He...um...knows where I keep the spare key."

Lucy remained silent for an uncharacteristically long time; Hannah could feel her gaze but she didn't dare meet it. "You're not wearing your wedding rings. Oh. My. God. You did the horizontal hokey pokey with him."

Hannah cringed and checked over her shoulders, but thankfully, her coworkers were busy. "Shhh. I didn't say that."

"No. But you won't look at me and your face is as red as that fire hydrant out front."

Hannah closed her work computer, grabbed her bag and headed for the door. "Hannah," her coworker Seth called out, "don't forget to bring those exercises you found on Monday."

Wincing, she nodded and waved and made a hasty exit before Lucy could say something about the fresh wave of heat scorching Hannah's face. She'd been so distracted...*after*...that she'd forgotten to put on her rings and download the workout Seth referred to, and this morning she'd been in such a rush to leave before Brandon arrived that she'd left her laptop behind. Then she'd had an emergency patient and hadn't been able to run home at lunch and pick it up. What a day.

Lucy caught up and accompanied her to the parking lot. "Girl, we have to at least have a glass of wine. I need details. Juicy, second by second details. Was he amazing?"

Hannah blanked her face to the best of her ability and dug for her car keys. "I need to go home, Lucy. He's ripping apart my kitchen."

"He was lousy?" Lucy squawked and dramatically covered her heart with her hand. "I'm so disappointed. I expected him to be like...a superhero or something. I should have known. All the gorgeous ones have a tiny di—"

"He doesn't." Then she realized what she'd admitted and sighed. "And he wasn't lousy."

Lucy blocked her path. "I can't believe you're holding out on me after all the goods I've given you."

Hannah sighed and forced herself to meet her friend's gaze. "Lucy, I love you like a sister. But there are some things I just can't discuss."

"But there *is* something to discuss. Right?"

Hannah bit her lip. "I don't know. We kind of left it…unsettled."

Lucy's teasing smile morphed into worry. "Oh, shit. You're not falling for him, are you? He's a cop. And you have a 'no-cop' rule. You're so paranoid you even have me avoiding cops."

Hannah's stomach churned. She was very afraid that what she'd experienced with Brandon wasn't just sex. Or therapy. But whatever "it" was, it certainly wasn't love.

"No, I'm not falling for him. We're just friends. Friends who've taken that relationship to a deeper level. That's all."

"He's great with your kids."

"Irrelevant."

"And really good with his hands and tools."

Very good with his hands, mouth and tool. Another wave of heat rolled through her—this one burning much lower than her face. Lord help her, now she was even thinking like Lucy. "I have to go."

But Brandon was waiting. She had to figure

out how last night changed their relationship before she got home.

"Do you want me to come with you?" Lucy asked, clearly reading Hannah's ambivalence.

Hiding behind her girlfriend, though tempting, would be cowardly. "I'm a big girl. I can handle it."

"Are you sure? Because I don't mind…"

Hannah hugged Lucy because her friend would, without a doubt, be there for her. And she was the only person Hannah could say that about. "Thank you. But I'll be okay."

"Will you? Are you sure? I mean… Sweetie, you're not me. I can do the you-scratch-my-itch-I'll-scratch-yours thing. But can you? Really?"

She'd thought so. But after Brandon had left, the doubts had flooded in. She'd showered, washed the sheets, and still she hadn't been able to escape thoughts of him. No matter which way she turned there were reminders of him in her house. And when she'd finally gone to bed she'd lain there replaying every heart-stopping moment in her head right up until the second he'd walked out.

It bothered her that she hadn't been able to interpret the expression on his face before he left. But she knew it hadn't been the easygoing, "Boy, wasn't that great? Let's do it again" she'd been hoping for. She hadn't been relaxed, either. In fact, she'd been more wound up *after* than she had *before*.

Did he hate her? Did he still want her? Would he be at her house waiting for her or had he written her off?

"I don't know where this is going. That's all I can tell you. Brandon and I will figure it out. Preferably before the kids return. But I appreciate you being there for me."

"Call me. For *anything*." Lucy mimed the phone sign, sticking out her thumb and pinkie, then waved and walked down the sidewalk.

Hannah drove home with anticipation and anxiety battling for supremacy inside her. When she saw Brandon's truck in her driveway she inadvertently tapped her brakes, startling the driver following too closely behind her into blowing the horn.

Hannah's hand shook as she reached for the garage door opener on her sun visor. Unless he swept her off her feet, dragged her straight to bed and made her forget her nervousness, the encounter ahead promised to be…awkward. An excited thrill ran through her as she considered the prospect of round two upstairs. Did she want that? Yes. She did. But she was also afraid of how deep-seated that want seemed to be.

She parked in the garage and sat in her car for a moment, trying to gather her courage. She had the same jittery feeling that she'd experienced in physical therapy school when she'd downed double espressos all night to cram for exams.

Best to get this over with and see where she stood. She entered the house through the laundry room, took one step into the kitchen and saw her den. Surprise stopped her. The wall was gone. The open concept she'd sketched on paper seven years ago was a reality. Excitement percolated through her.

"Good timing." She jumped at the sound of Brandon's voice. He stood to her right. "I could use your help."

He wore jeans, a yellow T-shirt that accentuated the gold flecks in his hazel eyes, and his tool belt. He'd shaved the beard that had erotically abraded her skin last night, but five o'clock shadow was already darkening his jaw. The memory sent lust hurtling through her. But if he felt the same, nothing on his somber face gave it away.

"Help with what?" she asked cautiously, still trying to gauge his mood. She'd braced herself for anything from regret to desire, but she hadn't expected him to act as if nothing had changed.

"Getting the new countertop inside."

She dragged her gaze from his neutral expression to the open tops of her cabinetry. "You've been busy."

"It's finished. Except for the counter. You might want to change first."

She glanced down at her white scrubs then back at him. Was that an invitation to go upstairs? If so, she didn't see even a hint of desire in his eyes. "I'll do that."

She left the kitchen. He didn't follow. With each tread she climbed something stirred within her. By the time she reached the landing, she identified the feeling as disappointment. Had last night meant nothing to him? She'd barely slept for worrying about it, thinking about it, replaying it. Would it happen again? Or had she been such a lousy lay that he didn't want her anymore? The latter possibility stung. Was this a "wham bam, thank you, ma'am" encounter? Lucy had been through a few of those and vented quite openly about how the dismissals made her feel. But Hannah never had. Rick had been her only lover. Before Brandon. Her father had watched her like a hawk from the time her mother disappeared until Hannah had gone to community college. And there she'd met Rick.

She tossed off her work clothes and changed into jeans, a T-shirt and sneakers, her ire building by the second. How dare Brandon act as if nothing had happened! She stomped back downstairs and confronted him in the kitchen. "Aren't you going to say anything?"

"About?" But the tension in his shoulders and his clamped tight lips belied the innocent question and blank expression.

"Last night."

A muscle twitched in his jaw. His fists clenched by his sides. "What do you want me to say, Hannah? Do you want me to tell you that you were the best I ever had? That I want to drag you to bed right now and do it all over again, only slower?"

Her lungs faltered. A flush filled her face then descended in a warm, tingling shower to her lower region. "Do you?"

His expression softened marginally. "Doesn't matter. It's not going to happen. I'm not the guy to call when you need your itch scratched. And I can never be more than that."

"Then last night…"

His fists clenched then released by his sides. "Shouldn't have happened. I'm sorry. I'll have better control of myself in the future. We need to get the kitchen finished before the kids get home. I have straps in the truck to lift the granite. We'll get that down tonight, then I'll come back tomorrow and paint."

He strode from the room before she could formulate a reply. The front door opened but didn't close—a clear signal that he expected her to follow.

Her lungs emptied along with the adrenaline that had kept her going all day. She had wanted to know what he thought. Now she wished she'd remained ignorant. And considering that all she'd wanted was a friend with benefits, his rejection hurt a lot more than it should have.

BRANDON FELT HANNAH'S gaze on him again Saturday evening, but he made a point of ignoring the attention—the same way he had each time she'd looked him over in the past twenty-four hours. He wasn't trying to be cruel, but he couldn't trust himself to look into her hunger-filled eyes and do the right thing. And the right thing was to resist the need to take her into his arms, carry her upstairs and replay last night, only slower.

Knowing what he did about Mason's computer activities complicated the situation. Hannah needed to know what her son was up to. But telling her that he'd been searching her computer without permission would only lead to trouble.

He'd talk to Mason and get all his facts straight. Then he'd go to Hannah. He had reservations about the strategy. But it was the best he had at the moment.

She'd worn her skimpy shorts again today and a shirt that had a habit of slipping off one shoulder to reveal a lace bra strap so fragile he could snap it with his fingers. But she wasn't wearing Rick's rings. A smear of white paint marked her thigh, and her toenails were painted the color of a ripe, juicy peach. She looked good enough to eat, and it was killing him not to take a bite.

Since he'd arrived he'd been silently reciting the reasons why they couldn't be together. The litany had done nothing to diminish his desire for her. As soon as he completed this final task he would wisely put a few miles between himself and temptation, and he wouldn't return to Hannah's house until the children were here to act as buffers and he could talk to Mason. Thinking about the kid and the potential trouble he was in was sobering.

He finished attaching the outlet cover beneath her new breakfast bar then put his screwdriver away. The job was finished and it looked good, if he did say so himself. But his opinion wasn't the one that mattered. Unable to delay any longer, he met her gaze.

"Is it what you expected?"

"No," she said quickly, then her face softened. "It's better. Thank you, Brandon. Can I buy you dinner to celebrate?"

Hunger raced through him like a pack of wild dogs. He opened his mouth to refuse her invitation, but the sound of slamming car doors outside halted the words. Footsteps hammered across the front porch then the door burst open. Mason rushed in with Belle on his heels.

"Mom! Mom! Can I get a model train?" Mason exclaimed.

Belle threw her arms around Hannah. "I missed you, Mommy."

Hannah embraced her daughter. "We'll put a train set on your wish list. Did you have fun?"

"Of course they did," Margaret Leith sniped in her usual irritated tone as she followed them in. "But they won't go to bed when they're told.

So we caught an earlier flight rather than endure another disruptive night."

Hannah's lips turned down. "I'm sorry. They have trouble settling down when they're excited," she explained to her mother-in-law, then turned to her children. "Did you enjoy the train and airplane rides?"

"They wouldn't stay in their seats," Mrs. Leith snapped before the children could reply. "And they bothered the stewards with too many questions."

Anger flushed Hannah's cheeks. She took a deep breath.

Brandon's anger flared. "It was their first trip by plane or train. It's natural for them to have questions, and if you couldn't or wouldn't answer them, then they had reason to ask the ones who would. Mason, help me get your suitcases."

The kid bolted out the door. Brandon took a moment to stare down the woman who'd made her son's life, and now apparently her grandkids' lives, difficult. The powerful surge of protectiveness he felt toward Belle and Mason surpassed what he'd felt for Rick. Margaret Leith looked away first.

Once she did Brandon headed outside. Mason stood by the open trunk of the car. Brandon detoured by the passenger seat. "Good evening, Dr. Leith."

"You're here again? You're spending too much time with my son's wife."

Brandon's temper reignited. Once more, he snuffed it. "I'm helping Hannah with some renovations." Then he joined Mason. "Which are yours?"

Mason yanked out two duffel bags. "These are mine. That one's Belle's. What're you doing here?"

"Taking down the kitchen wall. You walked right by it and didn't see the new island."

"For real?" Mason hustled back to the house. Brandon grabbed Belle's pink bag and followed. If he played his cards right he'd get to talk to the boy sooner than expected. He passed Mrs. Leith on her way out. "Have a safe trip home, Mrs. Leith."

She kept walking with her nose up in the air.

Belle was chattering nonstop about the trip. Brandon waited for her to pause for a breath. "Mason and I will go get dinner."

Hannah looked relieved. "Are you sure? We could do sandwiches."

"I'm too hungry for a sandwich. Let's go, Mason."

"Do I have to? I've been cooped up all day."

"Yeah. You can tell me what Belle will eat." He clamped a hand on the boy's shoulder and steered him out the door and to the truck. He put the vehicle on the road. "So how was the trip?"

"The train and plane rides and the model train

convention were awesome. But Grandmother and Grandfather bitched the whole time."

"Are you allowed to use that word?"

Mason rolled his eyes. "They say they want us around, then all they do is complain." A few moments later he protested, "Where are we going? This is a bad part of town. Mom never takes us here."

"The best fried chicken is sold in the heart of downtown. You and Belle eat fried chicken, don't you?"

"Yeah. Let me guess. It's somewhere you and my dad used to eat."

"Yes, we did."

Brandon turned into a parking lot in the roughest part of downtown. The chain-link fence surrounding the restaurant was sagging and rusty. It was a safe bet Mason wouldn't try to bolt here. He kept the windows up, the doors locked and the truck in Drive, and he kept an eye on his surroundings. "I had a look at your mom's laptop while you were gone."

Mason stiffened and gulped.

"How did you find the site with the kids on it?"

"I—I don't know what you're talking about."

He knew. Brandon could tell by the widening of his eyes and his increased respiratory rate. "Do you know any of them?"

No answer.

"I recovered your erased browsing history.

You've visited the site multiple times in the past three months. Why that site, Mason? Did someone send you the link?"

No answer.

"Do you know who runs it? Have they approached you?"

"I think I'm going to be sick."

The boy was pale and shaking. "I wouldn't recommend getting out of the truck here."

Brandon reached in the backseat and retrieved a bucket. He put it in Mason's lap. "It's an illegal site, Mason. Taking part in it is a federal offense." When the boy remained silent, Brandon added, "You can tell me what you know now, or we can wait and discuss this with your mom and the feds in my office. Right now it's just us guys talking. *There* it'll be a sworn statement."

"Did you tell Mom?"

"Not yet. I'm giving you a chance to do that. But if you don't, I will."

"I haven't done a video!" he blurted. "I mean… not really."

Apprehension rolled through Brandon. "Do you know someone who has?"

The boy's face scrunched up. He looked out the window, surveying the area as if he wanted to run, but then his shoulders slumped as he aborted the idea. "Yeah."

"Who?"

Another long stretch of silence filled the cab. "A kid from school."

"Is he the one who sent you the link and the note?"

Mason startled, his eyes stretching wide, then he blanched even more then finally nodded. He picked at his shirt, his pants and his shoe.

"How did you get involved?"

Mason kept his head low. Brandon counted to thirty before the boy looked his way. "Because he tricked me and he's threatening to tell Mom or the cops if I don't do what he says."

The warning prickle crawled across Brandon's neck. "Tricked you how?"

Mason picked at a fingernail until it broke off. "He asked me to take a movie of him and his girlfriend kissing. And then they...you know."

Dread filled his stomach. "No I don't. Tell me what they had you film."

He squirmed. "She...she...blew him. I didn't know she was going to. I've never seen that before. I mean I've heard of it, everybody has, but I never...watched it before then or did it, so I didn't know until she was going to do it until she was like...doing it, and then I kind of froze because we were at school! I couldn't believe she'd do that there. I mean, they could get caught! And then he said that because I watched them do it and I made the movie that I'm in trouble."

The words had poured out too fast and too earnestly for him to be making it up. "'Do it. Or else.' What does that mean?"

"He wants me to give him something."

"Give him what?"

"A movie or pictures of me and…somebody. I told him I don't know anybody to do *that* with. But he said he'd get somebody. If I do it, he'll leave me alone."

"You know that's a lie, right? Once you give in, they'll have an even bigger hold over you."

The boy nodded. "But what am I supposed to do? He said if I told anybody he'd turn me in to the cops and say I took the video and posted it without their permission."

Brandon's protective instincts roared, but he kept his voice calm. "Did you post it online?"

"No. He did that. I don't even know how. I keep stalling, hoping he'll leave me alone. But he won't."

"What excuses have you given him?"

"I told him I didn't have a camera, and I don't. Except for Mom's laptop. And I can't get that out of the house when she's there. But he's getting real ugly. He had some other guy—older, I think— call me. And it scared me. That's the only reason I agreed to go with my grandparents. To get out of town."

"Is this kid why you missed the bus that day?"

"Yeah. Promise me you won't tell my mom,"

he repeated. "I won't go on the web page again. Not ever!"

"I can't promise that, Mason. There are close to a hundred other kids on that site. It has to come down and the people behind it need to be caught and punished. Underage porn is a federal offence."

Silence filled the cab, then, "What will happen to me?"

Good question. "If you're telling the truth, then you're a victim, not a criminal. Are you telling the truth, Mason?"

"Yeah. I am. I swear."

Brandon looked into the eyes so like Rick's. He didn't think the kid was lying. But if he was wrong and Mason was more deeply involved than he'd admitted, the case and the media attention that it would draw, could very well destroy Hannah and her family. And there would be nothing Brandon could do to prevent it.

This was the dilemma his father had warned him about. Putting away the bad guys might mean prosecuting Rick's son.

CHAPTER SIXTEEN

"I LOVE THE breakfast bar, Mommy," Belle said as she carried her plate to the sink. "When can we eat there?"

"I'll have to get some stools, sweetie. Go upstairs and unpack your suitcase. Dump your dirty clothes down the laundry chute. Then get ready for your bath."

Belle skipped off. Hannah couldn't recall a more tense meal, and she was glad it had finally ended. She looked from Mason, who'd eaten practically nothing, to Brandon and back, trying to figure out what had happened while they were out picking up dinner. "What's going on between you two?"

Mason slumped in his chair without answering, but he had guilt written all over his face.

"We'll talk after Belle goes to bed," Brandon replied when her son didn't. "Mason, you have time to unpack. Then come back downstairs."

The boy bolted. Hannah's concern grew. "Did he argue with you? He's always cranky after he's been with the Leiths."

"I found out the reason for his bad behavior.

We'll discuss it when he's present. Get Belle to bed. I'm going to put away my tools." Then he grabbed his gear and stalked out.

With anxiety tying her stomach in knots, Hannah raced upstairs, rushed Belle through her bath then tucked her in. "What about my book, Mommy?"

"It's late. We'll read two tomorrow." She forced a smile, but it felt like her face might crack. When Hannah returned to the kitchen the dishes had been washed and were in the drying rack and Brandon was seated at the table with her laptop and a pad of paper.

Mason, his face pasty, sat slumped across from him. Brandon pointed to a chair for her to sit down in, much the same way he'd direct a suspect. Anxiety tightened Hannah's throat.

"You want to tell her?" Brandon asked and Mason shook his head. "Mason has been visiting a porn site approximately twice a week for the past three months."

Shocked, Hannah looked at her son, whose chin couldn't be tucked any tighter. "How? I had parental controls."

"That are easily bypassed," Brandon stated.

"He told you this?"

"When I confronted him with the evidence, yes."

What had Brandon done? It was like her father's snooping all over again. "What evidence? And where did you get it?"

Brandon went still, his eyes guarded. "I installed software on your computer when Mason went missing. It alerted me to his online activity."

"You did that after I specifically asked you not to?"

"I promised you I wouldn't unless he was in danger. When he went missing, I thought he was. I wanted to bring him home safely and that meant retracing his movements."

"You had no right—"

"Hannah, Mason is in serious trouble."

Dumbfounded, she gaped at him. "For looking at porn? You bet he is. I'll take away the computer and ground him—"

He shook his head. "Bigger trouble than that. He installed an anonymous web browser to get onto a dark web site with flicks of underage kids doing very adult things."

"The dark web?" She searched her brain, retrieving snippets of conversations she'd overheard between Rick and Brandon. "That's the hidden internet, right?"

"Right. Because the encryption makes it difficult to trace IP addresses. He says a friend sent him a link to download the TOR software and another link to access the site. That same friend has been trying to coerce Mason into providing a video of himself committing a sexual act, which he claims he hasn't done."

Horrified, she searched Mason's face. "Is this true? Why didn't you tell me?"

"The guy threatened to turn me over to the cops if I did."

"That doesn't make sense, Mason. Why would he turn *you* over to the police if *he* was in the wrong?" When Mason didn't respond she looked at Brandon.

"Mason shot a video for that friend—a sex video—on the school campus. The boy is using Mason's involvement in that for leverage."

"I didn't know it was going to be that kind of video," Mason defended. "He was supposed to just kiss her."

This was so far out of Hannah's realm of normal, she didn't know what to say. "Who?"

Mason slid farther down in his chair until Brandon shot him a look. "A new kid. An eighth grader. He was one of the cool kids. He didn't treat me like an egghead. I thought he was my friend. Guess I was just stupid."

"You weren't stupid, Mason," Brandon said. "Bullies know how to find a victim. What's his name?"

Mason's face scrunched, then he folded under Brandon's stare. "Jonas Owens."

"Where does he live?"

Mason shrank even more. "Two streets over. On Dixon."

Hannah stiffened. "That's where you were going the night you snuck out?"

"Yeah."

"You'll need to surrender your computer," Brandon told Hannah.

By surrendering her laptop she could be providing evidence against her son. She hadn't been a cop's wife without picking up a few things over the years. "Don't you need a warrant for that?"

Brandon's lips tightened. "I'll get one. If Mason isn't leveling with me, then he's going to be in serious trouble and you'll need a good lawyer."

A good lawyer. Something she couldn't afford unless— "I'd have to sell the house to pay for one."

The gravity of the situation sank in. Her son had been watching porn. Child porn. On the dark web. And he'd been threatened. And she hadn't known. Maybe she really was a bad mother. And if the Leiths found out they could use this against her.

If that wasn't bad enough, Brandon had been tracking Mason's online activity behind her back even while he'd been intimate with her. How was she supposed to trust him?

Fear for Mason made her heart race, and betrayal over Brandon's actions burned the back of her throat. She knew Brandon's ruthless reputation for solving a case regardless of the costs. Would her child be hurt in the process?

She'd invited Brandon into their lives, and now he could destroy her son. "Mason, go take your shower and get ready for bed."

For once, he didn't whine about being sent upstairs. She waited until she heard the bathroom door close. "Why didn't you uninstall the software when he was found?"

"I didn't get the chance before it alerted me to a visit to a porn site—"

"When? When did it notify you?"

He exhaled. "Last Friday."

"A week ago? The night I had the sitter? I asked you what was wrong when I got home and you didn't tell me."

"He had the laptop upstairs in his room. I caught him looking at porn that night—not the illegal site. He slipped up and used your regular browser to access that site. That's the only reason I was pinged. When I asked Mason about it, he swore he was only interested in learning about sex, and he was too embarrassed to ask you. It's normal for boys to be inquisitive. I took pity on him. He doesn't have a father he can go to with his questions. He gave me his word that he'd stay off porn sites in the future."

"You're not his father. Talking to him was not your job."

"Hannah, you won't ask the difficult questions. Somebody has to."

Would she have been able to prevent this if she had asked those questions instead of running to Brandon? "You should have told me. When did you find this child site?"

"Yesterday."

A chill ran over her. "You slept with me Thursday night then searched my computer Friday while I was at work?"

"Mason was too nervous at my parents' for a kid who'd only been curious. I had to find out why. You asked for my help, Hannah. Reading people and busting computer criminals is what I do."

"I know what you do. But my son is not a criminal. Was renovating my kitchen just an excuse to gain access to my computer?" Guilty color flagged his cheekbones, and her stomach sank. "Was sleeping with me part of your plan, too?"

"No."

She didn't know if she could believe him. "Gathering evidence is all you care about. Your obsession for closing cases is what got Rick killed." She ignored his flinch. "And now you're trying to destroy my son."

"Hannah, these pedophiles have to be caught and stopped. There were dozens of other victims on that site."

"I'm not arguing with that. I just can't believe

you'd keep this kind of secret about Mason from me! I invited you into my home, my life, my family and even my bed, and all the while you were sneaking around behind my back? Get out, Brandon. Get out and don't come back."

"Hannah—"

"I don't want to hear your excuses. I can't trust you anymore."

She marched to the front door and opened it. Brandon held her gaze for torturous long seconds, then nodded and walked out into the darkness. She slammed the door behind him, staggered to the stairs and sank down on the bottom tread. Panic, pain and fear filled her chest, making it difficult to breathe. She was terrified for Mason's sake.

But the agony she felt over Brandon's betrayal made one thing very clear. Somehow she'd made the mistake of letting him become more than just a friend with benefits.

She was—*had been*—falling in love with him.

"WELL? ARE YOU going to talk or make me drag it out of you?" Rebecca Martin asked Sunday afternoon as soon as Brandon shut down the tiller.

He met his mother's gaze across the garden row. She'd asked him to come over after church and help her get her summer garden planted. Brandon had jumped at the task because he couldn't stand his own company. He shouldn't be surprised she'd guessed there was more to the visit than just a desire for her companionship.

"I'm facing the biggest bust of my career."

"That should be exciting news. But I gather it's not."

"Busting the case could implicate Hannah's son. She asked me to help her find the cause of Mason's bad behavior. The investigation led me to an underage porn page that Mason's been visiting and a ring of kids that have been coerced into committing sexual acts they shouldn't and uploading the videos."

His mother's eyebrows arched then she shook her head. "Times have changed from the days boys ogled naked girls in magazines stored in an old tobacco barn."

He jerked in surprise. "You knew about that?"

"Your father saw you and Rick. He decided it was better for you to look at pictures than the real thing. Can you talk to Mason about his viewing habits and let it go?"

"I have talked to him, but I can't look the other way because of the other victims. The site needs to come down, and the ones peddling the children need to be prosecuted. But if news of the investigation gets out the media blitz could cost Hannah her job—and if she has to hire a lawyer—her home. It's the only real home she's ever had."

"You're very adept at reading people. Do you think Mason's involved enough to need a lawyer?"

"No. I think he's leveling with me."

"Are you sure enough to base your reputation on that?"

Brandon replayed all the signals the kid had been giving then added his gut feeling into the mix. "Yes."

"What did Hannah say when you told her what you suspected of Mason?"

The question hit the bull's-eye. "I didn't tell her until after I'd talked to Mason."

"Brandon, you are an excellent investigator, and I'm proud of you for figuring out this one. But sometimes, you get so hot on the trail that you don't see the real costs to families involved in a bust. Innocent people get hurt."

"You're saying I don't see collateral damage?"

His mother nodded. "When Hannah attacked you at Rick's funeral, she was wrong. In that instance. But she was making the accusations based on what she'd seen in the past. That's why we didn't intervene. We were hoping her outburst might make you aware of your…single-mindedness. But it didn't. If anything, you've become even more ruthless. Don't get me wrong. There's nothing wrong with excelling at your job, and some detachment is required for the nasty business you deal with. But you need to have compassion, too.

"Families are like fruit trees. You don't cut down the whole tree just because it has one bad limb. You prune the limb and let the rest of the tree recover. The same way you'd remove a criminal and let the family mend."

The truth hit hard. "I hear what you're saying."

"Is there a way to take down your bad guys without damaging the families of these children any more than they've already been hurt?"

Brandon frowned as he considered her question. "In a bust of this size the feds will be all over it and I'll be cut out. I don't know how I can protect the kids. I don't even know if I can protect Mason."

"In all the years you've been in law enforcement and all the times you've coordinated with the FBI, I don't believe you can't find a way to stay involved. And if you do, then you can look out for Hannah and her family. Because I think you care for them more than you're willing to admit. Don't you?"

He did. But he was afraid to follow that path. Afraid for himself. But more afraid for Hannah. "Even if I did, Mom, there are other variables beyond my control."

"You mean the possibility that you might develop Parkinson's?"

As astute as ever, she'd hit on one. Brandon nodded.

His mother peeled off her gardening gloves and hit him with that look—the one mothers employed to get difficult answers to their difficult questions.

"If I developed cancer or any other slow, debilitating disease, do you think your father would abandon me?"

"Hell, no."

"Don't swear on Sunday. But exactly. I married your father for better or worse, and I will be right by his side, trying to make every day he has left the best it can be—the same way he would be for me if I were the one afflicted. That's what people who truly love each other do, son. They don't run when the going gets tough.

"Life isn't easy, Brandon. When it is, God's only giving you a rest before the next test. If you care for Hannah, then you have to confess your bullheadedness and allow her—and only her—to decide whether or not she wants to forgive you and be a part of your future. The question is, are you man enough to do that?"

BRANDON FACED THE team of three other investigators at the conference room table Monday afternoon. "The feds are letting us run this one. Their agents are tied up with other cases. I want to bust this wide open, but I also want to minimalize collateral damage. That means no talking to the media. They'd turn this into a witch hunt and camp on these kids' lawns. These children, if they were coerced like Mason, are already victims who've been exploited. We're after the bad guys and that's it.

"When we scoured the school's yearbook this morning and compared the pictures to those on the website, we identified the Owens boy Mason had named, as well as two others.

"Toby, Zack," he addressed his team, "you'll follow up with those kids. Mason claims Jonas Owens had an older man call and pressure him. It was a burner phone, so I couldn't track it. But it's possible the Owens boy's father could be linked to the site. If that's the case, he won't be happy to see you. See if he has any priors before you go knocking."

"Got it," Toby said. "We'll wait for the go-ahead from you before hitting their house."

"Check for identifying landmarks in the videos and pictures and try to identify as many of the kids involved as possible. We'll have to notify their respective police departments. And in your spare time," he said with a smile because they wouldn't have any, "try to track the traffic to and from the site.

"Joe, I'll contact you as soon as I'm linked to Mason's laptop—if that happens tonight." He checked his watch then rose. "Time for me to roll. I'll talk to you guys later."

Brandon drove to Hannah's. Her garage door stood open. Her vehicle was inside. He'd timed his arrival to be just minutes behind hers. If he played his cards right, he'd solve the case and teach Mason the importance of Rick's job in the process.

He climbed the stairs and rang the doorbell with his usual exhilaration over making a bust conspicuously absent. Instead, the look of fear and betrayal on Hannah's face Saturday night still haunted him. She wasn't going to be happy to see him.

Belle opened the door. "Uncle Brandon!"

She launched herself at him. He set down his computer bag and scooped her up. She wrapped him in a stranglehold. Then Hannah appeared behind her. She had circles under her eyes, and her colorless lips were compressed—the way they were when she dealt with her in-laws. The clothes she wore didn't match Belle's today, as they had every other time he'd seen them together. That said a lot about her mental state. Pressure squeezed his chest.

"I need to talk to you and Mason. It's official business this time."

"Belle, go start your homework, sweetie."

Brandon put the girl down and she skipped off, throwing him kisses over her shoulder. He'd missed that. Just as he'd missed the desire in Hannah's eyes. His next move wasn't going to inspire it to return. He handed her the warrant.

She took it and glanced at it then her frown deepened. "Do we need a lawyer?"

"I'm not after Mason. I'm after the ones behind the site. But call one if you want."

She considered it then said, "We'll go ahead. For now. I'll get Lucy to keep Belle and I'll meet you downtown."

"If you come downtown you risk the media picking up the story. There's less chance of that if we do it here."

Frowning, she backed up, opening the door, but she was by no means welcoming. Mason stood in the foyer behind her, fear in his eyes. Hannah didn't ask Brandon to have a seat, but instead remained in place with her arms folded and pain shadowing her eyes. Her wedding rings sparkled on her finger.

"I need the laptop. Mason, your mother found one note. If you have others I want them."

"I got two more notes." Mason ran upstairs.

Hannah's lips parted in surprise at the revelation. "I didn't know he had more."

"Did you ask?"

Her lips compressed. She didn't respond, which gave him his answer. "So you're leading the investigation,'" she said, changing the topic. "Still chasing your own glory?"

Hannah's bitter quip hit like a bullet—especially coming on the heels of his mother's frank talk. "I want to make sure Mason and your family aren't collateral damage."

He'd earned her skeptical expression.

Mason returned and dumped the folded papers in the plastic bag Brandon held open. "Thanks."

Hannah put her arm around her son's shoulders. "Mason will help because I want the perverts who masterminded the page and tried to take advantage of him caught. But I insist on being present for every interview. There will be no more secret conversations behind my back." Another round hit its mark.

"And when we're done, Brandon, I don't want you anywhere near me or my children ever again."

If she'd emptied a clip of ammo into Brandon's chest he couldn't hurt more. Nor could he blame her for hating his guts. But the idea of not seeing Hannah, Mason or Belle again was intolerable. Not because of a sense of duty. But because he cared for them. Mason. Belle. And Hannah. Especially Hannah.

What he felt for her was more than desire. More than friendship. What was it if not those two? He knew her better than he knew anyone. He remembered her favorite things. And her smile had a way of making his chest feel full of…something. Something good and warm. And the pain and distrust he saw now hurt.

The answer hit him like an armor-piercing round, shattering the protective shield he'd worn over his heart. At some point his subconscious had jumped the track, and he'd gone from seeing

Hannah as Rick's girl to wanting her for his own. Exactly as his father had said.

He didn't just like Hannah. He'd fallen in love with her. And her children. But Hannah, Mason and Belle deserved much more than a man with an uncertain future and one who often put his professional goals ahead of anything and anyone else. Could he make himself into that man?

For them, yes. But it would take careful planning to win Hannah back, and he was very afraid that he'd burned all his bridges, or that if he hadn't, this investigation would finish the job.

Hannah and Mason eyed him with identical wary expressions.

"Can we sit down?" Brandon asked.

She motioned him toward the den. He put Hannah's laptop on the coffee table then sat on the edge of the cushion, with his forearms on his knees.

A pleat creased Hannah's brow. "If we're giving you the laptop, why do you need Mason?"

"Because I want his help with this investigation."

"Mine? What can I do?"

"If I tell you the plan, can you keep it under wraps? You can't talk about it at school or work. Got it?" He looked from Mason to Hannah. Each nodded.

He turned to Mason. "I need you to contact someone on the site and tell them that you've made your video but you need help uploading it. I'm hoping someone higher up in the food chain will respond. I'll have my computer linked to yours. That way one of the guys back in the lab can read everything that comes through my computer and see if he can track the traffic."

"Is that safe?" Hannah asked.

"Your IP address is encrypted as long as Mason enters using the software he downloaded."

"Yet you're going to track the other IP addresses involved?"

"We have some pretty sophisticated software in the lab that will allow us to do that. I wouldn't put him in danger, Hannah. The dark net is susceptible to viruses. I have a video with a virus embedded in it. When we get the uploading information, that virus will hit the computers of anyone who views it. That in turn will help us identify and locate people watching the illegal files. Got it?"

"Okay," Mason said, his eyes sparking with interest. "Is this the kind of stuff my dad did?"

Brandon welcomed the question. "It's the kind of stuff your dad did better than anyone I've ever met. He could write code and slip commands into files that were almost impossible to detect."

"Cool."

Brandon glanced up and caught a sad smile on Hannah's face, then he focused on getting the connections he needed. Once he had, he sent a message back to Joe at SLED.

"Go ahead, Mason."

Mason logged in to the site. Hannah stood behind him, her eyes rounding with shock at how easily he'd bypassed her parental controls.

"They learn more than keyboarding in computer classes these days, and there's no limit to the information available on YouTube," Brandon told her. "Like I told you when all this started, you can't watch them every second. So don't beat yourself up. You did nothing wrong."

When the page popped up, Hannah gasped and covered her mouth with her hand.

"Send a message, Mason. There's the link."

Mason typed. "Is that okay? Does it sound stupid?"

Brandon read it without commenting on the misspelled word. That would only make it more authentic. "It's perfect. Send it." Mason did and Brandon sat back. "The cheese is in the trap. Now we wait for the rat. Have you finished your homework?"

"Nah."

"Get started on it. This part can be quick or it can take days or weeks. I'll let you know if you get a hit."

"I kinda need the computer to write my paper."

Brandon had anticipated that, so he'd purchased another one and had already uploaded the necessary software. He dug the second laptop out of his bag. "I thought you might need it for homework. I brought one from home. You can use it while we have yours."

"You're really taking my computer?" Mason asked.

"Yes. Your laptop has a pathway mapped out to reach the site. We want to locate those node owners."

"Node?"

"A node is a server that receives and forwards your files or your connection to the illegal site. We want to catch the people who operate the nodes in the network."

"Gotcha." Mason went after his backpack. Hannah hovered as if she didn't trust Brandon out of her sight. And that was his own fault.

"Hannah, I'm sorry I went behind your back. You're right. I get tunnel vision when I'm working a case. But I swear, the night Rick died was not one of those instances. I would never have deliberately hurt him, and I will do my best to protect you and Mason."

"Nice words, but that's not what I've seen."

Changing her mind wouldn't be a quick fix.

"Mommy," Belle called from the kitchen, "I need help."

"Go. All I'm going to do is sit here and watch the screen."

Brandon spent an hour waiting in vain for someone to respond to Mason's query and wishing he could be a part of the kids' bedtime routine.

Belle skipped over and kissed him on the cheek. "I love you, Uncle Brandon."

Emotion squeezed his throat. "Love you, too, princess."

She beamed and headed upstairs. He missed reading to her. When the clock signaled Mason's bedtime Brandon shut down the computers. "I'm going to call it a night."

"What?" Hannah asked in surprise. "You're quitting?"

"Mason has school tomorrow. He'll be too excited to sleep if I'm here."

"And you're going to let that stop you?"

Her skepticism was well deserved. "Mason's a week out from final exams. I don't want to screw up his grade point average."

Her eyes narrowed. "Since when has something like that impeded your investigations?"

Guilt punched him. "Since I started caring about the victims. Tell Mason I said good-night."

He packed up both computers. "And you're right. At this point I could finish this without him, but I'd like for him to see what Rick did and how important his job was. If at some point Mason wants to come to the lab, I'd be happy to show him around. And Hannah, if you end up needing a lawyer, I'll pay for it."

"I would never let you do that."

"The offer's on the table. Call me if you want to bring him by SLED."

She searched his face, her distrust evident. "I'll think about it. But I think a clean break is best."

And that was no better than he deserved. Winning Hannah back might be an uphill battle. But bad odds had never stopped him before. He would find a way to have her in his life.

CHAPTER SEVENTEEN

"THIS IS YOUR fourth Wednesday without Brandon. Are you telling me he just disappeared?" Lucy asked during dance class.

Hannah kept her eyes on Belle, who was dancing her little heart out on the other side of the viewing window. She refused to admit that she'd missed Brandon. "He's working a case."

"And he hasn't called or anything?"

Mason looked up from his book. "He emails me."

Hannah nearly gave herself whiplash turning to gape at her son. "About what?"

He rolled his eyes. "You know."

The case. Hannah's pulse accelerated and curiosity swelled inside her. But she couldn't ask for details. Mason's private conversations were just that. Private. "Why didn't you say so?"

"Cuz you didn't ask. And you're mad at him."

Lucy's eyes went wide. "Mad at him? For what? What did he do?"

Hannah hadn't said anything to Lucy about the child porn ring or Mason's part in it. "Nothing."

Lucy's eyes narrowed. "I need to pee. Come with me."

"The girls—"

"If they need us Mason can tell them where we are." She clamped her hand around Hannah's and dragged her from the parent waiting area and into the bathroom. "Did he sleep with you then dump you? Because if he did, I'm going to kick his tight ass."

And Lucy would. She was that loyal of a friend. And if Hannah didn't tell her the truth—or at least part of it—Lucy would show up at Brandon's house within the hour. "He's gone because I sent him away."

Lucy's mouth dropped open. "Hannah, why would you do that? You're crazy about him! And he's amazing with your kids."

"I...had to. He kept secrets from me about Mason and he...snooped through my computer without telling me. And that's all I can say about that, so don't ask."

Lucy's lips pursed and her brow furrowed. "Is he the reason you moved back to the old master suite?"

She endeavored to keep her expression blank. "The children don't need me upstairs anymore."

"Your chest is red," Lucy pointed out. "Hannah Leith, you're fibbing."

Hannah stared at her best friend, and the weight of pretending everything was okay suddenly became too much to bear. "You're right. The truth is I can't go into the bedroom upstairs without remembering the day we made lo—*had sex*. In fact, there are so many reminders of Brandon in that house I'm thinking of selling it. I need to move to a place that requires less maintenance anyway."

Lucy's eyes filled with sympathy. "Honey, moving won't help."

"Why not?"

"Because you'll take him with you. He's in here." Lucy tapped Hannah's chest over her heart. "And until you deal with that, you're never going to be free."

"He can't be. He's a cop. And I will never let myself care for another cop."

"You can tell your heart who to love all you want to. But it's deaf and it doesn't read lips. Talk to Brandon. I'm sure he had a very good reason for what he did."

He did, but she couldn't tell Lucy that. "It wouldn't do any good. He's anti-relationship. Because of his father's Parkinson's disease."

"If Rick had survived the shooting and been severely disabled, would you have still loved him?"

"Of course."

"Maybe you need to explain that to Brandon. Make sure the big lug knows that real love doesn't quit when the road gets rough."

"I never said I loved him."

Lucy laughed. "You didn't have to. Your tail's

been dragging since he left, and you had an energy when he was around that I've never seen in you before. And I'm not talking about the sexual awareness that made me want to blindfold the kids. Then there's the way you perked up when Mason said he'd heard from him...like you were hungry for any news. Let's just say, I don't need to be psychic to read you. Call the man!"

HANNAH REPLAYED LUCY'S words on the drive home and all through dinner. She wanted to deny everything her friend had said. But she couldn't. Brandon had a way of making Hannah nervous and comfortable simultaneously. But could she live with knowing that each day he went to work might be his last? If her work had taught her one thing, it was that anyone could be hurt anytime anywhere, doing even the most innocuous things.

"Mommy, why are you making that face?" Belle asked over her plate of macaroni and cheese.

She'd begged for the pasta, so they were bypassing a meal out and eating at the breakfast bar Brandon had built. She'd found a set of four used stools cheap at a yard sale and she, Mason and Belle had refinished them, painting one in each of their favorite colors. The fourth chair was in the attic.

"I'm thinking hard, sweetie, and wondering if I made a mistake."

"It's okay, Mommy. We all make mistakes. Ya just hafta fix 'em."

When did Belle become so smart?

Then Hannah studied Mason. Curiosity over what Brandon and Mason talked about over email was driving her crazy, but that was her son's personal business.

Ask the difficult questions, Hannah, she heard Brandon's voice say. If she wanted to know what was going on with her son, she had to ask. And she should. She needed to know what Brandon was telling Mason. As far as difficult questions went, this one was beginner level. But she had to start somewhere.

"What has Brandon been emailing you about?"

"He mostly asks how we're doing, if Belle has lost any more teeth, and if Rocky has learned any new tricks. He wanted to know my dart score and if you'd been climbing the rope."

Then Mason smacked his forehead. "He sent me a file for you. I downloaded it but I forgot about it. He said you'd need a password to open it. But he didn't tell me what it was."

"A file? For me?" Her mouth was so dry it was hard to form the simple words.

"Yeah. Hold on." Mason put his plate in the sink then took off for the den to retrieve the laptop Brandon had loaned them. He returned, booted up then pushed the device toward Hannah. "Here it is. You can read the email if you want. He said the password is something you should never order on a first date if you want to impress a girl."

She laughed. On their first date Rick had taken her to a fancy French restaurant. The waiter had convinced him to order Tête de Veau. After Rick had eaten half of the dish he'd asked the waiter what it was. The answer—cow brains—had sent him racing to the bathroom. Was that the password? If so, it was one only she, Rick and Brandon had known.

"Are you sure you don't mind if I read your email? I don't like butting into your business."

"You're my mom. Brandon says moms are supposed to do that. It means they love you and want you to be okay."

Thank you, Brandon. "Thanks."

She pulled the computer closer and read Brandon's email. He asked the kinds of questions a friend would ask, and friends were something of which Mason didn't have many. As she read Brandon's words, she could hear his voice. He ended the piece with, "Take care of your mom and Belle for me. You're the man of the house now. Let me know if you need *anything*. Love, Brandon."

The emptiness she'd experienced since sending him away welled inside her. It was as bad if not worse than the way she'd felt after losing Rick. Because this time the loss was her choice. Her fault.

Then she clicked on the attached file. A box

popped up. She typed in Tête de Veau and the page opened.

Hannah,

Thanks to Mason, the team has apprehended the mastermind behind the site, and after seizing his computers, we've tracked leads to several of the administrators and moderators. In the process, we discovered that the members-only internet plat-form was much larger than first believed. I'll give Mason—and you—a heads-up when to tune in to the news.

I miss you. Take care.

Love, Brandon

Did he mean he missed them all? And was his signature no different than how he'd signed Mason's email?

She closed the laptop. The investigation was scary. She sent up a silent prayer of thanks that Mason hadn't become any more of a victim. She had Brandon to thank for that. Because he hadn't been afraid to talk to her son.

"You miss him, too," Mason said.

She debated denying it. But she couldn't lie to Mason and expect honesty from him in return. "Yes. I do."

And then to distract him, she forced herself to ask another question that had hovered on her lips over the past weeks. "Have you heard anything else from the bully?"

"Nah. He moved the last week of school. One day he was there and then he wasn't. He didn't even take exams. I heard he and his mom went to live with his aunt, or something. I kinda wonder if his dad isn't the mastermind Brandon wrote about."

A shiver of fear skated over her. What if he had been? "Why didn't you tell me when all this started?" Then she held up her hand. "I know, I didn't ask. I'll have to work on that. I… I don't want you to think I don't trust you."

Mason ducked his head. "I kinda gave you reason not to."

His remorse was heartfelt. "But you know I still love you, right?"

He nodded. "And I didn't tell ya' cuz I was scared you'd send me away to the boarding school Grandpa always talks about. I don't wanna go there. I need to stay here and take care of you and Belle."

Her little man. She hugged him tight. And he hugged her back. "There's no chance of me sending you away."

Her father… She'd called last week and asked him why he'd refused to tell her the truth about her mother. He claimed it was because her mother had failed as a parent and therefore needed to be discharged of duty.

Military jargon for a very personal matter. To him, that was perfectly logical.

"Will you do me a huge favor, Mason? Come to me next time you have a problem. I can't promise I'll have the answer or that it will be easy to talk about—whatever it is. But I do promise I will always love you. No matter what. And I will never leave you voluntarily."

"I know that."

She ruffled his hair. Then remembered he was too old for that. But he hadn't pulled away. "I wish I'd been as smart as you when I was your age."

"How could you be? All you had to learn from was books and teachers. We've got Google and YouTube."

That made her smile. "Yes. You do. For better or worse."

That made her think of Brandon. She owed him an apology. He'd done what she'd asked him to do and found the root of Mason's behavior issues. And he'd been there for Mason, willing to talk about the uncomfortable things she'd avoided.

"My tax refund check came today. That means we can buy a new laptop tomorrow and return this one to Brandon."

"Why wait until tomorrow? I know where he is tonight. It's Wednesday. Wing night."

Her pulse tripped into double-time. "It's almost your bedtime."

"School's out for summer. And I won't fall

asleep in science camp. It's awesome." The Leiths, in their usual way, had enrolled Mason in a very expensive science camp without asking. But her son loved it, and she wasn't going to refuse to let him go out of spite.

"You're not afraid of meeting the other officers?"

"Not anymore. They're on my side now."

"I want to see Uncle Brandon, too, Mommy."

A cocktail of fear and anticipation raced through her. "Then I guess we need to go and find Uncle Brandon."

TOBY SLAPPED BRANDON on the back. "Man, you've gotten rusty. The only way you're going to win tonight is if we award points for missing the board. But keep it up. When you lose, my bar tab is low."

Smiling, Brandon flipped his buddy the bird. He knew he should be celebrating with the rest of his team. They'd broken the biggest case any of them had ever seen. But the evening felt flat.

What had it cost him? Hannah, Mason and Belle. His phone vibrated in his pocket. He pulled it out and checked the message. Hannah's name popped up as the contact. His heart slammed his rib cage. Then he read the message.

It's Mason. I borrowed Mom's phone. Is the offer of wings still open?

Anytime, he typed back without hesitation. But would Hannah let him pick up the kid? She hadn't brought Mason by headquarters in the four weeks since Brandon had seen her, and she hadn't responded to the email he'd sent six days ago. He guessed when she'd said clean break, she'd meant it.

A phone played a Disney song behind him. He didn't know which song, but he recognized the tune as one his niece and sister sang all the time. In a room full of men playing darts, somebody's ass was going to get chewed for that. He turned, curious to see which one of the guys had been pranked by having his text tone changed.

Hannah stood in the doorway. Mason and Belle flanked her. Exhilaration filled him like a helium balloon, quickly followed by deflating concern. He crossed the room in three fast strides. "What's wrong?"

"What makes you assume something's wrong?" Hannah replied.

"Because you said you never wanted to see me again."

She wrinkled her nose—adorably. "I have a bad habit of that, don't I?"

She looked good. But nervous. Seeing her bite her lip made him want to do the same. He transferred his attention to the mini-Hannah by her side. Belle wore the same short yellow skirt, same white daisy-dotted shirt, same sandals and even the same gold glitter toenail polish. But she didn't have her mother's curves or any front teeth.

"How's my snaggletooth ballerina?"

"Uncle Brandon," Belle exclaimed and leaped. He caught her, lifted her and gave her a hug. Something warm suffused him, filling a void he hadn't realized he carried.

"How's the man of the house?" he asked Mason. Shifting Belle to one arm, he offered his fist. The kid bumped it then jumped forward and banded his arms around Brandon's waist like a boa constrictor. Brandon's throat clogged as he returned the hug.

Then Mason stepped back. "I'm building my bank account by walking the neighbors' dogs while they're on vacation."

"Good for you." Then his gaze returned to Hannah. "How are you doing?"

She took a deep breath, moving the flowered cotton in ways he didn't need to notice. "Mason, why don't you show Belle how to play darts?"

"Sure thing."

Belle wiggled. Brandon set her down, noting Hannah had avoided answering his question. The kids scampered to a recently vacated board in the corner.

"We brought back your laptop." She held it out.

Given the way she'd objected to his other purchases, he couldn't tell her he'd bought it for them. "You didn't have to do that."

"My tax refund came in. I'll buy a new one tomorrow…unless you're finished with my old one?"

"I am. I was going to call and ask if I could bring it by later this week and tell Mason how we used it to trap the gatekeeper of the website."

"How did you?"

"We infiltrated the members-only private network then employed an NIT—network investigative technique—to track the IP addresses. We found more than 150,000 members globally. We nailed the kingpin and his top two assistant administrators then the feds took over. This is too big for us." A line formed between her eyebrows. "Sorry. Technical mumbo jumbo."

"I haven't seen it in the news. I've been watching."

"We tried to keep it low-key. We didn't want any of the children to be further victimized by the media."

A smile twitched the corners of her mouth. "I appreciate that. The boy who was bothering Mason…was he related to any of the bad guys?"

"His father was one of the assistant administrators."

She rocked back on her heels and curled her glitter-tipped toes in her sandals. Then she inhaled and slowly exhaled. "So Mason was in real danger. Because I avoided asking difficult questions."

"He could have been, but he's okay because you

caught him sneaking out that first night. That's what you need to focus on."

"You always make me feel like I'm a good mom—even when I make mistakes." Then her smile drooped and she shifted in her sandals. "You know how hard questions are for me. But I need to ask you one."

The warning hairs on the back of his neck rose. "Shoot."

She took another deep breath then blurted, "Have you missed us—me?"

"Hell, yes." He hadn't meant to let it burst out like that, but the smile that flitted across her lips was worth it.

Relief filled her eyes. "Good. We've—*I've* missed you, too."

He glanced around the room, noting the guys were giving him space—which he appreciated. Brandon indicated an empty table in the back corner. "Let's sit."

She followed him and perched on the edge of the stool, then set down his laptop and gripped the edge without meeting his gaze. Her left hand was bare.

"I've taught Mason and Belle to admit when they've made a mistake and to apologize." Then she lifted her lids. "I owe you an apology, Brandon."

The pain in her eyes made his brain grind to

a halt like rough-shifting gears. "No, Hannah, you don't."

"You did exactly what I asked you to do, and because of my emotional baggage I misinterpreted you keeping Mason's confidences as spying. You were a friend to him the same way you were to Rick. I'm sorry."

He covered her fidgeting hand and a comet of heat shot from his palm to his chest. But she didn't pull away. "I'm glad I could help."

"It seems like that's all you've done. You've been like a guardian angel to us since Rick died. And I've never said thank you because I blamed you. I go to church every week and I know I'm supposed to forgive. But I didn't forgive you. And then to find out that I've been holding hatred in my heart that you didn't even deserve... I'm not proud of that."

He couldn't stand her berating herself. "Hannah, don't—"

"Please. Let me finish before I lose my nerve. I have another question. If Rick had survived the gunshot wound to the head, he would have no doubt suffered brain damage. Would you have abandoned him?"

"Of course not."

"Do you think I would have?"

Where was she going with this? "No. Never. You were his rock."

"Then what makes you think that you—with

your slim possibility of contracting Parkinson's—would deserve any less loyalty?"

He couldn't do that to her. "It's being a burden physically that I'm concerned about. I've taken steps to get around that by buying a long-term care policy that will insure that whomever I choose to spend the rest of my days with won't be saddled with my care—if it ever comes to that. I'm hoping I can find someone willing to risk it."

Disappointment clouded her face. His pulse kicked up. If that disappointment meant what he hoped it meant, then his luck was going to turn around tonight. And he didn't mean with darts. He checked on the kids and noticed his team had joined them, and it looked like Zack was giving throwing pointers.

His gaze returned to the woman in front of him. "I thought you'd sworn off cops."

"I um…might have been a little hasty in that decision."

Good to know. "Hannah, when Rick first brought you to our apartment I saw the kind of woman I wanted to find. Smart, funny, spunky, attractive."

Her eyes widened and she caught her breath.

"Don't get me wrong. I never thought of you as anything but Rick's girl when he was alive. You two were perfect for each other. But I realized something when you came back into my life. You had become the yardstick by which I measured all the women I dated. And my dates always fell short."

She sat up a little straighter and her breathing shallowed. Hope brightened her eyes and parted her lips. He knew his people-reading skills were top notch, but that didn't mean he wasn't ever wrong. Nerves tied his gut in knots because if he was misinterpreting the signs, laying his cards on the table would blow up in his face.

He tightened his grip on the hand he covered. "I never expected to fall in love with anyone—let alone a woman and her two children. But I have, Hannah. I've fallen in love with you, and I don't want to go through the rest of my life without you, Mason and Belle by my side.

"But I want more than friendship with benefits. I want more than to be Uncle Brandon. If you're not ready for that, then I'll give you time for the idea to grow on you. But I'm hoping you want more, too."

Love glowed from her and he basked in the light. "I do. I do want more. And I do want you, Brandon. Because I've fallen in love with you, too."

The helium feeling returned to his chest, swelling until he thought he might burst. He cupped her face, stroked her soft skin then gently brushed his lips across the ones she loved to bite. When he lifted his head, her lids fluttered open.

"Marry me?" Then he shook his head. "Maybe I should ask the man of the house first?"

Her grin took his breath. "You're welcome to ask Mason, but I want you to know I would be honored to marry you, Brandon Martin." Then her glow dimmed and her teeth pinched her tender lip. Doubt creased her forehead. "If you want, we could sell the house and start over fresh somewhere," she said so quickly the words almost ran together.

The house meant so much to her he hadn't seen that coming. "Hannah, there's a lot of you in that house. Are you sure you want to do that?"

"There's a lot of you there, too."

He nodded. "And Rick. There are a lot of great memories of projects the three of us did together—you, him and me. I'd hate to lose those."

"You wouldn't mind staying?"

"I'd rather stay there than uproot you from the only real home you've ever known."

A smile bloomed on her lips. "Thank you. I hope I can make it into your home, too."

"You'll do that just by being there."

He felt a tug on his pant leg and looked down to see Belle with Mason right behind her. "Does this mean you'll go to church with us?"

Belle was channeling his mother again.

"Yes, he will," Hannah answered before he could, then her warm brown eyes lifted to him. She winked. "I'll explain later. But the answer is most definitely, yes."

* * * * *

Get 2 Free Books,
Plus 2 Free Gifts—
just for trying the Reader Service!

Get 2 Free Books,
Plus 2 Free Gifts—
just for trying the
Reader Service!

Get 2 Free Books,

Plus 2 Free Gifts— just for trying the Reader Service!

HARLEQUIN

SPECIAL EDITION